KNUCKLEHEAD

KNUCKLEHEAD

A NOVEL

Matt Lennox

HarperCollinsPublishersLtd

Published by HarperCollins Publishers Ltd

First edition

HarperCollins books may be purchased for educational, business,
or sales promotional use through our Special Markets Department.

HarperCollins Publishers Ltd
2 Bloor Street East, 20th Floor
Toronto, Ontario, Canada
M4W 1A8

www.harpercollins.ca

Library and Archives Canada Cataloguing in Publication
information is available upon request

ISBN 978-1-44343-252-8

Printed and bound in the United States of America
RRD 9 8 7 6 5 4 3 2 1

Dedicated to my wife,
Natalie Jacyk

It's all over for you, I think, as I imagine I am Superfly; my mind is
    what I want it to be,
the Man is tired and suddenly he looks

old, very, very old as he turns away from me, the things he cannot
    dream—
my brazen plans, my *body full of love.*
    —LYNN CROSBIE, "SUPERFLY"

We never do anything anymore
One on the telephone, one on the door
Somebody said revenge was served sweeter cold
I told ya, I told ya . . .
    —NICKELBACK, "WORTHY TO SAY"

ONE

This one time when we were kids, me and Darren and Chass did some minor arson. It was the first legit knucklehead thing I remember doing. The first thing that could've had consequences attached to it. Consequences in the legal sense, you know? Like possibly a record or probation or community service. But we never got caught, and we never told anybody.

WE WERE ALL TWELVE AT THE TIME, HALF THE AGE I AM now. I was living with Darren and his mom, Barb. They had a house down on Free Street, near the ravine in the south part of town. I remember how their place had a propane fridge on the front porch and some gnomes in the garden, those cheery little motherfuckers that push around wheelbarrows and grin about god knows what. A dozen places up the street from D's place was Hausner Meats, this pig slaughterhouse that had been stinking up the neighbourhood air for a century or more.

I had to live with Darren because I couldn't be at home for a while. My mom and my old man were working on some serious things. In the spring of that year my old man had been fired from his job as a machinist and shop supervisor at Lars Fabrication. Another man had been fired too, this accountant named Greg. Something about a secret video camera the management had put in the men's room. I'm not gonna say much more about that right now, but it made things pretty bad for us for a while, let's put it that way.

My older sister, Lori, was able to go away and work at a summer camp, but that left me. So D's mom, Barb, who was a secretary out at Lars and knew what had happened, offered to take me in while everything got figured out. As soon as school was finished, I packed up and moved in with my best pal.

Living with Darren was way freer than living at home. Barb let us camp out in the basement rec room. There was a bathroom and a crawlspace off the rec room, and the crawlspace used to scare the shit out of me in the middle of the night, like if I woke up to piss or something, but otherwise me and Darren were kings down there. We'd wrestle and eat junk food and watch movies until three in the goddamn morning.

At the same time, Darren's older brother, Seth, was in juvenile detention for the summer, on account of an assault charge, so we were safe to go into his room, look at his *Penthouse* magazines, listen to his hip-hop and hard rock tapes.

The rest of the time we just cruised around on our bikes, all over Altena. It was good. It was really good. It could've been the best summer of my life, never mind what was happening at home. It stayed like that until Darren's dad, DB, came back up from the States, and then it got weird, but that's something else I'll talk about another time.

Chastity hung around with us too, when she wasn't working. She had her first job that summer, picking vegetables on one of the big farms outside of Altena. She was learning funny-sounding swear words, come mierda and maricón and chinga tu madre, from the Amigos who worked out there with her. She was the only girl me and D were really friends with, maybe because she was also my first cousin, so for our whole lives up to that point we'd had to be friends, you know, by default. Her mother and my dad were brother and sister. With everything that had happened, Chastity's mom, my aunt Glenna, wanted her to keep clear of me, as if my old man's problems were somehow mine too. But Chass didn't seem to care about that, or anything else her mother told her to do. If I ever asked her, she'd say, You think that crazy bitch runs my life? Don't be stupid, Ashley. Nobody runs my life.

Truth is, I think I was in love with her even way back then.

ANYWAYS, THE ARSON.

Missionary Park, which everybody calls Missionary Position Park, is between the middle of Altena and the south end, but it's the kind of place that feels cut off from the rest of the world. You can go there and feel alone. It's got a lot of trees. In the centre is one big grassy area where they have this monument. It's a statue of the old-time German missionary who passed through here, I don't know, two hundred fucking years ago. He's standing up on a big pillar of stone, and beneath him are three or four Indian warriors in their crotch-cloths and feathers, and they're staring up at him and he's staring down at them, and supposedly he's bringing them knowledge and wisdom and Jesus and everything else you need to be civilized.

Past the monument, on the edge of the grassy area, is where they used to have these porta-potties. Three or four of them, back in the day. The blue plastic ones you see around concerts and construction sites and everywhere else. The porta-potties aren't there anymore, but whether or not they got removed because of what we did, I don't know.

I remember it was late in the evening, right around the time when the July sun finishes going down and full dark comes up. The three of us were screwing around with some firecrackers we'd stolen from Seth's room. Black cats and Roman candles. With the Roman candles, we'd stand fifty paces apart and hold them by their sticks and light them and shoot them at each other, as if we were gunfighters in the Wild West. We never got close to hitting each other, but you were a pussy if you flinched or ducked. With the black cats, we'd string them up together and light the fuse and watch them go, bang bang bang, like a machine gun in a war movie. They made little red flashes in the dark grass.

When it came to the porta-potty, I don't think we planned anything, which is to say we didn't have intent. I know now how serious a word that is, intent, and how big a difference it makes if you have it when you do something. What I remember is at one point I fired a Roman candle at the monument, and when I turned around there was Darren, inside the porta-potty, stringing up some black cats in the TP box. He was laughing his crazy laugh, kind of bouncing foot to foot. He kept saying, This is gonna be great, this is gonna be great.

Chass was standing back a little, watching him, shaking her head. She was saying, What do you even think's gonna happen, D, you moron?

Darren lit the fuse and came running out of the porta-potty and yelled to us to hit the deck. We did. Well, he and I did. Chastity didn't. She always was a little cooler-headed about shit, even when we were kids.

I think me and Darren wanted to believe some big fuck-off explosion was going to happen, maybe from the black cats being detonated in a tight space or something, but there wasn't an explosion. All that happened was another bang bang bang, same as when we threw the black cats in the grass, only this time the noise was muffled and we couldn't see any flashes at all.

We got up and rubbed the dirt off our clothes. I remember Darren saying, Just like in the Nam, motherfucker, and I remember Chass saying, You're both morons.

It was five or ten minutes later, as we were getting on our bikes over at the other side of the grassy area. First it was the smell. Burning plastic. You can burn wood or weed or incense and it smells good, right? But you burn plastic and it's not right. It's not natural, and you know that, soon as you smell it. When we realized what was happening we turned to look. Right then there wasn't much to see except for grey smoke coming out of the top of the porta-potty door. Then the smoke turned black. Orange flames followed, quickly getting big. Before long the flames and the smoke, thick and black by then, stood straight up into the dark sky. The plastic walls and roof drooped inwards, and then all at once they collapsed. A huge fireball rolled out and up. Intent or not, that was as close to the awesome explosion as we were gonna get, just like in the Nam, motherfucker, and that was when we got the hell out of there, me on my bike, Chastity doubling on Darren's.

We were three blocks away, almost back to Darren's house, before we heard the sirens, but we never saw the firetrucks or the cops or whoever it was they sent. Like I said, we never got caught. We never had consequences.

I'M WALKING OVER IT NOW, THE GRASSY AREA IN THE MIDdle of Missionary Position Park. The whole park is smaller than how I remember it as a kid. That's always how it goes. You get bigger and the shit around you shrinks. From where I'm standing I can see both the place where the porta-potties used to be and the monument. Somebody's spray-painted a big yellow spot on the German missionary's crotch. It makes me laugh to look at it. Laughing hurts.

Torching that porta-potty seems pretty minor now. Kids doing something stupid, nothing more. But let's say we had've got caught. Let's say we had've done community service for a while. That would've put our names in the system, you know? Which maybe would mean we wouldn't've had the chances we had to do the things we did as we got older, the more serious shit. Maybe we would've been stopped before we even started. Who knows. This is one of the things I think about lately, how certain things in the past—things you don't even think about at the time, things you don't have any real *intent* about—have a way of setting things up for the future. You know what I mean? There are these moments, here in the present day, where everything's happening, bang bang bang, like those black cats going off, and what's happening makes you remember, fully, that moment in the past, whatever it was, minor at the time, that put you here now, exactly here. That's on my mind a lot.

The thing is, people have started to ask. No no, not about the porta-potty way back in the day. That's ancient history. People are asking about the last couple months. They waited for a while, like a grace period or whatever, and then they started asking. They want to know what happened with me and Darren and Darren's dad and Seth and that shitty old house down on Free Street.

Some people, if they think they know a little bit more than the average, if they think they have the inside information, they ask about the Amigos, or they ask about the crank.

If people think they know everything, they ask me about Chastity.

Of course they ask. How can they not? It's curiosity, a.k.a. sticking your nose up in somebody's business. Human nature. Altena is technically a city, but it isn't much of one, and you don't have to go far to find out how you're connected to this person or that person. Word always gets around quick, and the quicker word gets around, the more it changes. I've heard versions of the events in question that are fucking insane. Legitimately. I'm, like, you think that's how it went down? But I don't explain much. I don't correct them. Partly because I can't talk about it—the Crown is still putting the official bits together—so until it all comes out, the stuff I know is, like, confidential. And partly, mainly, I'm too tired, more or less, too burned out from everything to explain the facts to every nosy asshole who wants to know.

So when they ask, all I say is, It is what it is, bro.

But in my own head, where I've got nobody but myself to talk to, sometimes I think I'm the main one who fucked up everything. Sometimes I think, here I am, twenty-four years old, and what I did has fucked up everything. Sometimes I think it's all on me.

Then other times I think it's not on me, none of it, or at least not the parts that count. The Crown calls it the culpability, which is for sure a hard-gainer word, but whatever. The Crown is saying the culpability isn't on me, and sometimes in my head I can agree with them. When I'm leaning this way I think what I did was because I was backed up in a corner, you know? And I had to do something. The MAFD rule, Make A Fucking Decision. I was following the MAFD rule.

Either way, on me or not, it's serious shit and that's the truth, and the lives of the people I care about have been or are currently fucked up, and that's also the truth. I don't know what to make of it all. I keep going back and forth, and when I try to sleep at night my head gets filled up with some of the specific shit I've seen. It can get bad like this. It can make me feel like I don't know if I'm having a nightmare or if I'm fully awake. I know that doesn't make much sense, but I can't break it down much better than that.

I keep walking. I have news to tell. Shit I found out yesterday. It's been burning me up ever since. I have this news to tell, and other than that I have this need for a painkiller, a Percocet, starting to take hold. What a goddamn mess.

Anyways, I was told to go past the monument and I'd see it, the place where we're supposed to meet up. It'll be good to sit down. They took the cast off my arm and the stupid plastic boot off my foot a month ago, but getting around is still a pain in the ass. I miss my Ninja, and I miss the iron. I'm getting fat. Jesus am I getting fat. I can barely stand the sight of myself in the mirror. But I know, no matter how I'm feeling about it on a given day, no matter about the intent or culpability or all the shit the past sets up for the present, I know I put myself exactly where I am today.

It is what it is, bro.

TWO

I got the job through a buddy two weeks after I graduated grade twelve, and I kept it up till late April of this year. The job was bouncing at the Balmoral, the only real nightclub in Altena. The other guys on the crew were TJ Lemay and Brice O'Halloran and Trevon Rudder. Solid dudes, all. I'd lived with Trey for a couple years. He had a townhouse, and I rented the second bedroom for four-fifty a month.

Some people don't like the word bouncer. They prefer doorman or venue security or this or that. Softer-sounding words. The Balmoral's manager, Marcel, was part of this group. He called us his security staff. I guess him and the people like him think the term bouncer implies that you're basically a professional gorilla. Which, let's face it, you are. In this province, the bouncer or doorman or security staff or whatever gets to use reasonable force to expel intoxicated or aggressive patrons from the premises. It's been upheld in the courts a bunch of times. Reasonable force. Sometimes how you define reasonable can be pretty open-ended, you know? Open-ended depending on who's looking. Ha.

But don't get the idea that I was redefining reasonable force at the club every night. I learned early on in my job that you have to know how to hold back. You have to learn how to talk people down before you start manhandling them. You have to learn that it's the implication that does the work for you. That's why bouncers are usually big hardcase-looking motherfuckers like me. Most people, unless they're really drunk or unless they're really flexing nuts, they'll buy the implication. They'll walk out when you tell them to. Their pride will be bruised, but they'll sleep it off, forget it, and be back the next night. No problemo.

I'll say I was good at the job. I kept up on my first-aid qualification, got it renewed yearly or so, and I never had any serious trouble with complaints or lawsuits or any of that shit. And if things ever did come down to a battle, I never flinched. See the scar in my eyebrow? That's from when a guy with a ring sucker-punched me after I had to kick his girlfriend out. See the scar on my shoulder, right here? That was a guy swinging around a broken pool cue. I don't remember what his issue was. Like I say, I never flinched, and I was usually the one to end the battle, even before the other bouncers jumped in.

Look. Straight-up? I'd be lying if I said I don't kind of miss it.

You probably know what kind of club the Balmoral is. It's open from Thursday to Saturday. The weekend is the busy time. The DJ plays the Top 40, the dance music I hate but what gets the gals moving. The gals in their makeup and short skirts and heels or fake leather fuck-me boots. Where the gals are dressed like that, moving like that, the boys all follow, maybe try to move with them, maybe hang around the edges of the dance floor. Either way, they're spending money. Way too much money, I think, on marked-up beer or mixed drinks in plastic cups or glow-in-the-dark shots in glasses that look like test tubes. You know what I mean. You've been there, too, I bet, halfway hoping you'll have a good time, maybe pick somebody up for the night, at least get a phone number, halfway wondering why the fuck you keep coming back.

The Balmoral itself has been around for a long time. It's got a brown-brick exterior, sort of old-fashioned. It was a hotel for, like, fifty years, and a tavern off and on. When I was a kid it was an arcade. I wasn't allowed to go into it. It's right on Bicentennial Street, at the edge of downtown, and it shares the block with a bakery and a video rental place and a tiny Legion branch where old men play shuffleboard and talk about war. Past this area is the rest of Altena. The commercial buildings, the odd apartment mid-rise, the schools, the uptown neighbourhoods, a few strips of fast-food joints, a mall, a big-box plaza, a dozen churches, a bunch of identical townhouse developments. Surrounding the whole town are the greenhouses and farm fields that most of Altena lives on. Out there are the rundown bunkhouses where the Amigos live when they're up here working, eight or nine months of the year. Nobody wants you to see those places. They don't make it onto the postcards.

SO THIS ONE SPRING NIGHT, THIRTY MINUTES AFTER LAST call, we'd gotten most of the final two dozen patrons out. If I'd been outside, I know exactly what the scene would have looked like. Those last patrons would be slumming around on the sidewalk, smoking, laughing, talking on their cell phones, heading off, only slowly. Some gal would be sitting on the curb, crying about something. Two guys would look like they were about to fight, but then they'd be hugging and laughing about shit. Up in front of the bakery, you'd have the two cop cars you always have for the last hour or two of the night. And in the other direction, you'd have the Amigos.

They're always there, the Amigos, hanging around the same sidewalk bench. They change up night to night, but they're always there, and there's almost always four of them. Young guys. Jeans and jean jackets and tucked-in shirts. They stand there sucking on soft drinks and smoking darts and just watching the front of the club. They never bother anybody, and they usually split if a fight breaks out. Me and the other bouncers always figured they wanted to come into the club but didn't quite have the nerve to. It would be weird for them, I guess. Weird for them and weird for the locals. It's not mistrust. Not exactly. It's more like these are two worlds that don't cross over more than they have to. Trust me on this.

I wasn't outside that night. I was downstairs in the men's washroom. I had the very last patron of the night with me. He was a skinny guy I kind of remembered from high school. I'd run into him at a quarter to three. He was coming up the stairs from the washrooms, red-eyed and dragging his hand across his mouth. Puke was stuck to his chin and the front of his shirt.

I blocked his way and I said to him, Hey, bro, you're not trying to sneak away from any nasty business down there, are you?

The guy shook his head.

Let's go take a look, I said. You and me, because if there's puke in there, let me tell you who's not cleaning it up.

I'd long before developed an instinct for these things, and sure enough, out of the four stalls in the men's washroom, one of them had a pool of upchuck six inches short of the toilet bowl. There was a real thick stink to it. It reminded me of how the air from the slaughterhouse down on Free Street, Darren's old hood, sometimes smelled.

By the letter of the law, nobody could make the guy stay to clean up, but if he, like, volunteered, if I explained to him that he'd be banned for life if he didn't . . .

So before long I had him spreading the mess around with a mop. He was dry-heaving. I was supervising, sitting on the counter, kind of distracted by a game on my cell phone. I've never been real bothered by the sight or smell of puke, but I also wasn't going near it if I didn't have to. I was also, I'll admit, enjoying myself a little. In a club like the Balmoral, people will puke and spit on the floor as much as they can get away with. They'd fucking piss on it, too, I'd bet. But once in a while we catch them, and catching them almost makes it worth it.

The guy finally said, Am I done?

I looked up from my phone. All he'd managed was to thin the mess out a bit, turn it into an ugly spiral. He was wobbling on his feet. I said to him, Does it look like you're done? What does that look like to you?

The guy said something about abuse of power, but he went back to his mopping. Then after a minute or two, he said, I remember you. From high school.

Is that right, I said.

Yeah. I remember that time you knocked out Chris Hagar at a bush party. Do you remember that?

Nope, I said.

I was lying about that. I did remember knocking out Chris Hagar at a bush party. That was in grade eleven or grade twelve. I remembered knocking out Chris Hagar, and I remembered knocking out Dominic Zubrek, and I remembered knocking out Gummer Harrison. For whatever reason, I remembered every single battle I'd had in high school, and thanks to who my old man was, all the things that were said about him to my face, battles were a pretty common thing back then.

The guy was rambling on, as ass-kissing now as he was drunk. He said, And your buddy Darren. Darren What's-his-name. Your buddy. Or Derek? Whatever. My older brother, he used to buy weed from Darren all the time. And this one time he owed Darren money, and when Darren came to get it, he brought you.

I said, I don't know what the fuck you're talking about.

You guys came over to our parents' house. Ha. My brother almost shit his pants—

I slipped off the counter and moved across the floor and pushed the guy up against the wall. With one hand I held the front of his shirt. I pushed my other forearm against the guy's throat, hard enough to make his face turn red. I realized, too late, that I'd planted one of my boots in the middle of the puke.

It's none of your business, I said. I don't know you, you don't know me. It's none of your goddamn business.

The guy tried to say something, but he couldn't get the words out. His breath was goddamn horrible.

Then I heard Trey's voice from outside the washroom, up the stairs, saying, Hey, Ash, you down there still?

I called back, Just dealing with something. I'll be done in a minute.

I relaxed my grip on the skinny guy. I was shaking all over and there was a cold sweat under my clothes.

Get lost, I said.

The guy hesitated, and then he stumbled toward the washroom door. He blinked at me and as he turned to leave he said, Asshole. You're lucky I don't get a lawyer. I won't come back here.

I just smiled at him. I didn't feel like going any further.

The guy would be back, of course he would, probably as early as the next night. It was the Balmoral, the only show in town. Everybody came back.

THREE

On the eleventh of April, middle of the day, just as I'd been getting out of bed, my cell phone vibrated. The call display said *Pro Choice Electronics*, the electronics store at the mall. Darren's straight job. Darren liked using the office phone there, because a lot of other people used it too. In other words, you couldn't nail that phone down to any one user. D didn't have a phone of his own, only a pager. He was pretty careful about shit like that.

I answered. I could hear all the other noises in the background, the sounds of the store and the mall beyond it and everything. Darren didn't say much, didn't talk for long. All he said was, Hey, stranger. How's it going? Listen, can you maybe help me out this afternoon? There's something that needs to get got. Nothing big.

He wasn't specific, which was fine, because I never wanted to know much.

Before I'd even thought about it, I said yes. Yeah, D, I'll help you.

We settled on where and when he'd pick me up, and that was all there was to it.

I put the phone down and propped myself up on my elbows

and looked around my bedroom. I always said yes to Darren. Even now, when I'd barely spoken to or seen him in a bunch of months. He'd asked for my help and I'd said yes, just like that.

THERE WERE A FEW HOURS TO KILL. THIS WAS GOOD, BECAUSE I had my Ritual to take care of. I was barely out of bed and it was already eating me up.

First part of the Ritual was in the bathroom, where I stepped naked onto the scales.

236 lbs

I stepped off the scales and looked in the mirror. My chest and shoulders and arms were looking thick and powerful, but with only a bit of definition. Same deal with my legs. Heavy quadriceps and glutes, thick calves, but little shredding. My abs were totally hidden under a layer of fat I could pinch with my fingers. Looking at it depressed the hell out of me.

Back in October I'd done my first bodybuilding competition, the D'Amours Classic, in Toronto. Men's heavyweight open. I'd never worked so hard for anything, and believe me when I say I'd looked like a fucking god going into it. But I hadn't placed top three. I don't know why. Chastity, who'd been there in the audience, later told me the judges must've been idiots or on somebody's take or something. They couldn't've seen what she'd seen, she said, and not placed me in the top three.

Anyways, it was what it was. There was another regional open show, a qualifier for the provincials, coming up in August. I had the poster for it tacked to the wall in my bedroom.

This was April. August wasn't so far away.

My gear stood on the counter beside the sink. First was a plain white bottle, unmarked, with a month's worth of d-bol tablets in it, 30 mg a pop. For six weeks at a time I would take one every day after breakfast, before I headed to the gym, to start packing on the mass. I was a week into this cycle and I was feeling it, bro. Get me on the iron and I'd be fucking ferocious, you know? To go along with the d-bol was a bottle of milk thistle supplements, for my liver, and a little blister-pack of Nolvadex, to keep away the tits. If you're going to gear, you've got to be scientific about it. There aren't any shortcuts.

The gear was all pills, which was good because I hate needles. I popped the pills in my mouth and washed them down with tap water. The bathroom door was closed, so as far as Trey would know I was either jerking off or taking a shit. Trey smoked a lot of weed but he wouldn't tolerate any other illegal substances in the house. He really hated gear, said it made you all for show and not for go. That was a point where we'd just have to agree to disagree. Trey was a big guy, but he'd never stood up under the spotlights in a tiny pair of briefs in front of a room full of strangers and judges. He didn't know.

When I was finished gearing I stood back and looked at the mirror again. I slapped myself in the face a couple times, hard enough to bring the tears. Weakness, I said to my reflection, my fat, soft reflection. In the world I knew, there was nothing worse, nothing more disrespected, nothing more dangerous, than being weak. But I'd done it before. I'd fallen into that trap. Every day had to be a reminder of how easy it was to let myself fail. I slapped myself in the face one more time.

By two o'clock I was repping out some barbell curls. This was the second and most important part of the Ritual. The iron. Two hours a day, five days a week.

I watched myself in the wall mirrors, trying to focus less on my midsection and more on my form. I studied my biceps as they worked. Slow eccentric move downward to full extension, power back up, exhaling on the way. At the top, hold, squeeze. Then slow eccentric move downward to full extension. Repeat to failure. There was good thick vascularity happening all through my arms. Blood vessels as thick and round as pencils.

The gym was called Champ Fitness. It had been crowded at lunch, and would be crowded again after work and through the evening, but now was the middle of the afternoon and I had it almost to myself. This was the second best time of day to come. The best was late in the evening, right around closing time, or even later whenever I could talk the staff into it.

I did one more repetition of the curls, hissing through my teeth. At the bottom of the final downward movement I let the barbell drop onto the floor. The plates clanged together. My arms hung like lead. It hurt to try to lift them.

Fifteen feet away, some middle-aged lady was working out on the Smith machine. Quietly coaching the middle-aged lady was Chris Hagar, the very same Chris Hagar I'd punched out at the bush party all those years ago for saying something about my dad. Chris worked for the gym, so I saw him a lot. We would talk about exercising and nutrition, and sometimes he'd let me work out after-hours. We had a peaceable thing going. He never ever mentioned the bush party. I guess he'd learned his place. He nodded to me, gave me a two-finger wave. I nodded back.

The lady he was coaching wasn't looking at me. She was just doing her set, repping the nothing-weight up and down. She wanted to be looking at me, though. I could feel it. There's an energy I give off when I'm working the iron. Laugh all you want, bro, but there is.

I got down and did a set of sit-ups. I kept going until my abs twitched and clenched and forced me to stop. For a short time I just lay on my back, staring up at the ceiling, too gassed out to do anything more.

Ending like this—sore and beat and hungry—was the only right way to do the Ritual. Anything less was a waste of time, like that lady on the Smith machine. Like, why even bother.

FIFTEEN MINUTES LATER, I WAS SHOWERING IN THE MEN'S LOCKER room. I rinsed, dried off and wrapped the towel around my hips. I got my gym bag from my locker. Inside my bag was a plastic shaker-cup and a Ziploc of powdered whey protein, fifty grams of it. I dumped the powder into the shaker-cup and took the cup over to the sink. I filled it, screwed on the lid, shook it hard for ten full seconds and then choked the mixture down. I hated the taste of these fucking things, but I needed what they gave me. So I had four of them every day, on top of packing down my regular three square meals.

After I finished, I rinsed out the cup with cold water and filled it again and poured it in my mouth to get rid of that gritty, not-vanilla taste.

I set the cup to the side and looked at my upper body and arms in the mirror over the sink. I was alone in the locker room, so I struck a few show poses. I thought about the D'Amours Classic in the fall, and then I made myself think ahead to the next show, the one in August. This time I would place. I would. I had to treat it as a certainty. I'd heard the universe had a way of bringing things right to your feet if you just concentrated on them enough, you know, focused your energy.

I was about to flex my triceps when a man came into the locker room. I grabbed the shaker-cup and stepped away quick from the mirror.

I said, Still raining out there, or what?

Cats and dogs, said the man.

AFTER I'D DRESSED, I SAT OUT ON THE WOODEN BENCH BESIDE the gym's front door, sheltered from the rain by the eaves of the building. Darren was supposed to show up any minute now.

My body was cooling down but my anxiety was heating up. Before Christmas was the last time I'd helped Darren with anything. I hadn't spent much time with him since then. Darren or Chastity. I'd been laying low, on purpose but not having the balls to say anything about it, knowing all along it would only take the call, Darren asking for my help, to bring me out again. Today was that day. I leaned back on the bench, massaging a sore spot on my shoulder, looking at the puddles on the parking lot.

The gym was part of a small strip mall across from an endless line of greenhouses, located outside of town on a long road that everybody called White Bike Way. This was a nickname that came from a bicycle chained to a telephone pole five hundred yards down from me. The bike was spray-painted white and decorated with plastic flowers and rosary beads. Some Amigo had put it there to honour the dozen of his kind who'd been killed on their own bikes over the years, riding late at night or early in the morning, hit by farm trucks or drunks. The bike had been in place for at least four years. Nobody had ever vandalized it. From where I was sitting, I could just see it through the rainfall, a small but bright white dot.

I took out my phone and looked at it. No missed calls. As I was putting it back in my pocket I heard a car horn honk, the sound of a bass beat, getting closer. I looked up. Darren's car, this tricked-out blue Subaru, was pulling across the parking lot in front of the gym. The bass beat got louder. Darren braked, squealing to a stop only a few feet short of where I was sitting. I could see him grinning at me through the windshield.

There were two other people in the car. One of them was in the back seat and one in the passenger seat. I could see her slim shoulders. I could see the blond highlights in her hair, which was hanging out from beneath an oversized trucker cap. I sucked in my breath.

Three years they'd been together, Chastity and Darren, my cousin and my best buddy. Three years. Darren said it was always meant to be. He said she was his soulmate. They lived together in his apartment.

The passenger door opened and she got out. She was wearing bright blue sneakers and tight jeans and a light jacket. A small denim purse with brown leather straps hung from one shoulder. She looked skinnier than when I'd last seen her, and she'd been tanning too much, but all the same the sight of her made me weak in the knees.

Take the front seat, she said to me.

No no, I said as I stood up.

Yes yes. You haven't gotten any smaller.

I came close to the car. I could feel the rain on my hood and shoulders. Chastity opened the back door, but before she got in, she reached her arms out to me. Bracelets jangled on her wrists. I pulled her in and held her close, feeling her small body against mine, my thoughts going crazy.

This wasn't supposed to be happening, her here. Chass had always kept herself even more ignorant of D's business than I was.

We separated. I held her at arms' length and said, Since when do you come along?

Her green eyes narrowed to slits and fixed on me. Her mouth tightened. A moment passed. But then she hugged me again and put her lips right up to my ear and said, It's good to see you, Ash. Let's just leave it at that.

She took my gym bag and put it in the back seat and got in and closed the door. I sat down in the passenger seat. Southern rap was banging loud from the speakers. Behind the steering wheel, Darren was wearing a crisp white polo shirt and a pair of baggy jeans. He'd shaved his head down to a copper-coloured stubble. He'd always been short, slim, but now he looked skinny, same as Chastity. Bony even. The edges of his collarbone poked against the inside of his shirt. He was wearing too much cologne.

The other person in the car was Seth, sitting behind the driver's seat, wearing a blue two-piece Adidas track suit. He was bigger than Darren, almost as big as me, but his size was mostly fat. He had fat in his face and belly. I hadn't seen him in a few years. Last I'd heard, he was down in the States with their dad, DB.

I said, What's the good word, Seth?

Seth barely glanced at me. He said, Yeah, hey.

I looked at Darren. Darren grinned crazily and grabbed my head with both hands and put a loud kiss directly on my eyebrow. He said, I finally managed to get you out of hiding. Where the fuck have you been all my life?

I've been around, D.

Lies, lies, said Darren.

I'm here now, bro.

Yes, you are. Let's go.

He pulled out of the parking lot and back onto White Bike Way. He geared up to fourth, floored it until the rpm started to redline, and popped into fifth. The telephone poles on the side of the road blurred past. The white bicycle appeared and disappeared.

Over the stereo I said, Where we going?

Darren weaved around a pickup truck. He was leaning forward in his seat, holding on to the steering wheel with both hands. Every so often he would scratch at a little red patch, maybe a razor-burn, on the side of his jaw.

D, I said.

Hmm?

Where are we going?

Oh, just to see a guy I know. I gotta pick something up from him.

Like a TV, right? I said. Or something heavy?

Darren turned his attention away from the road and looked at me. Grinning, he said, Come on, brother. This guy's just a little late is all. It's no problem, straight-up.

FROM THE BACK SEAT, SETH SAID, I STILL DON'T KNOW, DARREN.

You still don't know what? said Darren.

Why you think we need the extra hand. No offence or nothing, Ashley.

Darren looked back at his older brother, started to reply, but before he got anything out, Chastity said, Darren, Christ. Look where you're going.

Darren looked forward in time to see that he was drifting. Three or four hundred yards up, coming our way, was a tractor-trailer, laying on its air horn. Darren swerved back into his lane, laughing, scratching at his jaw again.

I felt uneasy. I didn't like the way Darren was driving, and I'd never liked Seth all that much to begin with. Darren didn't usually bring extra people along on a collection. And definitely not Chass. Never Chass. Why now?

So? said Darren.

So what? I said.

So you want to tell us why you've been hiding out for a while?

Yeah, said Chass. You don't call, you don't write.

I glanced back at her in the side mirror, but she was looking out at the passing fields, her window partway down, dart in hand. I pulled my eyes away, tried to get a hold of my mind. A real bitter sense of guilt went through me. That was for Darren.

After a few seconds I said, I haven't been meaning to hide out. I don't know. Winter hit, and I just didn't feel like doing anything.

It's okay as long as it wasn't something I did, brother, said Darren.

It wasn't, I said. It wasn't anything at all.

Everybody needs a change of scenery from time to time, said Darren. But then, it's funny, you end up right back where you started. It's, what's that word, inevitable.

You want to know what's inevitable? said Chastity. You getting us into a fucking car accident.

Yeah, D, I said. Slow it down a bit, will you?

You guys, said Darren, laughing, slowing down a little. But soon he accelerated again, weaving around another slow-moving truck, and then had to give a wide berth to an Amigo bicycling along the road. Darren honked his horn in irritation.

Once we were past the Amigo, he said, Did I tell you my dad's back in town?

A cold feeling went through me. I said, Your dad.

The Travellin' Man himself, said Darren. He's been back here since, I don't know, late January? He's fixing up my mom's old place.

Hey, Darren, said Seth. Why don't you shut the hell up.

I had no idea your dad was back, I said.

Well, I haven't seen you, said Darren. Have I? Anyways, I think he's here to stay for a while, if you can believe that shit. You should come see him, Ash. Hang out, have a couple beers. He always liked you.

IF THERE WAS ONE THING IN THAT CAR RIDE THAT COULD get my mind off Chastity, it was this talk about Darren's dad.

Remember a while ago I told you how I've been thinking about the past, like, how things that happen at one time set up the things that happen later on. You don't see the set-up, really, until it's too late. His name was Don Braemer, but everybody called him DB. That summer I lived with Darren, back when we were kids, DB wasn't around at first. He hadn't been around for a while, and there was no sign that he'd be coming back anytime soon. Otherwise there was no way in hell my own parents would've let me stay with Darren and his mom. To them, Seth was bad enough, but DB was another deal altogether. He was what my mom called bad news, what my dad would shake his head about and say, Well, he's not my kind of guy, anyhow.

Back then, based on the few times I'd met DB, I thought my parents were unfair, uncool, way too judgmental. Back then I thought DB was kind of awesome. Especially compared to my own dad, at the time DB was like a goddamn movie star.

Kids, bro, don't know shit.

Anyways, DB came home one evening that summer, about a week after me and Darren and Chass had torched the porta-potty. It was after supper, and Barb was about to take me and Darren to the Dairy Queen uptown. We were heading out the door when we saw DB's Eldorado in the driveway, parked behind Barb's Topaz.

I knew how this was a big surprise. Barb and Darren never really knew when DB was coming back from the States, where he had his different business interests. Sometimes he'd just show up, and then he'd be gone again for a long time, two months or three months or four or six. He called himself the Travellin' Man, like in that old Tommy Hunter country song. He'd sing about following the breeze and gathering memories . . . Barb would shake her head, but she'd crack a grin about it too, which encouraged DB, and he'd sing some more. His voice was a not-bad tenor.

It made me wonder if that was what being in love really was. Something where you could be away for a long time, and you don't even call, and then you just show back up out of nowhere and get taken in like nothing's changed.

DB's Eldorado was big and boxy, with a hardtop and a taupe finish. DB called it his pimp car. It was ten years old but in beautiful condition, and it had California licence plates. I remember how he was just stepping out of it. He had dark red hair, thick and long enough to hide his ears and touch his collar. He wasn't tall but his arms were big and his legs were strong. Darren shouted out to him and then ran forward.

My two favouritist people in the world, said DB.

Barb stood on her porch beside me for a little while. Then she went down the steps and across the yard to him, and he gave her a big hug and a kiss on her mouth and he reached down and squeezed her butt, which made Darren and me look at each other in disgust.

Then DB saw me. He walked up on the porch and shook my hand, and he said, Jesus, kid, you get bigger every time I see you. If I was a psychic, I'd say linebacker is in your future.

Barb told DB that I was crashing with them for the summer. She didn't say anything about my dad, which was good. I didn't want DB to know what my dad was. Around DB, thinking about my dad made me ashamed.

Fair enough, said DB. I'll be happy to have Ashley keep Darren outta trouble. Anyhow, goddamn am I ever hungry.

DB must have already known about Seth being in juvenile, because he didn't say anything about it, and neither did Barb. None of us ended up going to Dairy Queen that night, but DB introduced us to his version of Monopoly. It consisted of dealing out all the properties and utilities and railroads, randomly, at the beginning of the game, as well as a bunch of different allotments of start-up cash. He explained his rules like this. In life, he said, nobody starts out at the same place. At school they'll tell you you do, that everybody is equal and starts out the same, but it's a lie. Everybody starts out different, and you got to win or lose on whatever you've been given and whatever you can make, you know, the hard way. Nothing's fair, not at the beginning, the middle, or the end. So let's play it like that. Let's play it true.

My phone call to my parents that night, which I did every night while I was staying at Darren's, was short. Two minutes talking to my mom, two minutes talking to my dad, not saying much at all, and then back to the game as fast as I could get there. I didn't tell my parents anything about DB being back home. I wasn't going to take that chance.

Over the next few days, DB taught me and Darren how to open a beer with a lighter. He showed us some wrestling and weightlifting techniques. He took us fishing twice, and he gave Darren a fat Swiss Army knife with two dozen functions.

I didn't know why DB was in town again. I didn't know what DB's business interests really were, although, even as a kid, I knew they were probably a little bit fucked up and shady. The truth was, I didn't mind. I thought it was kind of badass.

DB was pretty nice to me too. He took extra time to show me the weightlifting stuff, because Darren didn't really care about that. DB also liked a lot of historical shit, mostly war. Same as with the weightlifting, Darren wasn't interested, so it was always me asking. I'd ask DB about Vikings and knights and things like that. DB answered all the questions. He talked about the Crusades and he talked about the samurai of Japan and he talked about tank battles in World War II. He talked about the Apache Indians of the Southwest, who were so deadly and dangerous that it took the U.S. Army to finally beat them, way back in the Western days, and he talked about the Mohawks who lived up around Altena and were some of the most skilled fighters in all of history. I listened carefully, hanging on to everything Darren's dad told me.

At the time, I couldn't imagine anybody using the same words for DB they used for my dad. You know, cocksucker and faggot. Words like that. This was a big deal. A really big deal. I don't know if you can understand that.

I'm talking about DB because I was wrong about him, okay? And it's, like, important that I get that out there. I was wrong about him. I learned that a little later, not even all that much later, after all the good stuff, the weightlifting and the Monopoly and the stories about tank battles. I learned it the day DB hired me and Darren—we were kids at the time, for fuck sake—to do a little job for him.

Paid knucklehead shit. I'll talk about it another time, but trust me when I say it was the set-up, bro. That thing in the past you remember in the present, when everything starts to go wrong around you.

Twenty-five minutes after Darren picked me up at the gym, we pulled into the King's Court Motor Inn, west of the city limits. The King's Court had one row of suites, maybe ten in all, next to a swimming pool that was either still closed from the winter or closed for good. I guessed for good. The joint did not look like it was doing well. The whitewash was peeling off the cinderblock walls and the front windows of two of the units were covered by plywood. The office was dark, and the only vehicle in the parking lot was an old station wagon. I had passed this place a million times in my life and never given it any thought.

Darren parked on the far side of the swimming pool. He told Chastity to stay with the car. She gave him a look, one I couldn't really make sense of, but she made no moves to join us.

Me and Darren and Seth got out of the car. Darren led the way, whistling as he walked. If the cold bothered him in his polo shirt, he didn't let on. The rain had quit and the smell of wet pavement was heavy on the air. Traffic on the road beside the motel was almost dead. That suited me fine.

The suite on the far left side of the row had the metal numbers *01* screwed onto the door. The blinds were all the way down in the window, but there was some kind of on-again off-again music coming from the inside. Broken riffs of electric guitar. Darren pressed his eyes to the window, cupping the sides of his face with his hands to block out the daylight. He started to say something, but before he got out more than two words, Seth pounded on the door with his fist.

Little pig, little pig, said Seth.

Go easy, said Darren. Junior's alright.

There was a moment of silence. Then the guitar started up again. Seth pounded the door twice more. I looked back over the barren parking lot and the swimming pool. Darren's car looked far away. Chastity couldn't be seen.

The door opened an inch. A voice from behind it said, Ahh . . .

Hey, Junior, said Darren.

We're coming in, said Seth.

Seth shouldered the door open and entered. The voice said, Ahh . . . Okay, okay.

Darren and I followed. I closed the door behind us. The suite we were in was bigger than it looked from the outside, big enough for two queen-sized beds and a kitchenette and a small sitting area. It had been lived in for a while, and not real cleanly. There were clothes all over the floor and furniture, two stacks of dishes jammed into the sink, and an aquarium full of dark green water sitting on one of the dressers. The smells of the room hit me hard. Dirty B.O., but something else too. Kind of a chemical smell. It reminded me of that burning porta-potty, the strong stink of melting plastic.

The man who'd opened the door was tall and skinny, maybe thirty years old, with lank hair and a narrow face and bad skin. There was a hairy brown birthmark next to one of his eyes. He stood in the middle of the room, shifting from foot to foot. He was wearing grimy sweatpants and a T-shirt. Behind him, on one of the beds, was an electric guitar attached to a small amplifier sitting on the floor.

Darren, said the man. What brings you guys out here?

Come on, Junior, said Darren. Don't be a dumb-ass.

Seth sat down on the end of one of the beds. He looked around the room and said, Fuck, it reeks in here.

Not far from the suite's front door was a television, propped up on a metal stand. On top of the television was a large square of tinfoil. Sitting on the tinfoil was a light bulb. A plastic straw had been snaked through the top of the light bulb and secured with duct tape.

This isn't the way you were supposed to be doing things, said Darren. You're the retailer.

I know, said Junior. I know.

He sounded miserable. Almost like he was about to cry. I didn't want him to. Crying, that kind of weakness out in the open, really made me uncomfortable.

So how much is even left? said Darren.

I was still looking at the light bulb. There was a dark patch in the glass. Something had been burned inside of it. Beside the light bulb were two or three little plastic pouches, each with a cartoon elf printed on them. I had this urge, out of nowhere, to reach out and pick one up. I resisted. Fingerprints, bro, for one thing, and for another thing, I didn't like how anything in that room felt.

The thing is, okay? said Junior. The thing is—

Seth said, The thing is an ounce, you dirty fucking door-knobber—

The door not far from the kitchenette—I hadn't even paid attention to it—clapped open and a woman busted out, wide eyes, wide mouth, hair all fucked up, half again as skinny as Junior. She was in her late fifties at least, and in both hands above her head she held a clothes iron. The cord was flapping behind her. There was no way of knowing if the iron was hot or not, but I could feel every inch of exposed skin on my body.

The woman cried, You assholes!

I flattened myself against the wall. She came to a stop beside Junior, bringing the iron down and thrusting it out in front of her. Seth jumped off the bed and crowded in next to me. Darren was backing away too, and reaching one hand around to the small of his back as if he had an itch to scratch just above his ass.

He said, Norma, what are you doing?

The woman cried, You assholes! I'll burn you alive, I swear to Jesus. How about it?

Junior blocked her with his arm. He said, It's okay. Listen.

How about it, how about it? said the woman, staring directly at me. You think you're so big and tough, boy? You want to get burned alive?

Jesus, bro, I said to Junior. Is your mother crazy or what?

Mother? she screamed, and she lunged forward. Junior's arm did not even slow her down, but in one stride she'd either lost her balance or tripped on something. She fell forward into me and Seth. Seth managed to bat the iron aside with his hand, but he let out a yelp. The woman writhed against us, both her hands free now, clawing and cursing and trying to bite. She smelled terrible. I couldn't believe this was happening. I managed to grab each of her wrists, but she wrenched her arms back and forth. She was ten times stronger than she looked, and way stronger than any young gal I might kick out of the Balmoral. I felt a dangerous twitch all through my own arms, still repped out from the gym. The woman gnashed her teeth at me.

But then Junior was on her from behind, whispering in her ear, pulling her backwards. He managed to break her free from me. She gave me a last half-hearted kick, and then Junior had yanked her to the sitting area.

Junior had this real scared expression, directed not at the woman, and not at me or Seth, but at Darren. He said, You don't need that.

I looked over. I saw the little gun in Darren's hand. It was canted sideways and pointed at Junior and the woman. Darren said, Knock it the hell off, Junior. Jesus fucking Christ.

It's okay, said Junior. It's okay. No more trouble.

Norma, said Darren. Are you paying attention?

I'll burn you alive, said the woman.

I'll take that as a yes, said Darren. Listen up. We're going to talk about what you owe. And that's all we're going to talk about, because I'm done doing business with you. You're blacklisted. I didn't want it to go this way, Junior, but that's on you.

IT WAS A STRANGE WALK BACK ACROSS THE PARKING LOT. Darren was doing another count of the greasy bundle of cash

Junior had scraped together for him. Just over six hundred dollars, half of what was owed for the ounce he'd smoked instead of sold. Seth kept cursing and looking at his hand where he'd swatted the iron away. There was a blister, a little smaller than a dime, on the edge of his palm.

Up till that day, from what I knew, the majority of Darren's business was weed. He'd started back when we were in grade ten, and he'd been smart about it. Like, for instance he kept his profits levelled to where they wouldn't draw attention. Also he had his legit job at Pro Choice Electronics, thirty hours a week, so that all his taxes and whatever else were sorted out. He lived in his own place, this nice condo-style two-bedroom apartment with new appliances, in a quiet building where most of the other residents were retired people.

He'd told me once, about a year ago, that he'd squirrelled away close to a hundred grand. He said there was no reason not to keep going, playing it safe and smart and modest, until he had enough money to retire down to Mexico or somewhere like that, live like a king among the Amigos. He said he would take me and Chastity with him, make good on our childhood promise that we'd someday get out of Altena.

But that shit in the motel suite was not weed. It was crank, and it was apparently crank by the ounce, if what Seth had said was true. It wasn't some one-time, one-off hook-up. Worse than that, this wasn't the States, where I'd heard you could score it just about everywhere, all the time. Any sign of crank around here would draw the heat real fast. There were these two cousins, the Yoders, from the Old Order Amish community outside of Altena, who'd been picked up with three ounces of crank on the near side of the border. Even without any priors, the Yoders had drawn five-year sentences. It'd even turned into a local joke, the two bearded Amish kids having their coming-of-age in maximum security.

I'd laughed about those sorry assholes myself, but it didn't feel like a joke right now. None of it. Especially not that gun coming out. I couldn't stop picturing it in Darren's hand. I'd seen him flash a knife a few times before, and once a baseball bat, but nothing more serious. Now the gun was tucked back into the waist of his jeans and hidden underneath his shirt.

Trying to keep my voice easygoing, I said, Is it even real?

Is what real? said Darren.

The gun, bro.

He gave me a look, eyebrows raised.

I said, It's just an Airsoft, right? Like the ones they sell at Canadian Tire?

Sure it is, said Darren. You pull the trigger and a little flag pops out with *Bang!* wrote on it.

I wondered then, kind of for the first time, what side of the good guy–bad guy divide my best pal was standing on these days. I know what I'd always believed about him—that is, good guy, way down at the core, doing what he had to do to get by, same's everybody else—but I'd never figured him to be, like, dangerous.

Darren's dad was dangerous. That I knew. But Darren? His business was shady, okay, but he wasn't following in DB's shoes at all. He didn't have it in him.

So right there, right then, I pushed the thought out of my head. The gun was an Airsoft, a toy. Was all for show. And the crank was none of my business. Oh, and DB being back in town, that wasn't anything that should bother me. Nothing I should care about at all.

We walked a little farther. Darren started laughing about something. I looked at him. His mother, said Darren. His mother.

What? I said.

You thought Norma was Junior's mother.

She isn't?

True love comes in all shapes and sizes and ages, brother.

I looked down at my forearm. I'd taken a long but shallow scratch from the woman's fingernails.

It was kind of on you, wasn't it, said Seth. Everything going to hell in there.

I bit my tongue, didn't say anything.

Halfway to the car, Darren grabbed my wrist and lifted it. He stuffed some money into my hand. A hundred bucks. I closed my hand around the money and put it into my own pocket. I could feel it in there, like it had weight or heat or something.

As we passed the swimming pool, we could see Chastity leaning against the trunk of the car, smoking another dart and talking on her cell phone.

I hate when she leans on the spoiler, said Darren. Hey, baby—

She held up two fingers, the cigarette between them. Darren shut up. We were close enough now to hear what she was saying. She was talking part in English, part in Spanish. The Spanish sounded like nonsense to me, but I heard her say, in English, Never mind what Bailador said. Look, I have to go . . . No puedo hablar ahora.

Listen to her talk that wetback talk, said Seth. Cerveza puta taco, blah blah blah.

She took the phone away from her ear and folded it closed. Her face was troubled. She looked at me first and then at Darren.

What's the deal? said Darren.

He just got some bad news from home is all, said Chastity.

Who, what's-his-name, Ra—

We'll talk about it later, Darren.

Darren turned to me and said, She's still friends with a bunch of them, the Amigos. From when she was a kid, working on that farm. She can talk to them and everything, you know, more than just que pasa or olé or chinga tu madre. Hey, remember that? Chinga tu madre?

Darren, said Chastity. I told you. We'll talk about it later.

Yeah yeah, said Darren. I hear you, boss.

He went to the back of his car, gently guided Chastity away from the spoiler. He popped open the trunk. He was doing something, maybe stashing the gun. I couldn't tell for sure with the trunk-lid in the way.

Chastity came around the side. She passed me and the smell of her filled my nose. The perfume, I remembered, was called White Diamonds. It was the only kind she ever wore.

She said, Can we please just go now?

Yeah, D, I said. Let's get out of here.

Alright, said Darren, shaking his head. Let's go, you guys.

He closed the trunk. We all got back into the car, the same seats as before. I looked at Chastity again. Darren had no clue. No clue. Nobody did. Except for me and her. She met my eyes, held the stare until I broke it.

I settled forward in my seat and found Darren looking at me. He said, Thanks for helping me out today, brother.

We didn't need the extra hand, said Seth. I told you.

Shut the fuck up, Darren said softly.

FOUR

Front of the bike to the back, son. That's how you turn it.

I know that.

And it helps if you've got the ratchet set to reverse.

My dad and I were in his garage, crouched down beside my bike. I had this Ninja 500, an '01 I'd saved up for and bought new, with seventeen-inch wheels and badass custom red paint and an after-market exhaust that made the thing roar like a monster. Altena is mainly Harley country, and even my old man, back in the day, had one—a vintage knucklehead, funny enough—but I fucking loved my Ninja. Wherever it is now, bro, what's left of it . . . ah, breaks my heart to think about.

Anyways, I had a long socket wrench on the drain-plug bolt on the underside. On the floor below was a plastic jug to catch the old oil. I pulled on the wrench. The bolt was tight enough to make the veins in my forearm stand out. The scratch given to me by that crazy tweaker, Norma or whatever, was half healed. I pulled on the socket wrench harder, feeling my dad's eyes on me.

You put it back on too tight last time, he said. Doesn't have to go on so tight.

I said, Yeah, well, here it goes.

The bolt loosened. The oil began to drain out into the jug below. It was hot and free-flowing because we'd run the engine for a few minutes before we'd set to work. My dad nodded once. He had a beer in his hand. He lifted it and took a sip.

He was fifty years old, and he wasn't nearly the size he'd been when I was a little kid. I had forty pounds on him. But he was in good shape all the same. He did distance running four or five times a week and still worked the iron every couple of days.

The garage, detached from my dad's house, was big and new, with a high roof and insulated walls that kept it warm through the cold months. Each of his tools was assigned to its own spot, outlined in black marker. My dad had built the garage three years ago. He said he'd been waiting his whole life to have it.

His house was on a five-acre property out on Grace Road, away from the centre of Altena. Away from the people who lived there. My dad had never left the area completely, in spite of what had happened to him. At this point, I guessed he never would. Maybe it was like Darren had said, how Altena had a way of keeping people around no matter how things went down.

Outside the garage, the late afternoon was warm and sunny, definitely spring. I'd hammered through a leg workout before my dad had picked me up and brought me out to the house. We were going to get my bike ready for the road, then we'd have dinner.

After the old oil had slowed to a drip, I ratcheted the bolt back in, trying not to overtighten it. Me and my dad were replacing the filter when we heard a voice behind us saying, Dinner's ready in twenty-five minutes.

Greg was standing at the back door of the garage.

We'll be there, said my dad.

Greg had this face like a child's, I don't know, twenty or thirty years younger than he actually was. He always looked kind of surprised. I didn't like his face. I can't explain why. Sometimes when I looked at Greg, those old words came into my mind—faggot queer faggot faggot—whether I wanted them to or not. The same words I'd knock you the fuck out for saying about my dad.

Hello, Ashley, said Greg. I didn't see you when you got here.

Hey, I said.

Greg hung around for a little while, watching us work on the bike, and then he disappeared back to the house. I was glad to see him go.

We finished replacing the filter. Then we started to put the new 10W-40 in. My dad broke the quiet, saying, He wants to be on good terms with you, son. You know that, right?

I said, We're on fine terms. I don't know why you're worried about it.

I'm not worried, said my dad. But I know it's not easy for you. It can't be. Shit, it's not easy for us. But we live way the hell out here, and we just stopped caring a while back. That doesn't mean I'm not interested in how it affects your sister or you. Do people still give you a hard time?

I said, No, they don't. Nobody does. They all know better.

I wish that had ended when you finished high school, he said.

It is what it is, I said. Life's a battle. I'm realistic about that shit, Dad. Nobody gives me a hard time.

Hey, come on. I'll give you a hard time if you don't hold that funnel steady. Half that quart just went on the floor.

We finished up with the bike a few minutes later. My dad stood first, his knees popping as he straightened up. He set his beer bottle down on the workbench and picked up a rag and cleaned the grease off his hands.

As I went to stand up, my hamstrings cramped hard. I rocked

backwards, dropped onto my ass. I shot my legs out in front of me, kicking aside the funnel we'd been using. I grabbed and pounded at my legs, each in turn, until the cramps subsided. For a few seconds I just sat there, massaging my hamstrings, hissing. I looked up to see my dad looking at me with amusement.

He said, That was interesting.

I'll bet it was.

You been hitting the weights hard again?

Trying to get back into it.

You don't mess around with any steroids, do you?

No, Dad.

Don't try to pull one over on your old man. I knew a guy in college. He was on the wrestling team and he was experimenting with them. This was back before they were real popular, you know? Back before people knew about the side effects. Anyways, this guy, holy smokes, he was squatting a thousand pounds when he was at his prime. The bar would bend over his shoulders. Like a bow. But I'll tell you, son, it went bad for him. Kidney failure at age twenty-three. He lived, but he had to be hooked up to one of those machines, what's it called, dialysis. That's what steroids will do for you.

I said, Well, don't worry about me.

My dad laughed. He said, You can't tell me not to worry about you. It's in my contract. But if you tell me you're keeping clean, then I believe you.

IT WAS GOOD WITH ME AND MY DAD, BUT IT HADN'T ALWAYS been good. Whether my dad liked it or not, who he was had made high school a war for me. Like I told you before, grade nine, grade ten, grade eleven, grade twelve, I'd fought my way through all of them. Even after I had my growth spurt at the beginning of grade eleven, and then did my first cycle of gear and got really big, even then I still had to fight all the time. I'd hear the words as I walked in the hallway or through the cafeteria at lunch. Your dad, Ashley, homo faggot cocksucker.

I wasn't really talking to my dad at that time. I guess I still figured it was all on him that our family got broken up. But what was I going to do when people mouthed off about him? Was I supposed to back down? Where I live, bro, disrespect isn't something you can just ignore. Allowing disrespect to go unaccounted for is weakness.

I remember all the battles, it's true, god knows why I remember them all, but a few stand out more than the others. The first was in the locker room after a rugby game our team had lost. This was grade nine or early grade ten. Tom Downford, a big starting second-row, said my dad was a faggot. I was just a substitute flanker at the time, but I called Tom out. To Tom's credit he manned up, I guess not thinking much of me and maybe just wanting a scrap for the fun of it. He didn't even get a punch in before I'd put him down with one shot square in the mouth. Busted his lip wide open. I remember the spots of blood all over the white tiles of the locker room floor, Tom sitting there bleeding down his chin, looking more confused than hurt, like he couldn't figure out what the fuck had just happened. I never had a problem on the team again.

About a year after that first battle, some guys from a different school were in the cafeteria at lunch one day. They'd come to see Chastity. Something had gone down with one of them and her, god knew what, and Chass being Chass, she'd blown him off and he'd got his heart broke and blah blah blah next thing you know this guy and his buds are over at our school looking to—what?—confront her I guess, the way dumb-ass young bucks with broken hearts like to do. Anyways, I saw it happening when I came out of the meal line, and when I went over to side with her, these guys started talking shit about my dad. Oh, aren't you the dude whose dad is a fuckin' homo, et cetera, et cetera. It was strange, because I didn't know how these guys even knew my dad or knew me. Fucking small town, word gets around. Aren't you the dude whose dad blows other men at the bus station? No sooner had those words come out of buddy's mouth than Chastity smacked him right across the face, loud like a handclap. I punched out the other two, one after the other, because they were standing in, like, single file between a couple tables. Down they went. Their first friend standing there with his eyes all full of tears and a red print of Chass's hand on his cheek. Ha, what a bitch. The guy, whoever he was, not Chastity. That was the first time I ended up in the VP's office for fighting, but nobody could prove anything, nobody in the cafeteria snitched, so I got let off.

Then in grade eleven Chris Hagar and Raj Kumar both called my dad a fudge-packer. To be clear, these were separate occasions—Raj and Chris weren't friends as far as I knew—but with the same results. I called Chris out and beat his ass at that bush party. The battle with Raj went down in the school parking lot outside a dance. Raj even had a couple friends with him, but Darren jumped in on one of them and the other ran off. I have to give credit to Darren. He wasn't there for all the battles, but he always had my back when he was. He was never a big guy, but he wouldn't back down, no matter how many guys were chirping me. It definitely cost him, like, at least a couple black eyes and one chipped tooth if I remember right. But after the battles, he'd laugh about it, like it was nothing. He'd find us a joint to smoke or a drink to drink and he wouldn't bitch or moan or give me advice I didn't need.

And he never, not once, said anything disrespectful about my old man.

That's something, bro. You know? That's something I'd almost rather not even think about, kind of in light of the shit that's happened since those days.

Anyways, the last time I battled in high school happened in January of my grade twelve year, and neither Darren or Chastity was there for it. The battle went down in the school weight room. It was between me and Brian Kozak, this well-off uptown kid who'd sized out over the last year. I wouldn't have had a problem with him if he hadn't started telling me how to bench-press better.

I was on the bench press, working on my max lift, 205 pounds in those days. Not huge but not bad for a high school guy, and a bigger max than anybody else could do. I did a couple single-rep sets and then rested. And then Brian Kozak, doing some biceps curls, asked me if I wanted advice on how to do a more efficient bench-press. He said it was all in the breathing and the posture. I asked him what was he, some kind of expert? I'd been pumping iron for three years at that time. Brian had been doing it for, what, five or six months? Brian said that didn't mean he hadn't learned the technical science of it, and that I could benefit from his knowledge. I shook my head and told him no thanks, no offence, but I wasn't interested. There wasn't a teacher supervising in the weight room at the time, but the two or three other guys present were starting to pay attention, which pissed me off. I didn't like being examined. So I got off the bench and went over to do a set of squats, hoping Brian would leave it there.

But then Brian said, I guess not taking advice runs in your family.

I said, What do you mean?

And Brian said, Because obviously your dad doesn't take advice either, otherwise he would've moved away a long time ago.

Looking back, I think Brian wanted it. He'd sized out over the summer and he wanted to try it on. That comes when you fight your way to the top of the hill, you know? Like it's one thing to get up there, but you also got to stay up there. You'll have your challengers, bro. I did. Brian Kozak, perfect example. He wasn't a complete pussy, either. As we got going he caught me with a punch that blackened my eye for a few days. Took me by surprise, if I'm honest, and I might've even had a half-chance of losing it right there, but Brian, I think, was just as surprised that he'd landed it. So I hip-tossed him to the weight room floor and got on top of his chest and punched him in the mouth a couple times. I held him in a chokehold until he, like, verbally admitted that he was giving up the fight. Saying uncle. Then I made him take back what he'd said about my dad. That was it.

I went about my business in peace for two weeks after that. I didn't see Brian Kozak in the weight room, and I didn't give him much thought. My black eye faded. Purple to yellow to nothing. But then one day I got called down to the VP's office.

Yet again, Mr. Rosco, said the VP, I have a problem to which your name connects.

My name, sir?

Yes. There's a student who reports that you assaulted him in the weight room not long ago. He has witnesses. And his parents are seriously considering pressing charges.

I couldn't think of anything to say. Brian Kozak had snitched. Had gone running to the VP like some whiny little punk.

You know what I'm starting to believe about you, Mr. Rosco? said the VP.

I don't have any idea, sir.

I believe you are a bully.

A bully. For standing my ground, fighting my battles, fair and straight-up. I didn't say how it really went down, what Brian had said to antagonize me, because it wouldn't've made any sense to someone like the VP. I just took the written warning I was given, which the VP said was the last before serious action would follow. He never said what that serious action would be, but he did tell me he'd called my dad to discuss the problem. I wanted to jump over the desk and pound in the VP's face when he said that. Talking to my dad about my problems was not up to the VP or anybody else. It was my business and my business alone.

Bully. The word kept repeating in my mind. A bully is a cowardly motherfucker who picks on weaker people for no real reason, other than they can't fight back, so it's a guaranteed win without really having to put nothing up. Yes, I am a battler when the cause is there, when it's honourable and when respect is at stake, but no, I am not, and never was, a goddamn bully.

But . . . Pissed off as I was, the way things worked out, the VP's call was the start of my dad getting back into my life. It wasn't easy. It was hard as hell at first. But it was a beginning.

It was too cold for supper in the backyard, so we ate in the dining room. Me, my sister, Lori, her husband, Ben, and my dad and Greg. Supper was beef medallions wrapped in bacon and a green salad, the kind of meal you see in one of those house-and-home magazines. That was Greg's kind of thing, trying to class everything up a little. College teacher or not, queer or not, my old man still drank beer and watched Sunday football and wore his hat at the table, no matter how much Greg busted his balls about it. Not that Greg should have been worried about classing shit up either—I know the shirts and ties he wore were the kind you bought pre-packaged together for, like, twenty bucks in the discount menswear store. Uptowners, bro, we were not, and never would be.

Also on the table that night was this good homemade corn-bread that Lori had brought over. She was six months pregnant, had gained a bunch of extra weight. She and Ben lived in London, not far from where our mother had ended up, four years ago, at the end of her divorce from my dad. Since then, our family had managed this kind of working balance. Back in high school, I wouldn't't've believed it was possible, but things have a way of moving on, I've learned. Things evolve, change over time. That was about the only thing you can count on.

We passed the platters of food around the table. Two tender-loins had been cooked for me, on account of all the extra food I needed to eat day to day. I unloaded them onto my plate and dug in. Down the table, Lori was talking about this stage in her pregnancy. She said the baby was kicking a lot. She said she and Ben had signed up for a birth class, which was to start the following week. She said her skin itched, her head ached, her back ached, and she was bunged up a lot of the time. Each of these things she said in this upbeat way, as if they made her happy. Maybe they did. She kept repeating how it was real now, it was really real. My dad and Greg listened close to everything she said. At one point Lori told them they were going to be great granddads. They didn't reply, but they did hold each other's hands on the tabletop.

I felt a sharp twist in my gut. I had to look away. I met Ben's eyes across the table, but same as ever I couldn't read him. Ben was a quiet dude. He would usually get totally silent whenever Lori started blabbing on about something. I wondered if Ben was okay with this, the idea of his son or daughter having two granddads who lived together, who were . . .

You're zoned right the hell out, aren't you? said Lori.

I looked at my sister. What?

I said you're zoned right out, brother. You're not even here.

Oh. No, I'm here.

You looked kind of pale there for a minute, said Lori. I thought you were choking on something.

Nope, I said.

So how's it going, anyways? I haven't even talked to you for like a month.

I'm good, I said. Really. Nothing much is going on. You know what I mean? Everything is the status quote right now.

The status quote? said Greg.

Yeah, you know. Normal.

Greg smiled and said, I think you mean the status quo, Ash.

I felt my cheeks burn. I said, Sure. Whatever. What's a quo, anyways?

I couldn't help it, my eyes drifted down to my dad's and Greg's hands, still together on the tabletop. My dad slipped his away, apparently to lift his beer.

Still working at the club? said Lori.

I nodded. I am, I said. It's getting busy again. It'll be crazy in the summer.

And are you gonna try college in September, or what?

I don't know, Lori. I don't really know. But I'll figure it out soon.

When? said Lori.

Soon, okay?

Have you been seeing much of Darren and Chass? said my dad.

My food went down rough and I coughed against it. I hoped none of them noticed. I see them a bit, I said. They're doing okay. Status quo for them too, I guess.

Let me guess, said Lori. Chastity has decided to become,

what, a kindergarten teacher? And Darren, how's med school treating him?

I said, Screw off, Lori. You don't give anybody a chance.

Hey, I just call it like I see it. Darren's a skid, Ashley. Honestly.

Go easy, Lori, said my dad. Darren's okay. He's had a rough go, but he made out okay. He's always real pleasant to me if I see him. Me and Greg both.

Chastity is a right little bitch though, said Lori. You have to admit that much. White trash. And the apple doesn't fall far from the tree, right? When's the last time you heard from Aunt Glenna?

A long time, said my dad, looking down at his plate.

I bit my tongue. I didn't want to talk about Chastity. Since I'd seen her with Darren, she'd been back on my mind constantly. I had thought I'd got past it all, but I hadn't. All those feelings, the hot stuff and the fun and the panic and the guilt, all those feelings were digging right into me, worse than ever.

Lori was saying, I'm telling you, Dad, when this kid is born, I'm not even gonna tell him, ever, about that side of our family—

Maybe, said Greg, we should change the subject?

There's a damn good idea, said Ben.

Everybody looked at him. In my company, those were the most words Ben had ever said at once. I glanced at him, maybe to share a nod, like the kind between two allies, but he'd already gone back to his meal.

AFTER SUPPER THERE WAS DESSERT AND COFFEE. LORI AND Ben left at seven o'clock. Ben gave me a quick handshake, the same thing he gave me every time we said hello or goodbye to each other. Lori hugged me and kissed me on the cheek and said she was sorry if I thought she'd been busting my chops too much. She said she just wanted me to do right for myself.

I got ready to leave ten minutes later. I went into the kitchen first, where Greg was loading the dishwasher. Every couple dishes he would stop and sip a cup of coffee. I told him so long and thanks for the good meal.

Greg turned and for a few seconds looked at me. He picked up his coffee cup and held it below his chin. Then he said, It's good to have you out here, Ashley. Your dad loves seeing you. I do too. You're not even far away from us, so let's try to do this more often, yeah?

Faggot faggot faggot, I thought. I smiled and nodded and said, Yeah, that sounds good. Well, I'll see you.

Before you go, said Greg, there's two things I didn't get a chance to talk to you about at the table.

What's up?

Well, first thing is a favour, I suppose, but sometime soon would you show me a few things in the gym? I need to start getting back into shape.

I nodded, said no problem, knowing already how much I hated the idea of being with Greg at the gym. The gym was my territory. Why did Greg have to screw around with that?

The other thing is kind of a job opportunity, said Greg.

I said, A job opportunity.

Yeah. A good friend of mine owns a custodial services company. He's always looking for reliable guys. There's benefits, vacation time. It won't make you rich but it's steady. He said he'd be happy to hear from you if you give him a call.

Custodial services, I said. That's, what, janitor work?

Well, that's definitely one way of putting it, said Greg.

I was about to say one thing but I thought better of it, and instead I said, I'll give it some thought. Okay?

Sure, said Greg.

Faggot, said my brain.

I went to the front door. My dad was just coming from the bathroom off the vestibule. We went together out to the garage. The sky had stayed clear and was heading toward last light. The days were getting longer. It was a good thing to see.

In the back of the garage was a storage locker where my dad had stored my riding gear, my helmet, gloves and padded jacket. I slipped the jacket on. I hadn't worn it since the previous fall, right around the time I was in the final work-up stages for the D'Amours Classic. Now I winced at the way the jacket felt loose in the shoulders and tight across the gut.

I guess it's too much to ask you to buy something brighter, said my dad.

I'll be fine.

The black jacket and the black helmet don't show up so good after dark, son.

I'll be fine, Dad. People can see the bike. And if they can't, they're blind and shouldn't be driving anyways.

More your problem than theirs, don't you think?

I will be fine, I said. For real.

We walked the bike out to the driveway. I was eager to climb onto it and start riding. I started to say goodbye, but my dad interrupted me. He said, Ashley, I don't want you to think we're on your case.

I said, Who's we? You and Greg?

No, son. Me and your mom. Believe it or not, we talk pretty often. There's not much that'll ever be fixed between us, as I'm sure is pretty goddamn obvious by now, but we do share a lot about our kids. We have to. Your mom is worried about you. Which you know.

She's just overreacting, I said. Things are okay with me.

Well, to be honest, I'm worried about you too. At least a little bit. I'm worried that you've maybe got yourself stuck in a loop here, and you can't really see your way out. And it happens. It happens. I know. I was there too a few times in my life.

I'm figuring things out, I said. That's all.

Sometimes a guy needs help figuring things out. Did Greg talk to you about his buddy's outfit?

You mean the janitor job?

My dad's eyes narrowed. His mouth took on the shape of a weird little not-quite smile. He said, For your information, my son, it's a good job. Not too heavy on the hours, full benefits, vacation time. Greg's friend started out on the crew, same as anybody else. Now he owns his own house and he goes to the Caribbean once a year. So don't be so quick to turn up your nose just because you might get your hands dirty.

I said, A janitor, Dad. Shit.

My dad inhaled, and then shook his head. He said, Look, just an option, okay? Something with a little more security than working the door at the nightclub. That's all. Can you give it some thought for your old man?

Yes, I can give it some thought.

That's all I can ask for. And the steroids too. Don't muck around with those. Okay?

Okay, Dad. God.

Okay. Enough of all the serious talk. Get home safe. Say hi to Darren and Chastity if you see them.

I will, I said.

My dad gave me a quick hug. Then I put on my helmet and mounted my bike and started it. I flashed him a wave and navigated out of the driveway.

I waited until I was at least half a klick away from the house to really open the bike up. The speedometer soared up to 140 kilometres per hour, and my head spun with that feeling, the one that has no name. It can only come from going real fast, being totally free for just that one moment in time. Maybe you know that feeling, maybe you don't. Anyways.

FIVE

So, sometimes the cops would come into the club, maybe once a month. They'd come in and they'd poke around, make sure nobody was drinking underage or finger-banging on the dance floor or slinging dope in the bathroom or was otherwise fucked up or fucking something up.

I was patrolling near the dance floor when I saw them. Their badges and handcuffs and belt buckles reflected the purple spotlights. One was a cop I'd never seen before. The other was a lady cop, Constable Casey, a regular face in this part of town. They were with the manager, Marcel. He was showing them around the bar. They were shining their little flashlights into the darker corners and on shelves and in the space underneath the cash register.

Chances were the cops wouldn't find anything. After all, me and the other guys on the security crew ran a pretty tight professional operation. The cops just liked to make their presence known, liked to do community relations. That was what the lady cop, Constable Casey, called it.

I watched. I didn't like cops at all, which I bet doesn't surprise you. Yeah, laugh all you want. I'd ended up in the drunk tank once when I was twenty, and I'd been stopped on the street or at house parties a few times, but I'd never had serious trouble—never mind the shit I did for Darren occasionally. Still, I'd interacted with the cops more than once in the course of my job, usually whenever I had to eject a patron who wouldn't go quietly. We'd get those kinds of guys out to the street and the cops would take it from there. Having seen the way they handled those late-night pickups, I'd come to believe the cops were mostly gorillas too, same as me. Gorillas with the courts and the lawyers and the whole system behind them.

The cops left the bar and did a circuit of the dance floor, Marcel following at their heels. The people dancing all made room. A minute later the cops appeared to be on their way back to the front door. Then they stopped in front of me.

Remind me, said Constable Casey.

Ashley, I said.

Right, Ashley. How you doing tonight, Ashley? All good?

Yeah, everything's cool. What are you guys up to?

Oh, you know. Community relations.

Despite how I felt about most cops, I thought Casey was okay. Maybe lady cops are calmer or something. The other cop with her, though, was the kind that loved to be working on Saturday nights. Big, trouble-hungry–looking, the kind who wanted a bar fight to spill out onto the street. I could feel this guy sizing me up. I didn't bother making eye contact. I didn't want the asshole to have the satisfaction.

Casey shined her flashlight around my feet. At least she didn't shine it in my face. Then she turned it off and said, Well, stay safe tonight. If you have any problems, you know where to find us.

She and the other cop passed me by. Marcel hung back. He clapped me on the arm and said, Don't mind them, big guy. You just keep doing what you're doing.

JUST BEFORE LAST CALL, I FELT MY CELL PHONE VIBRATING in my pocket. I took it out and saw Chastity's name on the display. I paused for a second, feeling heavy. She hadn't called me since December. A lifetime ago.

I answered. Chass? I said. I'm inside the club. The music's loud. Hold on a second.

I moved across the dance floor and went down onto the club's lower patio, where I wouldn't be visible—talking on my phone—if Marcel came back out of the office. The crowd on the patio was just starting to thin out, but there were still forty or fifty people in small groups, smoking darts and talking and laughing. Past the patio, a single cop car was parked up the street a little ways, maybe Constable Casey and her pal. In the other direction, the usual group of lost-looking Amigos was hanging around their sidewalk bench.

I leaned on the rail at the edge of the patio. I looked at my phone. The counter on the display was ticking, showing forty-five seconds since I'd answered. The call was still connected. She hadn't hung up. I'd halfway—more than halfway—thought she would.

I put the phone to my ear and said her name. On the other end, her voice was hard to hear. I had to pay real close attention to it. She said my name twice.

I said, What do you want?

There were a few seconds of dead air before she spoke, and when she did, her words were still broken. She said, . . . just have . . . leave . . . I tried . . . to Cesar, but he . . .

I can't hear what you're saying, Chass.

She said, I fucked up.

What do you mean, you fucked up?

And then, totally clear, she said, Before I go, I have to make it right. And, I don't know, I thought maybe you could help me.

I closed my eyes. I leaned harder on the rail. She said my name again.

I said, I haven't heard from you in months. You know that, right? And remember what you told me the last time? How you don't need my help? How nobody needs my help? You remember that?

Out of the corner of my eye, I saw TJ Lemay come out onto the patio. He started clearing the patrons out. He looked at me and pointed to his watch. I held up my finger.

Ashley, said Chastity.

No, I said. Look. I don't know what you're up to, and I don't want to know. It was fucked up enough when you came out with Darren the other day, but like I said, I don't want to know. You told me you don't need my help, ever again, and that was the last time I heard a goddamn thing from you. So no. You're on your own, Chass. Sorry.

The words were good and strong. The words were everything I'd been waiting to say to her. You ever get a moment like that, bro? A moment to, like, take your stand, say your piece? It's one to remember, isn't it.

Ash, said TJ.

I nodded to show I was coming. TJ shook his head and turned to tell a girl she had to finish up her drink and start moving toward the exit.

Do you get me? I said into my phone.

I heard Chastity breathe out through her nose. I'd seen her do that a bunch of times before. It meant she was angry, on the edge of lashing out. Good. Let her be angry. Let her lash out—and what would she say for herself?

But she didn't say anything. She just hung up.

I GUESS BY NOW YOU'VE FIGURED IT OUT. SO ONE WAY OR THE other, here it is, straight-up, me admitting it. Chastity and I have some history.

Here's how it started. It was last October, a Saturday night. The D'Amours Classic.

First clear thing I remember about that night, looking back on it now, was hearing my name over the PA system, then coming out onto the stage, half blinded by the spotlights. The song I'd picked and given to the organizers ahead of time was howling out of the speakers. Fuck the judges, I was thinking. Finish strong. It's all I had left.

I moved to the front of the stage, able to make out only the edges of the faces in the audience. Just as well. I didn't really want to see the people who were seeing me. There was clapping, there was applause, but it was hard to hear over my music.

I struck my first pose, front double biceps flex.

The top three athletes had already been announced earlier that afternoon. I wasn't one of them, like I told you, but I still had my final posing routine to do. Everybody got a chance to do that—a final routine. Doesn't matter if you place or not, the organizers said. You still get to finish on a positive note. Bullshit.

I posed side chest, then back lat spread.

My skin was tanning-bed bronzed and covered with posing oil. I'd bought the cheaper stuff and was regretting it, hating the way it felt on me. My chest and legs and armpits were completely shaved, and the shorts I was wearing were tiny. I'd done a hundred push-ups backstage before my final routine, and my muscles were all bulging. Fully striated, bro, just the way you want them to be when you go up under the spotlights. I weighed exactly 205 pounds, and had never before been this perfect.

But not perfect enough to place top three.

I posed side triceps. The spotlights were hot. The oil on my skin felt like it was boiling.

The show was being held in a big event room in a hotel in downtown Toronto, over a cold weekend. I'd registered in the spring, had started training hard right away. Everything had come to this, and I'd failed. I didn't yet know if I was heartbroken or fucking furious.

Failing to place at the regionals meant I couldn't go on to the provincials, not this year. Even now, on stage, I was sorting through what I might've done wrong. Maybe my earlier poses hadn't been good enough. I'd cycled off my gear a month before, early enough to not test positive, but maybe too soon. Maybe I'd lost just that much size and shape.

I struck my final pose, front abdominal-thigh isolation. My abs stood out hard. Before I exited the stage I took a final look at the half-visible crowd. There was only one person out there I knew, one person who had come to the show with me, one person who'd witnessed the whole goddamn disappointment.

Chastity.

LATER THAT NIGHT I WAS DRINKING AND EATING IN THE bar of the hotel where me and Chass were staying. It was not the same hotel as the show, where most of the athletes and the people they'd brought had rented rooms, since I wasn't able to afford the rates there. I was just as happy to be away from it all anyways.

I was knocking down chicken wings and french fries, chasing the food with beer. All the things I'd obsessively avoided for the three months leading up to the show. Chastity watched me with amusement, eyebrows lifted, until I asked her if the sight of me stuffing my face bothered her. She said it didn't bother her at all, she liked to see a big man eat a big meal. She said she didn't do self-denial, and she took a salty french fry from the basket and grinned as she ate it and washed it down with a mouthful of my beer. Then she ordered us a round of vodka shots, two each. We were in the city, she said, and we were gonna go dancing.

The shots came. She passed me my two. We clinked the little glasses together and tipped them back, one after the other, without a pause. The vodka burned my throat and hit my head hard. But it was good. Being alone with Chastity was better than anything I could think of, almost enough to fix my disappointment about the show.

It wasn't supposed to have been just the two of us. My dad had wanted to come, but he had previous plans with Greg's family. Darren was also supposed to have been with us, but had had to bail at the last minute. Business issues, he'd said, and he was sorry as fuck he wouldn't be able to make it. He'd be there in, like, spirit, he said. And then he told me to kill the show, and he told Chastity to take a million pictures. He was supposed to have driven, too, so at least he'd loaned us his car.

Chastity was happy to come, even without anyone else. She didn't get to the city much, and there were some stores she wanted to visit.

We had a few more drinks. She helped me with the food. We talked about Altena and the people we knew, but Darren's name didn't come up. Me and Chass both seemed to be avoiding him as a topic. Weird.

After a little while, looking away, she said, I don't know if you know this, Ash, but I've been seeing Nevaeh. I've seen her three times since the summer.

Nevaeh. Chass's daughter. This was something I hadn't heard Chastity talk about in a long time. I didn't say anything.

Chastity lifted one of the last fries out of the basket, but then she put it back down. She went on, telling me she didn't want to make it public knowledge to everybody, because, as I knew, people loved to talk and draw all kinds of conclusions. Anyways, she said, she'd spent three afternoons with Nevaeh at the house in Chatham where her mom and dad lived.

I got a little tense. Her family was my family, in the extended way, but I didn't see them much. It was hard for me to deal with how Aunt Glenna had treated my dad when he was outed. Glenna hadn't been any better to Chastity, either, when Chass had got knocked up at eighteen, right when we were all finishing grade twelve.

It wasn't a simple situation. I mean, when is it ever? The guy who'd got Chass pregnant was named Adam—this was well before Chass and Darren hooked up. Adam was a bass player in an Aerosmith cover band from Windsor, but that was the only good thing about him. He was otherwise lazy, didn't have a day job and was addicted to painkillers, percs and oxys and some others. Hillbilly heroin, bro. Before long, Chastity was on them too. I don't know much about pregnancy and babies, but I do know you're not supposed to be popping 150 mg of oxys a day when you're, like, in the family way. Nevaeh was born two months before she was supposed to.

What happened after that was Aunt Glenna got custody of the kid pretty quick. Chass was another full year or more getting clean, and by the time she did, Nevaeh's dad had split out West somewhere. I don't believe anybody heard much from him after that. Big surprise, right? Certain guys can run away just as fast as they can blow their load and knock a gal up, but that's all besides the point.

Since Nevaeh was born, Chastity's relationship with her mom had been on and off. Mostly off, as far as I knew. The two of them were known to have huge fights from time to time. A couple years ago, Darren told me about how he'd been with Chass when they'd run into Glenna at a grocery store. Chass and her mom had got into it somehow, over god knows what, and their fight ranged from yelling to throwing things to all-out punches. It changed a little every time Darren told it, but I could believe any of the possibilities.

Carefully, I said, So, does this mean things are alright with you and your mom?

We're . . . okay, said Chastity. We're okay. I mean, it's for Nevy, right? That's what it's all about. My mom and me, we both get that, I think. She's a strong woman, Ash. I've gotta give her that credit. I just wish she could see the good in people more. Like your dad, you know? Her own brother. That was a mistake, but I don't know if she'll ever realize it.

It is what it is, I said. I'm just glad you get to see Nevaeh again. You're . . . you'd be a good mom. She deserves you.

You know what she calls me? Auntie Chastity. My little girl. She calls me Auntie.

But it's a start, right?

Yes. It's a start. Come on, big man. Enough of all this. You're gonna take me dancing now.

WAY LATER, I WOKE UP IN MY HOTEL ROOM. IT WAS FIVE o'clock in the morning and still dark. I was sobering up and it hurt. Bad. I stumbled into the bathroom and poured myself a glass of water and sucked it down.

Coming out of the bathroom, I realized I hadn't just dreamed it. It had happened, with her, and it couldn't be taken back.

We'd gone to a big nightclub. Some three-storeyed place that made the Balmoral look like a shitty, small-town dive bar—which I guess was pretty accurate. The security crew there had been at least two dozen strong, all of them huge black guys in suits. Me and Chastity danced and drank and danced, and I kept away any guys who circled too close to her, and she laughed. She put her arms around my neck and kissed my cheek and rubbed her hips against mine. She did this like a tease, you know, all in good fun. She laughed about it and I'd laughed too.

We were falling-down drunk by the time we left that club and took a taxi back to the hotel. When we got off the elevator on my floor, she followed me. She said if a room was going to be trashed, it would be mine, not hers.

We smoked some darts. We gossiped and we confessed some of the Altena people we'd slept with over the years. There wasn't any talk about Darren or Chastity's mother or Nevaeh or my dad. Chass had a little coke in her purse. We shared it, bumping it off her credit card. I hadn't done any coke in a long time, and it made me feel powerful enough to show her how many clapping push-ups I could do, or how I could lift her up with my one arm fully extended. She told me the show judges were obviously fucking idiots not to have placed me top three. Fucking idiots.

How things had gone from there, I couldn't quite recall. There'd been more talking, and another bump or two of coke, and then she stood up and pulled off her shirt to show me the new bra she was wearing, which she'd bought at the Eaton Centre earlier that day. The bra was black and lacy, and she wanted to know how cute I thought it was.

Then I took my own shirt off, laughing while I did it. She told me again what idiots the judges had been, couldn't they see what she saw, couldn't they see the perfection of my body, and she was saying this with a hand pressed flat on my stomach, low, just above my belt buckle, and the next thing I knew our clothes were off and her legs were around me and it was happening.

Later, after I came out of the bathroom, sobering up, realizing that it was real, I sat down on the edge of the bed and looked at my cousin's naked back. It was pale and thin and beautiful. I reached out and touched her. I ran my finger down her spine.

I wasn't ashamed about this. I didn't feel any guilt. All I felt was that nothing else mattered. I felt like I'd waited my whole life for this.

THE MORNING AFTER WAS DIFFERENT, WHICH ANYBODY could've predicted. At nine o'clock I woke up and saw Chastity dressing. I was looking at her back again, as I had during the night. She was re-clasping the new bra she'd shown me. I didn't say anything, and a minute or two later, she was slipping out the door and easing it closed behind her. I had no idea if she'd known I was awake or not.

At ten we met for breakfast in the hotel bar. We didn't talk much more than to say how hungover we both were. But Chastity still looked good. She'd showered and put on clean clothes and makeup. I'd also showered, and I'd put on track pants and my hoodie, but I could still smell booze coming out of my skin. I felt sick. I wanted to reach across the table and touch her face, but now there was doubt about it. I guess it was the reality of the situation settling in.

The drive back to Altena was just as quiet as breakfast. We stopped for a while at an outlet mall so she could look at a shoe store she liked. As she tried on a pair of leather boots, I hung around nearby, getting real uncomfortable. Thoughts of Darren had started to come to me. With the thoughts came the guilt. It was bad, bro, the guilt. As bad as you'd think. All those years we'd known each other, me and D, all those battles where he'd had my back, all those times he'd called me brother. It was burning me up, but it was made worse, somehow, for knowing I wouldn't take anything back. That I'd do it again without any hesitation at all. I looked at Chastity sliding one of those leather boots off her foot and I felt like the floor was dropping out from beneath me.

On the second part of our drive, I fell asleep for a while. I had a bad dream, but it didn't have any real shape or size or whatever. Then I woke up to the radio, to Chastity quietly singing along. She had a dart going and the window partway down. The air coming in was cold but it was good. It smelled like the fall, and it helped my headache.

For a while I just sat there, not saying anything, coming back to life a bit at a time. Then I realized Chass was taking sideways glimpses of me as she drove. When I met her eyes she asked me how I was feeling. I said I would survive.

She said, I mean, how's your pride?

How's my pride?

Don't be dense, bucko.

I said, If you mean the competition, I'm fine. I'll be fine. Fuck 'em.

That's right. You got nothing to regret about it, Ash. You worked your ass off, you got up on stage, put your money where your mouth is, you got nothing to regret. I'm proud of you irregardless.

She let the window down a little lower and pitched her dart out onto the highway. I took a chance then. I reached out and put my hand on her thigh. It was a quick move, and as soon as I did it I knew it was all wrong. But she was cool about it. She was, like, gentle. She reached down and squeezed my hand and held on for a couple of seconds, and then she lightly pushed my hand away.

She said, You know what you mean to me, right? You know you're the only one in my whole life who gets me, right?

I am?

Yeah, you are. I don't know why, but you are. You always were. Even Darren doesn't really get me. He's always thinking about other things, which is what it takes to do what he does, I guess, but . . . Anyways.

I said, Okay.

So I just need you to understand. Where we're at, you and me, and where we can be and where we can't be and everything else. Okay?

Okay.

I didn't really understand. All I knew was how much this hurt, whatever it was.

We weren't too far from home. The rest of the ride passed in silence, except for the radio, which she'd turned up. Pop song after pop song, the same shit they play at the club, cut with commercial breaks and some jackass DJ.

Chastity took me directly to Trey's place. I got out of the car and got my suitcase from the trunk. I was about to head inside when I heard her voice, calling me back to the driver's side window. I went. She told me she'd had a good time and thanks for bringing her along. She said we needed to get out of Altena more often. Then she told me to just keep on keeping on, the best way I knew how, and not let anyone stop me. She pulled me close and kissed me on the cheek, the same way she had a million times before, and then she backed up Darren's car and turned onto the street and drove away.

SIX

Early Sunday morning, my phone woke me up, vibrating on the floor beside my mattress. It took a while for me to come around, to know what was happening. It was early, two, even three, solid hours before I would've been getting out of bed. Coming awake, you never quite know what's what. I didn't know how long the phone had been buzzing. Ten seconds? A minute? I blinked at my alarm clock: 8:26.

I rolled over and picked up my phone. I was doing this more eagerly than I wanted to. The display said *Unknown*. That could mean anything. Anyone. I answered.

On the other end was Darren's voice, not Chastity's. He said, Ash, you awake?

I said his name, rubbing my eyes.

Shit, I'm glad I got you.

It's early, D—

He said, I'm at the fucking hospital.

I propped myself up on my elbows, more awake now, and said, What?

Yeah, said Darren. I'm at the hospital. I've been here over-night. My fucking car, Ash . . . Last night.

Jesus. What the hell happened? Was Chastity with you?

No, it was just me. One minute I'm driving, the next minute I'm spinning out like crazy, right? And I almost hit this fucking tree, but I didn't, but I did go down into the ditch, on the side of the fucking car. I don't know. I have no idea how it happened. This was around two-thirty. Some people in a car behind me, they saw it happen, and they called 911 and everything, so I got put up in the hospital overnight, for, like, observation, because I hit my head, but not bad, but enough to bleed, which of course made every-body lose their shit. And of course the car had to get towed . . .

I said, Were you drunk?

What? No. No, Ash. I swear to fucking god. Sober as anything. Legitimately. But the cops want to interview me sometime today. I can't get out of here till they do, which is why I'm calling you, waking you up, which . . . I'm sorry, but it's why I'm calling you.

I said, Slow down, Darren. Jesus Christ, I can't even think straight yet. Slow down.

Sorry, brother.

Okay. So what do you need?

I need a favour, okay?

BEFORE I LEFT TREY'S PLACE, I MANAGED TO EAT A BREAK-fast of instant oatmeal and five hard-boiled eggs and a protein shake, and then I took my gear, and then I had a long shower. I hoped the shower would wake me up from the few hours of sleep I'd had, but by the time I got to the hospital an hour later my eyes were still burning and my head was all over the place.

I went in through the visitor entrance. There was a lady in a little white booth behind a glass window. She told me where Darren's room was, up on the third floor.

When I turned away from the lady, I saw a couple of Amigos waiting behind me. They crowded up to the booth as I stepped away from it, and I heard one of them talking to the lady in broken English. Each had a ball cap in his hands. One of them was short. The other was tall, especially for an Amigo, and good-looking, with dark eyes and shining black hair.

Eight months of the year, the Amigos were all over town. Certain people got to know them pretty good, like Chastity, who'd worked with them out on the farm, but I could count on one hand the number of times I'd actually had anything to do with them. I would see them on their bicycles or hanging around a couple of cheap bars downtown or lined up at the Western Union on payday. Most times I saw them they were out working in the fields and greenhouses. Otherwise they were kind of invisible. I only noticed the two that morning because I'd never seen them in the hospital before, and because one of them was tall.

Amigos around here were easy to forget, let's put it that way.

I went up to the third floor and found Darren's room. There were four beds but D was the only patient. There was also a man nurse, which always looks weird to me, I don't know why, standing beside Darren's bed, serving him some pills in a little paper cup. Darren had the bed mostly upright. He had a bandage wrapped around his head, and there was gauze and tape on his nose. There were dark bruises under both of his eyes, like he'd been on the losing end of a battle. He saw me and grinned and held up a fist. An IV was taped to the back of his hand. I went over to the bed and bumped his fist with my own. I was careful about it, on account of the IV.

The man nurse nodded at me and turned his attention back to Darren. He said, And how many quarters in a dollar?

Ten, said Darren.

Ten? said the nurse.

Shit, man. Four. Come on.

Don't forget, said the nurse, you got it wrong an hour ago.

Four quarters in a buck, said Darren. I'm at Altena General Hospital. My name is Darren Scott Braemer.

The nurse smiled in a patient way. He gave Darren some water in a plastic cup and watched him swallow the pills down. Then he said, Okay, smartass, you're doing better, but you're not a hundred percent just yet. I'll be back later on, but if you need me, call. C'est bon?

Yes, boss, said Darren.

The nurse looked at me and said, Friend or family?

This guy? said Darren. He's both.

Okay, said the nurse. Enjoy your visit, but if Darren here has to go to the bathroom, you have to take him. If he tells you he can take himself, don't listen to him.

I said, I have to take him to the bathroom?

You don't have to hold it for him, but you'll have to walk him there. He's apt to fall on his face otherwise. You look like you might be able to manage it, but if it's absolutely out of the question, call me.

Don't worry about it, I said. I can do it.

The nurse nodded and gave me a thumbs-up, and then he was gone. I sat down in a chair beside Darren's bed. It bothered me to see him like this, never mind all the secret shit standing between us.

Darren, meanwhile, was using a remote to flip through the channels on a wall-mounted television not far from the bed. The sound was off. He didn't stay on any channel longer than a second. He said, Oxys, brother.

I said, What?

They got me on oxys. Whew. I feel great.

When are you gonna get out of here, D?

Ah, fuck. Probably not till tomorrow. They have to do X-rays and all of that. My neck is fine, but I hit my head on the window and busted my nose on the steering wheel. And the cops still haven't come by to talk to me.

How mangled is your car?

It's not too bad, said Darren. The window got busted, and I think the headlight got knocked out. There's probably a bunch of scratches along the side. I'll need to come down before I care about any of that cosmetic shit. I think I got it worse than the car. As long as there's no frame damage, and as long as the alignment's okay, it's drivable. Which reminds me.

Reminds you what?

If . . . if I need to go to Detroit, in a couple weeks' time, would you go with me?

Detroit? I said. What's in Detroit?

Just some guys I need to talk to, said Darren. It's not a for-sure thing yet, but if it happens, the only person I'd want with me is you.

Sounds shady.

It's not. It's just talk, Ash. I swear. And it's good talk. It's opportunity talk. There'd be money in it, for both of us. Real money.

I said, Jesus, D, slow down. One thing at a time.

Sorry, sorry. I'll bug you about it some other time.

I nodded, said, Has your mom been in to see you?

Darren looked at the TV screen. He said, Nah. She doesn't need to know about this.

Has anyone else been here? Seth? Your dad?

No.

I said, Or Chass? Has she been in?

Nope, said Darren. I haven't even talked to her. Have you?

I thought about the call from the night before. I looked at my shoes and said, I haven't talked to her at all, bro.

I guess you know, maybe, her and I aren't doing too good.

You and Chass?

Yeah, said Darren. It's a fight, all the time. A couple days ago we said we should spend some time apart. You know, with everything that's been going on.

I don't know. What's been going on?

Darren didn't answer. Instead he lowered his bandaged-up head to the pillow and said, That girl is my fucking soulmate, Ash, but she drives me crazier than anything. Anything. Sometimes she makes me so crazy I want to, I don't know, go on a rampage. Break things. Burn Altena to the fucking ground. That's love. That's what love is.

I licked my lips. They'd gotten pretty dry. I said, Do you want me to call her?

Don't worry about it. She doesn't need to know about this, either.

I can call her right now, D.

No, said Darren. I don't want that. Okay? Just back my play here. Please.

Alright, D. Your play.

A couple minutes went by. I kept quiet.

I wasn't drunk last night, said Darren. When I crashed. Everyone will think I was drunk, but I wasn't.

So how did it happen?

You know what? It's stupid, brother, but I dozed off. I fell asleep at the wheel. When people say that's dangerous shit, they're not lying. I was just so fucking tired, and I didn't even realize it. That's the thing.

Well, I said, all that matters is you're alright.

I am, said Darren. Also, I have to piss.

The dude said I have to take you.

Fuck, never mind that.

I have to take you. I'm not gonna let you fall on your face, dumb-ass, while I sit here watching. Let's go.

Shit, said Darren. Alright alright. Lead the way, sir. I won't cause any trouble.

He got out of the bed, all slow and careful. I took his arm. It amazed me how thin his arm felt, nothing but hot skin and a thin layer of muscle over the bone. I thought again how skinny he was looking. That little baggie of crank, the one with the elf on it, popped into my head. It was one thing if D was slinging that dope, but what if he was hitting it too?

I led him to a small washroom on the other side of the room. The door stayed open, and I kept an eye on him as he leaned against the wall above the toilet with one hand and handled his business with the other. When he was finished, he shuffled out and let me lead him back to the bed.

Once he was resettled, I cut to the chase. I said, So other than not telling anybody you're in the hospital, what's this favour?

He said, It's kind of a pain in the ass . . .

How so?

Well, look, you know Royal Towing? Where Jimmy Forrest ended up working?

Sure. Oak Street.

Royal towed my car last night. I got a hold of Jimmy before I talked to you. He said I could get it today.

I said, Okay . . .

I need to get my car over to my dad, said Darren. And I need to get it to him today.

A cold feeling filled my gut. I said, Where is he?

My mom's old place on Free Street. I think I told you, him and Seth are fixing it up. But the thing is, you know, my dad's keeping a bit of a low profile right now, which is . . . whatever. It's no big deal. But I need to get the car to him, like, ASAP. So I need your help, Ash. I hate even having to ask, but . . .

Darren was looking straight at me. He seemed almost desperate. I didn't like it. But I didn't really hesitate. I reached out and bumped my fist against his shoulder and told him okay.

THE ROYAL TOWING LOT WAS FIFTEEN MINUTES' WALKING distance from the hospital. I walked it, leaving my bike at the hospital. Along the way, I got myself a coffee. The day was sunny and cool. The streets were quiet. Church services wouldn't let out for another half an hour. I passed Saint Theresa's, the Catholic church. The sign in front showed times for both regular Mass and Spanish Mass, which the church put on for the Amigos.

I told myself I was walking to Royal Towing because I didn't know if they'd have parking for my bike, like they did at the hospital, which of course was bullshit. I was walking because I was delaying what was to come, namely seeing and talking to and dealing with Darren's old man. It had me uneasy, a little messed up already.

Anyways, I got to Royal Towing at ten minutes to noon. The lady in the office trailer confirmed that they had Darren's car, but she wanted me to pay the towing fee, a hundred bucks. I told her I was just picking the car up for my friend and didn't know anything about the fee. She said I'd only be able to get the car if I came up with the fee. We went back and forth a few times, until I was about to give up and leave, maybe try to call Darren at the hospital and ask him what the fuck, but then Jimmy Forrest came into the office and told the lady it was okay, it was all taken care of.

Jimmy led me out to the lot behind the office trailer. Parked close to the gate was Darren's car. The paint was badly scratched along one side and there were some shallow dents in the front fender. The driver's side window was missing.

I said, Oh man. Darren fucking loves this car. Look at it now.

I fixed up the mirror for him, said Jimmy. But if he wants the glass repaired and the scratches took care of, he's gonna have to take it to a shop. Good thing it drives fine. I don't think there's nothing wrong with the frame or the alignment.

I nodded. Jimmy was fat, strange-looking, and bald since high school. I didn't know him that well, even though it was obvious he and Darren had some kind of understanding. Business, I thought. What's that six degrees of separation thing? In Altena it's six degrees of Darren.

I hope Dare makes out alright, said Jimmy.

He'll be fine.

Jimmy might've kept talking, but right then the lady in the office trailer came out on the steps and yelled for him to come get a dispatch call. He dropped the car keys into my hand and walked away.

I unlocked the driver's door and sat down behind the wheel. The seat was set too far forward. My knees were practically pushed up against the wheel. I reached down beneath the seat and pulled the release and the seat slid all the way back.

Then I sat there for a full count to ten, not turning the ignition, not doing anything. It was strange enough to be in the driver's seat of Darren's car. He'd let me drive it once but he'd been in the car at the time. The only person I knew who'd driven it without him around was Chastity. The time she took me to the city for the D'Amours Classic, for example. And some of the times after that, our visits. Fuck, some of the things we'd done in that car . . .

But it wasn't the car, and it wasn't Darren, and, for now, it wasn't Chastity.

The longer I sat there behind the wheel, doing nothing, the more DB filled my mind.

DB PAID US TO DO THE JOB. DB FRONTED US.

This was yet another thing that happened the summer I was living with Darren. It went down after DB had been back in town for a while.

The way I remember it, me and Darren were sitting in the hot back seat of DB's Eldorado. DB had driven us downtown, telling us we were going to the Dairy Queen. Shit, bro, every time somebody told me we were going to the Dairy Queen that summer, it never actually came true. It was no different with DB. He drove us to a church parking lot on the edge of downtown. I remember how the leather upholstery in the back seat was covered with beach towels, and how the buckles of the seat belts were scorching. Up front, DB had his tape deck on, playing more of that country music he liked.

He was sitting behind the steering wheel and he had one arm stretched over to the headrest on the passenger seat. He was wearing jean shorts and a black T-shirt with a picture of a motorcycle on the chest. He had mirror sunglasses on his face. He kept peeking over the top of them whenever he talked to us.

He said, Hey, knuckleheads, do you know what fronting means?

I remember thinking Darren should answer first, since DB was his dad. But Darren was only interested in this canvas bag, which DB had passed back to us just before he'd asked us about fronting. The bag had leather straps and zippers. There was some machine oil on the side. It looked heavy.

Up front, DB was tapping his fingers on the passenger headrest in time to the music. *Love her like the devil when you get back home*, he sang along. The vibe he was giving off was patient, real patient. He was always good at that.

Finally it was me who said, What does fronting mean?

Fronting is a certain way of doing business with a guy, said DB. Or in this case, with two guys. It's where you give the guy, or the two guys, their product or their payment up front, you see? If it's the product you give 'em up front, you've given it to them before they've paid you for it. And if it's the payment you give 'em up front, you've given it to them before they've done whatever it is you're paying them to do. Roger dodger so far?

I nodded. Darren was still looking at the bag.

The thing about fronting is it takes faith, said DB. Trust. Why do you suppose that is?

Again, I waited for Darren to speak but he didn't. I kicked his foot. Darren looked at me. He was frowning, but he clearly didn't know what was being talked about.

So again it was me who answered. I said, I guess you have to trust the other guy to, like, do his part? Because you've already paid him for it?

Bang on, said DB. You have to trust the guy you're fronting to make good on whatever you're fronting him for. That's why, you know, as a rule of thumb, you shouldn't front, because when it comes to business, you can't trust ninety-nine percent of the people out there. Having said that, I'm going to front you guys.

Why? Because I trust you. I know you're not going to stick a fork in me over a business interest. Right?

DB was looking at me over the tops of his shades.

Right, I said.

What DB fronted us was a five-dollar bill each. Not a lot of money, but all the same, taking it from DB's hand, as part of a business deal, made me feel good, made me feel like a man. I remember that buzz, clear as anything.

Our instructions were pretty simple. We had to take the bag to a place called the Balmoral, which in those days was a video arcade. We had to find DB's friend, a guy named Mr. Kinkaid, and give him the bag. If Mr. Kinkaid wasn't there right away, we could spend our money on arcade games or a bite to eat while we waited. Once we were finished, we had to come back to DB's car. He said he would take us back home to carry on with the Monopoly tournament we'd had going for the last day.

Roger dodger, boys? said DB.

I said, Mr. Braemer?

I told you, it's DB. Mr. Braemer was my dad, and he's long gone and god rest his soul. Ha.

Kiss an angel good mornin', sang the song on the tape deck.

DB? I said. I don't want to sound stupid, but how'll we know who Mr. Kinkaid is?

You see that, Darren? said DB. Your best pal uses his head. That wasn't a stupid question at all. You'll know Mr. Kinkaid because he's big, big like you might end up if you keep doing those exercises I showed you. Kinny also has a tattoo on his neck. A green shamrock, like the ones you see on St. Patrick's Day. Don't stare at it when you see him. Alright, now. You're on the clock, so hup-to.

We got out of the car into the hot afternoon. The air was shimmering over the church parking lot. Darren was holding the canvas bag in both hands. He said, Man, this feels like it's full of rocks.

I'll carry it, I said.

I thought Darren might argue, but he just shrugged and put the bag down and told me to suit myself. I picked it up. It wasn't as heavy as Darren had let on, but it wasn't light. Maybe there were engine parts or electronics in the bag—maybe those were the things DB was giving to this buddy of his. No big deal. I looped the straps around my arms and over my shoulders so that it would sit on my back like a knapsack. DB was watching from the driver's side window of the Eldorado.

Darren and I started walking. We'd gone about half a block when Darren said, Five bucks. That's bullshit. We should've made him give us ten bucks each for this. That bag is heavy, and, like, who the fuck is Mr. Kinkaid?

I couldn't think of anything to say. I wanted to hit Darren. Instead I just spat on the ground and kept walking. If DB had asked, I would've done the job for free.

I HADN'T SEEN DARREN'S OLD HOUSE IN A LONG TIME. Darren's mother had moved out when Darren and I were still in high school, and not long after, Darren had moved into his own place. Pulling up now, in Darren's car, I saw that the outside of the house had gone to shit. The lawn was overgrown and the trim around the windows was peeling and the shingles on the roof were buckled and rotten. The front porch was completely missing, leaving a pale patch on the bricks where the ledger board had been. One of the old ceramic gnomes remained in the yard. It was the most colourful thing in sight.

Behind the house, someone had enclosed the backyard with a

tall board fence. A plywood gate, big enough to drive a car through, blocked the top of the driveway. The rest of Free Street, on either side of the old house, didn't look any better.

I parked Darren's car in the driveway. The asphalt was cracked and uneven. Outside, the air smelled bad. I looked up the street at the brick wall around the pig slaughterhouse. Darren used to say you could sometimes hear the pigs screaming. I'd never heard it myself and didn't know if it was true or not, but I can tell you that Darren had been a vegetarian since grade nine.

I walked to the top of the driveway and opened the gate. It was heavy but unlocked. Just like Darren had said it would be. I slipped through. Parked on the other side was DB's Eldorado, the same car as ever. The only straight-up difference was that the California licence plates—so, like, exotic back in the day—had been replaced with Michigan ones.

The grass in the backyard was uncut and long. There was a crooked metal shed near the top of the ravine. I went to the back of the house. The door there was new, the newest thing in sight. It was made of strong windowless steel, the kind you'd see fitted into the wall of a factory or something. I knocked and waited. A small breeze picked up and gave me a solid whiff of the slaughterhouse. I heard a rusty scraping noise from behind. I turned around. Coming out of the shed was Seth, wearing dirty cargo pants and an oversized basketball jersey and a pair of yellow dishwashing gloves.

He said, Ashley . . . what the fuck are you doing here?

Hi to you too, Seth.

Yeah, hi, whatever. You know people knock on doors, right? They don't just let themselves into someplace.

I said, Does it look like I was letting myself in? I was knocking.

What for?

I said, What for? I came down here for the memories, Seth. I came down because I like the way the pigshit smells. Jesus Christ. I drove your brother's car over here for him. He's in the hospital.

He's in the hospital, said Seth.

Yeah, he's . . . Look, is DB here or what? I don't feel like telling this story twice.

Wait here, said Seth. Right here.

Seth took a key out of his pocket and unlocked the steel door and went through and closed the door behind him. Out of curiosity, I tried the knob, expecting it to be locked. It was. I was annoyed and a little spooked. Uneasy, like I'd felt before, while walking from the hospital.

I took my phone out but right away realized I didn't know what I'd do with it. Darren didn't have a cell phone, and I had no idea if he had his pager with him at the hospital. What would I even ask him? In any case, looking at the screen I could see the signal here was almost nothing. I put the phone back in my pocket.

Business, I thought again. This all had to do with Darren's business in some way or other. Had to. And, same as always, I didn't want to know much more.

But I couldn't shake the question, no matter how much I didn't want to know, about what the hell DB had to do with all this—like, how much more serious shit Darren might've gotten into lately, and on his old man's watch to boot.

The steel door opened again. Seth stood on the other side. Behind him, two steps led up into the kitchen, which I could see was mostly gutted. A circular saw sat in the middle of the floor. There were a couple piles of sawdust and all the cupboards were gone. Another set of stairs led down to the basement.

Okay, said Seth. You're welcome to come in. So come in.

IT HAD TURNED OUT, IN ITS WAY, TO BE BULLSHIT, THE JOB DB fronted me and Darren to do all those years ago. Not that it hadn't, like, served some kind of purpose. Mainly for him. Whatever it did, whatever it was, it broke up how I saw him, you know? It changed my perspective. On a lot of things.

I never found out what Darren thought about it. I didn't ask him. Darren never had much to say about his old man, definitely nothing bad, and he'd always been quick to step up in DB's defence if he needed to. That, at least, is something I can understand, maybe better than anybody.

Anyways, that hot summer day it took us fifteen minutes to get to the Balmoral, with me carrying that heavy bag the whole fucking way. I'd sweated right through my shirt by the time we got there, and my shoulders and back were hurting. But I hadn't said anything. I hadn't asked Darren to take over. I was still, I don't know, pretty honoured, like, to be doing the job in the first place. Not that I didn't think there was something shady about it, because I wasn't that stupid, even as a kid.

We paused for a little while outside the joint. The same place where the gals in their short skirts and the farm boys playing dress-up now line up at night or hang around and puke on the curb at last call. I'd never been allowed to go into the Balmoral, the arcade, in those days, but right then I didn't really care about my parents' rules.

The marquee over the front door showed a picture of a grinning monkey in a tuxedo, holding a cane with one hand and tipping a top hat with the other. Me and Darren went inside. The place was air-conditioned and cold, and the carpeting on the floor had pictures of spaceships and planets and stars on it. In the far corner of the main room were a couple of coin-operated pool tables. The rest of the space was taken up by rows and blocks of pinball machines and arcade games. Raiden, Contra, Missile Command, Street Fighter, and a couple of classic games, Asteroids and Galaga. The air was heavy with the smell of popcorn and cigarette smoke, and there were voices and chimes and bells and electronic sounds.

I hadn't even noticed that Darren had wandered off until I saw him coming back my way, holding his arms out. He said, Well, I don't see anybody with a tattoo on his neck, so I don't know.

I nodded. When I look back on it now, I realize I was happy that Mr. Kinkaid, whoever he was, wasn't there yet, because that gave us time to have a go at some of the games. I went to the front counter and traded some of my money—my fronted money—for game tokens. Tokens were twenty-five cents apiece, but if you bought them by the dollar you got an extra one. We each bought three dollars' worth, and then used the rest of the cash to buy Cokes and chocolate bars.

We had to wait for a couple of older kids to finish with Street Fighter, but once we got it, we didn't let it go. I slipped the canvas bag off my back and put it at my feet and pushed it with my shins against the base of the machine. Darren had played a bunch of times before and was good at the combinations. I just jerked the joystick and mashed the buttons with my hand. I wasn't any good but the game sucked me in completely.

Eleven tokens later, I had to piss so bad I couldn't ignore it anymore. I told Darren where I was going.

Sure, said Darren.

Your dad's bag is right here. Watch it, okay?

Okay.

I pulled myself away from Street Fighter. Near the front counter, a sign said the washrooms were in the basement. I found the staircase and bounded down two steps at a time. I found the men's room, the very same place where a whole lot of years later I'd be supervising the pukers as they cleaned up their own messes.

When I came back up I saw a man hanging around the front counter. The man was big and strong-looking, older but not as old as my dad or DB. He had a black buzz cut and a thick black moustache. He was wearing a pair of jeans and engineer boots and a dark T-shirt, and, just as DB had said, there was this big green shamrock tattooed on his neck. He was scanning the arcade. Then he took a pack of smokes from his pocket and tapped one out and lit it up and took a drag.

I looked over to the Street Fighter machine, but Darren was gone. It took me a few seconds to spot him on the far side of the arcade, playing another game. I hurried over and told him there was a man here who had to be Mr. Kinkaid.

Okay, said Darren.

He was pretty distracted by the game.

I was about to pull him away by the sleeve, but then I noticed. I said, Where's the bag?

The bag? said Darren.

Darren, fuck.

I rushed back to Street Fighter. Two teenagers were at it now, banging away on the buttons and joysticks. At first I didn't see the canvas bag anywhere. I started to panic, but then I spotted it. It had been kicked around to the side of the machine. I grabbed it. All I got from the guys playing the game was an annoyed look, like I was a fly buzzing around them, but they didn't stop me or say anything.

I hung the bag over my shoulder and made my way to the front, not waiting for Darren. Near the counter, the big man with the shamrock tattoo was stubbing his smoke out in a foil ashtray. I stood in front of him. The man looked down. That was when

Darren fell in beside me. In spite of everything else, I remember being real fucking glad to have my buddy there.

I said, Are you Mr. Kinkaid?

Who's asking? said the man.

His voice was scratchy and soft. It didn't seem to match how he looked.

I didn't know how to answer. Saying DB's name felt like snitching, somehow. But it seemed the man already knew, because after a couple of seconds, he grinned. His teeth were big and blocky and a bit yellow. He said, Never mind. How about that. DB sends his kids.

Mr. Kinkaid led us into the alley behind the arcade, and yes, Jesus Christ, I know how creepy that sounds. Even then, as a kid, I knew it was bad. I think that was the exact moment when I had my first legit second thought about DB. Doing a job for him didn't seem so badass at that point.

So there we were in the alley. Mr. Kinkaid had a motorbike parked out there, a big Harley with blue trim and chrome pipes and leather saddlebags. The licence plate on it said *Michigan*.

There weren't any other people back there, and I couldn't see the street. I kept thinking I would just run. If anything went wrong or got weird, I would grab Darren and bolt. Easy as that.

Well, said Mr. Kinkaid, let's have a look at that bag. Drop it right there.

He was pointing to a spot five feet in front of him.

I said, Just drop it on the ground?

On the ground, kid, and then take a few steps back. I don't want you or your pal anywhere near me. You think I'm a pervert or something?

At least Mr. Kinkaid seemed to be worried about the same shit I was. If nothing else, there was that.

I walked forward and dropped the bag off my shoulder. I took a few steps back. Mr. Kinkaid picked up the bag and hefted it. He said, Lucky you got some meat on you. This is a heavy bastard.

He unzipped it. He seemed to want to show us what was inside, because he gestured for us to take a look. The bag was full of money, American, bundled up in tight little bricks. My mouth went dry. I'd never seen so much money in one place in my life.

Holy shit, said Darren.

Mr. Kinkaid looked at him. He said, I guess you didn't know your old man moved this kind of cash around, did you.

No, sir.

And to think, he gives it to you guys to carry for him. He's nothing if he isn't real careful, is he.

I had no idea what Mr. Kinkaid was talking about, so I didn't say anything. Neither did Darren. We just watched as the guy thumped the bag down on the ground and zipped it back up.

But then he hesitated. He scratched his throat, right next to the shamrock tattoo. He bent over and unzipped the bag a few inches, took out one of the bricks of money, peeled two bills off, and handed one to Darren and the other to me.

They weren't five-dollar bills. They were twenties. Crisp, green and white American twenty-dollar bills, with a picture of a pillared building on one side and some dead president's face on the other.

You can get those changed up to Canadian, said Mr. Kinkaid. Then you can play Pac-Man till your eyeballs drop out. But do something for me. Tell DB this isn't really the kind of crap I like to bring kids into. He can come his own self next time. I won't bite.

Right then I felt cold, all up and down my spine. Never mind the money, and never mind how it'd felt at first. This wasn't fun anymore, not at all.

I said, Can we go now, Mr. Kinkaid?

Yeah, said Mr. Kinkaid. You all can go.

ALL THAT ANCIENT HISTORY SHIT—THE FRONTED CASH, the Balmoral when it was an arcade, going into the alley out back with Mr. Kinkaid—was what I was thinking about as Seth led me down the basement stairs. Like I said, it's funny how things in the past set up what happens later on, and you don't realize it, like, you don't think about it, until it's happening. Until you're in the middle of it.

A sharp smell hung in the basement air. Cat piss, I thought. It got stronger as we went down.

The rec room was smaller than I remembered. There was the same shitty panelling on the walls and the same all-weather carpeting on the floor. A lamp stood in the corner. It was on, but it didn't give much light. There was no other furniture except for a stereo, which was playing old country and western music, no surprise there.

The two doors leading off the rec room, the crawlspace and the can, were both closed. I remembered how that crawlspace used to terrify me in the night, when I'd stayed there as a kid. I was glad it was closed now, but I couldn't help but think about what might be behind it, you know, like one of those homemade crank kitchens. The kind you read about in the paper or see on the news.

From the bathroom door, I heard the toilet flush and the sink run. Then the bathroom door opened and DB came out. His hair was greyer now than red, and there were lines around his eyes and on his forehead, but he otherwise looked the same. His right hand was wrapped up in bandages.

He sized me up and grinned and said, Ashley, Ashley. Sorry I can't shake your hand. Had a little renovation misfire.

How's it going, DB? I said.

Any better and there'd be two of me. You're still pumping iron, by the looks of it.

Yeah, I am.

Still, said DB, I guess you're not strong enough to protect my son from himself. What did he do this time?

He got in a car crash last night, ended up in the hospital.

What the fuck, said Seth. What in the fuck, Darren.

I said, He's still there now, but just for X-rays and all that. He hit his head and broke his nose, but he's okay. He wasn't drunk or nothing, either, so I don't think he's getting any heat from the cops. He just fell asleep at the wheel. That's all. Ended up in the ditch.

Well, call it a lesson learned, said DB. What about that piece of Jap crap he drives around?

It's scratched up and a window got knocked out, but I think it's okay. It drives fine. I brought it over here. He said you needed it for something.

Give Seth the keys, will you? said DB.

I turned. Seth was giving me a pissy look, as if Darren's accident had somehow been my fault. I looked him in the eyes and gave him the keys. Seth went back up the stairs.

You want a beer or anything? said DB.

I'm fine. Gotta work out later.

DB crossed his arms over his chest and leaned against the wall. Just like that, he had me on edge, even more than I already was. He seemed smug, somehow, like, pleased with himself. As if he'd just won a card game. He grinned again, said, So tell me how everything goes with you, Ashley. Darren says you're still working the door at the old hotel downtown.

Pretty much.

Perfect line of work for a guy like you.

How about you, DB? I said. Back in town to stay for a while, or what?

DB's grin faded, just a little. I'd maybe got half an inch under his skin. That felt good, but I'll tell you, bro, it was scary at the same time. Like that feeling you get when you've gone just a little further than you thought you could, and suddenly, where you're at, all bets are off. Anyways, before he could reply, Seth came back down. He said, The car'll drive, Dad. It's fine. It just looks like hell, which we should maybe fix up, because—

DB gave Seth a hard look and Seth shut up.

The cat piss smell in the air was making my eyes water. I said, Well, I should get going.

All that mattered was getting out of that basement.

Sure, said DB. Thanks for bringing the car over.

I said, No trouble. You, uh, want me to tell Darren anything? I might go back and see him later on.

No, said DB. I'll be there as soon as I can to see him my own self. Say, Ashley, you haven't seen that better half of his, have you?

Who, Chastity?

Unless he's got a different better half, said DB. You were always pretty close with her too, right?

We're cousins, I said, way too quickly, and then I said, But no. I haven't seen her.

DB pushed his lips together and nodded.

Beside me, Seth was shifting foot to foot. I had the feeling that he was just as uncomfortable as I was. I really wanted to be out of there. Like, I was starting to feel short of breath.

Then I found DB giving me this weird stare. He said, That shit with your dad.

What shit with my dad?

You know, your dad . . . Is that shit contagious?

What? I said. No, man, it's not contagious. It's not a cold.

So it's not something you got from him. Like, genetically.

No.

DB stared for a few seconds more. And then, once again, the grin. He said, You know I'm just hassling you, Ashley. No disrespect to you or your old man. It's modern times now, isn't it. Everybody accepts everybody.

It's all good, I said, forcing a grin of my own.

I LEFT THE HOUSE ON FREE STREET FEELING MESSED UP. Light-headed, for some reason, but also definitely relieved for being out of there. But also bugged and angry from seeing DB. *That shit with your dad . . . is it contagious?* Motherfucker.

I was also still sucked into the past. That hot day, that job. I hadn't really thought about it in years.

I remember me and Darren talking about our dads as we headed back uptown. I remember Darren saying he figured DB would probably head back down to California pretty soon, now that his business or whatever was done.

And I remember saying, Well, he can take my dad with him when he goes.

Your old man's alright, Darren said. He's always been pretty nice to me, you know?

Sure. I guess.

And he doesn't have friends like that Mr. Kinkaid asshole. That's a good thing right there.

I remember thinking that was a good point, but also how I was able to feel that American twenty-dollar bill in my pocket. I kept touching it, wondering what I would do with it. I even thought I should maybe give it to my mom and dad, like somehow more money would help them solve the situation they were in.

Thing is, I was missing them right then, my mom and my dad, more than I had at any time before, all summer long. Somehow, working for DB, for five fucking dollars, had made me realize how much I was missing them. I've never been able to figure that out.

So I guess you'd think, maybe, that whole day, way in the past, should've set me straight. I guess you'd think I shouldn't've been finding myself coming out of that basement, in the present, still doing shady business that I barely had any real knowledge of. And you'd be right. I wouldn't have anything to tell you to explain it, to justify it or whatever. Loyalty to Darren? Maybe. Playing at being a hardcase? Maybe. Knowing better but not *doing* better? Maybe. Probably.

It is what it is, same as always.

SEVEN

On the 14th of April, the scales told me I was 229 pounds. The mirror told me that both my biceps and triceps were showing their shape. My neck looked wide and strong. Fat veins stood out from my wrists, all the way up my arms and into the fronts of my shoulders. My legs were thicker too, with the quads showing their shape. But my stomach was still too padded. There was still too much beer and junk food going into it.

I did a few poses, watched my movement and form critically.

Then I took my d-bol and Nolvadex and milk thistle, and part one of the Ritual was done. I did part two, the workout itself, that night. Chris Hagar closed up the gym around me and left the back door unlocked so I could get out that way.

It was risky for Chris to let me stay behind and work out, so I knew it wasn't something I could ask for all that often. But once in a while, a night session, where I had the gym totally to myself, was just the thing. It was, like, what's the word, a meditation or something. A good way to get my head in order.

So I had my once-in-a-while night workout. I went hard, focused on my abs. I stayed at the gym until I'd done a thousand sit-ups. I'll admit, the last few sets weren't much more than ten or twelve reps at a time, with longer and longer rests in between. But the only way you get there is by slugging it out, doing your time. There aren't any shortcuts.

I was in the locker room, getting cleaned up, when my cell phone went off. The screen said *Unknown*. I answered, wondering if I'd hear Chastity's voice on the other end, but it was Darren's. We didn't talk for long. He asked me where I was and I told him out at the gym and he laughed that it was so late at night. Then he said he'd been let out of the hospital with no major issues, and had had no problems with the cops. He thanked me again for helping him with his car. He was talking fast, too fast for me to get much of a word in. He mentioned something about Detroit again, but before I could even ask, he said he had to get going and that we'd talk soon. That was it. Neither of us mentioned Chastity at all.

THE DAYS OF THAT WEEK PASSED BY. I RODE MY BIKE EVERY-where, happy to have it on the road again. From Monday through Wednesday the Balmoral was closed, so apart from the gym I didn't really have much to do. I played video games late into the nights and slept in every morning.

But Chastity, bro. Goddamn fucking Chastity. She was on my mind. I hated to admit it. I'd been right to tell her off when she called me. She'd had it coming. Still, she was on my mind, more and more every day. On Thursday, just after I ate breakfast and geared up, I broke and called her. I stood there in the bathroom, still on the scales, with the phone against my ear. There were two, three seconds of dead air while the call connected, and then a recording of her voice, *Hey, it's Chastity. You know what to do.* I ended the call real quick, not leaving a message.

I put the phone down on the counter, and what happened next kind of zapped me, kind of froze me to the spot. I thought, What if she was in trouble? For-real trouble, you know? What if . . . ?

I grunted and cleared my throat and shook my head. I wiped my sweaty palms on my thighs.

She was just holed up somewhere. She'd pulled disappearing acts in the past, one time as long as a month when she was twenty-one. She'd even tried stripping that time, some peeler joint in London. Later she'd told me and Darren how she lasted three nights taking her clothes off on stage before she knew she had to come back home. This, now, was just her usual bullshit, thinking about herself and nobody else, and I was right to have told her off. I was right.

I TOLD THE PATRON, IT'S NOT ME. IT'S THE LAW, BRO.

I don't accept this law, said the patron.

I said, What?

I don't accept this law. Laws work because everybody agrees about them. If we all rejected them, they wouldn't work. They wouldn't mean anything. So I don't accept this law.

This patron and I were standing inside the club at the top of the stairs that led out to the street. It was Thursday night, and Thursday nights were supposed to be for the college students. Half-price cover and three-dollar bar-rail shots for anybody with a valid student ID. It could get crazy fast. Nothing was harder to handle than an over-liquored college gal and the two or three guys trying to get her attention. But this patron I was talking to wasn't a college student. He was in his late thirties or early forties, with big thick glasses. He was one of a small number of middle-aged dudes who came alone to the club, especially on college nights like this. I'd seen this same guy working as a clerk at the video place down the block. Right now he was trying to leave with a plastic cup of beer in his hand.

I said, Well, the law is the law, I guess. Whether or not you accept it.

You're just conditioned to think that way, my friend, said the patron.

He didn't seem really drunk or hostile. If anything, he was kind of friendly. He creeped me out a bit.

I said, Look. Never mind the law. If I let you out with that beer, I lose my job. And I don't want to lose my job. Do you at least accept that, bro?

The patron looked like he was giving it some thought. After a few seconds, he nodded. He started to turn back to the club's interior, but then looked at me and said something. I couldn't hear him over the music. I asked the patron to repeat himself, and he said, Is it all you got, I said.

What are you talking about?

Your job, said the patron. Is it all you got?

I said, Yes. No. What the hell? What business is it of yours?

Because all these things, jobs and what-have-you, the only reason they mean anything, the only reason we have to do them, is because we agree to. Same with laws. So don't do it. Don't let them condition you. Don't become your job. Take it from me.

Before I could reply, the man had carried his cup of beer back into the crowd, back to creep around whatever twenty-year-old babe he'd set his sights on.

By twelve-thirty, the club was three-quarters full. I hadn't expected it to be quite this busy, although I knew that at least half of the crowd were just townies instead of actual college kids. I walked a circuit and then took up a post against the wall near the bar, where I could keep an eye on the dance floor.

I could still picture the club back when it was an arcade. In my mind I could see where all the video games and pinball machines had been. By the time I was sixteen, I'd spent way too much time here. But then the owners, whoever they were, went bankrupt. I remember the day when Darren and I and a couple of others, skipping class, watched from across the street as all the games were dollied out and loaded into a cube van. It was two years later when the place reopened as a nightclub, and a year after that when I got hired on with the security crew. The manager back then was this fat asshole named Angelo, who claimed to have Mafia ties. His first words to me were, Listen, tiny, your job here isn't to get all hot and horny and punch some guy out just because he drank too much. If you do that, you'll wind me up in a lawsuit and I will be forced to make your life a living hell. Got me?

Fat Angelo. Where the hell was he now? I couldn't even really remember when Angelo had disappeared and Marcel had taken over. Oh well. We'd traded up. Angelo had been a dick. Marcel was strictly by the book about everything, but he was otherwise alright.

Two fingers poked me in the ribs. I turned, and I swear I thought Chastity was standing next to me, holding a mixed drink. I almost said her name.

But it wasn't Chastity. It was her on-and-off best friend, Michelle Levy. Michelle was shorter than Chastity and not as skinny. Her face was rounder and her eyes were brown. The only similarities to Chass, really, were the blond streaks in her hair and the salon tan on her skin.

Rosco, said Michelle. Give me some love, you bastard. I haven't seen you . . .

I hugged her. She smelled good. She had these nice-sized tits, not even fake, and I liked the way they pushed up against me. I said, Hey, Michelle.

I haven't seen you in forever, she said. Where've you been?

I've been around. I've just, you know, been keeping a low profile.

That's fair, said Michelle, nodding, working on her drink. Sometimes you have to duck out of things for a while. I know that feeling. It's good to see you anyways.

So what brings you out on a Thursday night?

Nothing much. I'm with a girlfriend. She's from out of town, but she's taking a cosmetics course at the college. So it's at least kind of legit that we're here on college night.

Michelle talked about some other things. I couldn't hear her well with my earplugs in, so I had to lean close. She was wearing a low-cut black shirt, and beneath it, the visible edge of her bra glowed purple under the club's black lights. I'd fooled around with her a time or two but we'd never gone very far. There'd always been an unspoken thing between us. It was only in the last six months I'd really realized what, who, that unspoken thing was.

. . . but it's no big deal, Michelle was saying. That's what I told him, anyway. Guys never seem to get it, you know?

I had no idea what she was talking about. I said, Michelle, have you talked to—

But then, like, out of nowhere, there was this battle going down fifteen feet away. At first I thought it was two patrons, but then I saw it was only one patron, and the other guy was Brice O'Halloran. Brice wasn't doing great, either. He was sitting in a weird position, holding his face. The patron, smaller than Brice by at least fifty pounds, was crouched above him, taking wild swings at Brice's head. The crowd of spectators was getting bigger by the second.

I rushed forward, pushing people out of the way. I grabbed the patron by the backs of his arms. He was small but he had a solid build and he was fighting hard and he was laughing at everything. He twisted halfway around and put an elbow into my chin. It was a good shot. I had to blink the stars out of my eyes, but I stayed upright. Then I managed to get one of the guy's wrists back and slip him into a standing armlock. I put on a slight amount of pressure, enough to feel the guy squirm, and I leaned down and said into his ear, Give me a reason, motherfucker, and I'll break your arm.

The guy laughed some more. Then Trey was on top of us. Between him and me, we lifted the patron off his feet. We hauled him down to the front door. People were watching but were staying well clear, jumping out of the way as the two of us got this laughing, kicking jackass out of the club.

The lineup outside scattered and turned into spectators. At the bench a little farther up the block were the usual Amigos. I could feel them watching us. For once, there were no cop cars to be seen. I thought back to last weekend, when they'd come into the club, Constable Casey and the other cop, doing their community relations. I wondered where they were when I actually wanted them.

We got to the front edge of the club's property and shoved the patron to the curb. The guy went down hard, tripping over his own feet. But he was up again quick, still laughing. Me and Trey stood beside each other. I thought the patron might make a run at us, but he stood his ground on the sidewalk, shifting his weight from foot to foot, shaking his arms out to his sides. He was nineteen or twenty and didn't really look like anyone special. He could have been any of the college kids or farm boys or townies out for the night. His pupils were black and dilated wide open.

Take a walk, sir, said Trey. Go home.

You got no idea what I could do to you, said the patron. You're lucky. You're all lucky.

Go home, sir, said Trey.

I looked up the street. Still no cop cars. I looked back at the patron and said, Quit blowin' smoke, bro. Take a walk.

The patron rushed forward then, head down and leading, arms pumping. I was surprised, so much so that I might not've been ready if the guy hadn't made a hard right turn, his shoes scraping on the sidewalk, and run off, away from the crowds, past the Amigos and down the street. His laughter echoed after him.

DOWN NEAR THE BATHROOMS, SAID BRICE.

I thought you said *in* the bathroom, said Marcel.

I did? I meant near the bathrooms. You know, like, around the corner of the hallway there. That's where I caught him getting pushy with this chick.

Brice was holding a Ziploc of ice cubes against his face. His cheekbone was purple and swollen. Earlier, right after things had calmed down, he'd said the crazy patron had hit him with a bottle. It didn't break, he'd said, but it had put him down. I wondered if Brice had maybe just been sucker-punched by the guy. It was possible. Brice was not as tough as he talked.

It was three-thirty, and me and Trey and Brice were in Marcel's office, which was actually just a secondary storage room. We were sitting in front of his desk. Across from us, Marcel was writing in the incident logbook, going over each detail slowly and carefully, chain-smoking the whole time. On the wall behind him was a framed poster of Bob Marley, hanging crooked, with a caption that read *One Love*. The rest of the office was dimly lit, packed full of papers and files and a couple empty beer kegs.

And then? said Marcel.

Well, like I told you before, said Brice, I seen him getting pushy with this chick. He's trying to get her top off, he's trying to feel her up, she keeps telling him no. It was really brutal, Marcel. Really disrespecting of her. I don't put up with that shit, so I grab him and tell him to come upstairs, and at first he comes with me, and—

What did the girl do? said Marcel.

The girl?

The girl, Brice. The one the gentleman was getting pushy with.

Oh, said Brice. Man, she pretty much bolted as soon as I grabbed the guy. You know? Like, I never caught her name or anything. She bolted. I guess she was embarrassed, or maybe she was relieved that I was there to help her out.

Go on, said Marcel.

I listened as Brice went on to talk about how the patron went with him willingly, but as soon as they got to the top of the stairs, the patron got hold of a bottle and suckered Brice with it and then the battle was on. Brice didn't say anything about sitting on the floor, not fighting back, taking a dozen punches to the head.

At that point Marcel turned to me and Trey and gestured for us to pick up the story. We told him about hauling the guy out to the sidewalk, how there were no cops around, how it ended there, with the guy running off down the street.

He was messed up on something, said Trey.

What makes you say that? said Marcel.

The aggression, for one thing, said Trey. And his pupils were dilated. I know you saw it too, Ash.

I shifted in my chair. I had noticed the guy's pupils, and the way he'd been fighting was something else, but I didn't like making Marcel think there were drugs in the club. Marcel would get paranoid about shit like that. He would start to micromanage us, you know? Look at every single thing we were doing. Nobody wanted that.

Still, what Trey said had kind of put me in a corner. All I could do was nod and say, Yeah, Trey's probably right.

What do you think, Brice? said Marcel. Was the gentleman high, or what?

Well, I don't know about that, said Brice. I figured he was some drunk asshole, just like the rest of them. There's no dope on our watch, Marcel. I'm a hundred percent sure about that.

AFTER OUR MEETING IN THE OFFICE, TREY AND BRICE AND I left the club together. It was ten to four. A black Audi pulled up in the parking lot in front of us. All the windows were down. We saw a couple of girls in the back, including Dani Knox, who was one of the bartenders. Behind the steering wheel was Michelle Levy, waving her arm in time to the trance music playing from her stereo. She yelled, Hey, boys, we're going to the Dynasty. You want to come?

Michelle led the way in her car, Trey took Brice in his truck, and I went on my bike. I took my time, enjoying the empty streets and the cold air against my body. When I got to the restaurant I parked my bike beside Trey's truck. Across the street was a crummy bar and grill called Villagers, which was mostly frequented by the Amigos and the muffin-topped local slags who followed them around. But tonight was late, and a weeknight, and by this hour Villagers was closed, as was almost everything else in town.

I went into the Dynasty. The lights overhead were on full blast and crazy bright. There were fifteen or twenty other late-night diners at the Dynasty, stuffing their mouths with dim sum and roast duck and chow mein. I recognized most of them from the club. I wondered if the lunatic we'd kicked out might be here, but I didn't see him anywhere.

I found my friends at a big corner table. Brice was retelling the story of being slugged with the bottle. He was making it sound as if he'd rescued that gal, whoever she was, from getting raped in the bathroom. Right on with the heroics, bro, I thought, and for a moment I wondered if there'd ever been a gal in the first place.

I sat down next to Michelle and put my bike helmet on the floor beside me.

There were six of us at the table. Me, Michelle, Brice, Trey, Dani, and Michelle's girlfriend, the cosmetics student, whose name I think was Heather. We ordered a bunch of food, only half of which we would probably eat. The Chinese server, winking and laughing, also let us buy half a dozen beers. The girls were all pretty drunk already. They kept saying they wanted to see the sun come up. I didn't tell them how it was overcast outside. My eyes kept creeping back to Michelle. She'd always been a nice distraction, with or without what hung between us.

When the food came, I ate greedily until I felt full. I picked up a fortune cookie and crushed it in my hand. I opened my fingers. My fortune read, *Carry your troubles on your head and bow to honour.* Who knew what that shit was supposed to mean?

By the time we left the Dynasty, the first light of dawn was in the sky, although it was still clouded over. All six of us made our way back to Trey's place and crowded into the living room, talking and laughing. Dani got hold of a bottle of vodka and a jug of cranberry juice. She mixed some drinks. Trey put on some music and rolled a big joint.

I went into the kitchen and got myself a beer from the fridge and went back into the living room. Michelle was nowhere to be seen. Trey was trying to show Heather how to play a video game. Dani was knocking back a shot of straight vodka. Brice was on both knees, fiddling with something on the coffee table. I leaned in beside him to see what it was.

A little plastic baggie with an elf on it.

Through the elf, I could see the dope, coarse and kind of pink, almost a full gram. Without thinking about it, I reached down, but Brice snatched the baggie away.

He said, Tut-tut, mister. There's a little taste for everybody. Ladies?

Sure, said Dani. Whatever. But you have to keep me entertained.

Trey looked up from the video game lesson and saw what Brice was holding. He said, Hey, I won't have any of that door-knobber shit in my house, dude.

I said, Where'd you get it?

Hmm? said Brice.

Where'd you get it?

This is what I caught that stupid kid with, said Brice.

I said, Who, the one in the bathroom?

Yeah, said Brice. I caught him hitting a bump at the sink, and I busted his ass. Bam. Now, finders keepers.

I said, So there wasn't any girl.

Girl? said Brice.

Yeah. You said he was pushing some girl around.

Oh, yeah, no, there wasn't a girl, said Brice. I just told Marcel what he needed to hear. Anyway, all the rest of it's true. I took him upstairs and he came along and then he hit me with a bottle. Whatever. We took care of him, didn't we.

I'm serious, said Trey. You want to do that shit, you can't do it here.

Alright, said Brice. Alright. We'll save it. Okay, sweetie?

Whatever, said Dani. But if you call me sweetie again, I'll bust a bottle on the other side of your head.

I stood back from the coffee table, frowning. I was about to say something, about to ask Brice more, but I stopped myself. The old question was in my mind—the Darren question, and when did he start seriously slinging speed, and did I really want to know?

It didn't take much to decide. Just one look at that little baggie, that little elf on it, and just one second thinking about all the things I'd already seen—shook-down tweakers in shitty motel rooms, for example—and my mind made itself up. Ignorance equals bliss, always.

I WENT TO THE UPSTAIRS CAN AND TOOK A LEAK. WHEN I came out I saw my bedroom door was open. Michelle was in there, poking through my CDs. She glanced over her shoulder and said, What took you so long, Rosco?

I said, I didn't know you were waiting for me.

Sometimes I think you just play dumb, said Michelle. It works for you too. Big, tough, not so quick on the draw, pretty nice in spite of all that. It works for you. But I think you're way smarter than you let on. That's why I like talking to you. What are all the peasants doing downstairs?

Drinking, I said. Nothing else.

Good for them, she said.

Good for them, I said.

I didn't say anything else. Nothing about the baggie on the table, for instance. Maybe Michelle had known about that, maybe not. Ignorance, right?

Now, said Michelle, this isn't exactly the first time you've gotten me alone, is it.

Hey, you brought yourself up here. I thought you'd gone home.

She looked at me with half-closed eyes. I think it was supposed to be sexy, but it wasn't quite. Still, I already had a hard-on. Any other worries I had—about the present, the past, the future, my friends, Chastity—were slipping into the background. It was a relief, and I wanted it. I took a drink of beer.

So what now? said Michelle.

I said, Ah, fuck.

I pulled the bedroom door closed. Michelle stood grinning, waiting for me. She was the on-and-off best friend of the girl I loved, but I didn't care. Just then I didn't care about anything.

That temporary escape from your thoughts, bro, is one thing—maybe the only thing—a hard-on is really good for.

I FELL ASLEEP AFTERWARDS, LYING ON MY BACK, AND I dreamed that everything was black. I couldn't move, not a muscle, and I couldn't even breathe. Panic started to set in, and there wasn't a goddamn thing I could do about it—but then I was being shaken awake.

I sucked in air and raised myself on my elbows.

Michelle, it was Michelle shaking me awake, Michelle still in bed with me.

Ashley, she said.

I said, I'm awake.

You were snoring, then you stopped breathing. Fucking scary, man.

Sorry, I said. I just . . . What time is it?

No idea.

I leaned my head back on my pillow. That nightmare or whatever it was had been brutal. Choking in the total dark, like I was buried somewhere.

Weak grey light was filling out the shape of the window above us. A bass beat was playing, not too loud, from the living room below, but there were no other sounds.

Were you sleeping? I said.

Sort of. Your snoring woke me up.

I'm sorry.

Don't be, said Michelle. Real men snore. Ha. You know, it amazes me it took us this long.

Me too.

But even as I said it, I had mixed feelings. She wasn't who I wanted her to be. Funny how that kind of truth usually kicks in only after you've gotten off.

I'm glad we did, said Michelle. We could maybe make a habit of it.

Maybe we could.

I put my hand on her thigh and stroked it with my thumb. Her hips moved.

That's better, she said.

Can I ask you something?

Sure, whatever.

Do you think Chastity is okay?

Michelle's hips stopped moving.

Oh, Rosco. Really?

Really what?

She pulled away from me and said, Always, always with Chastity. You've got this thing about her—and can I tell you something? It's weird, man. This thing you have about her. She's your cousin, but if I didn't know better . . .

I said, Hey, come on, it's not—

I'm just breaking your balls. Kind of. But listen. It's great that you've always wanted to keep tabs on her and whatnot, but she's a grown-up. She's probably the most, like, independent person I know. Stubborn too. Nobody can keep tabs on her, and that's just how she likes it.

I said, I just want to know if you think she's okay.

I don't know if she's okay, said Michelle. She's Chastity. She's always got some kind of drama on the go.

So you're not, like, worried about her?

Well, I don't know. I haven't even talked to her in a week, maybe two.

I said, Did you have a fight?

No, said Michelle. Yes. It's none of your business, okay? It's the usual shit between us. We get into it over nothing and then we don't talk for a few weeks. I just think she could be more grateful, you know, since she was living at my place.

Living at your place? For how long? What about Darren?

Michelle was already getting off the mattress. She reached around for her clothes and began dressing in the semi-dark, laughing as she did it.

Michelle, I said. Hey, come on. Come back.

I gotta get going, Rosco. It was fun to finally do this. I only wish you could put everything to rest with Chastity. For your own sanity, man. Really.

I stood up. I was naked and the bedroom was chilly. I wrapped my arms around myself and then moved in front of the bedroom door, a second before Michelle reached for the knob. I said, Michelle . . .

I gotta get going.

I just want to know, Michelle, if Chastity's okay. You can think what you want about me and her, but I just want to know. Please.

I saw the outline of her shoulders drop. I heard her exhale. She said, Listen, Ashley, it's like I told you. I don't know if she's okay. She's been all over the place lately. I mean, did you know about her family?

Kind of.

They've been talking again, and . . . she's been giving them money. Lots of it. It's gotta be all the cash she has. I've seen her taking it to them in envelopes, like, every two weeks.

I said, For Nevaeh, right?

Yeah. I think so. I really want to get going, okay?

I stepped aside and opened the door for her. She went through, out into the darkness of the hallway.

I'll call you, I said. Maybe we can hang out.

Sure. Give me a call. I'm around.

I stood in the bedroom doorway, thinking Michelle had gone, but after maybe five or ten seconds she spoke out of the dark, completely invisible. She said, Ashley? Listen. There's one more thing, and I really don't know much about it, so don't ask me more than what I'm gonna tell you. I don't even know if Darren knows. I don't know if I'd tell him, either, if I were you, because he's . . . he's Darren, and I'd be lying if I said I totally trust him. But that's neither here nor there, because this thing doesn't really have much to do with him.

I said, What is it? What thing?

Michelle came back into the bedroom. She pitched her voice low, and said, Well, listen. I know I said I hadn't talked to her in maybe two weeks, but that's not exactly true. Two weeks ago we had a fight. I don't really want to talk about it, and I don't think it even matters. But we had a fight. A bad one. She fucking punched me. So I basically kicked her out—she'd been staying with me for a little while before the fight happened—and she left, but she didn't take any of her stuff. And I didn't really want to just throw it out, no matter how pissed off I was. So I left her stuff where it was, in my spare room. Anyways, like, a week goes by, and I don't hear from her, I don't talk to her, nothing. But then last weekend I got a call from her. It was, I don't know, Saturday night, I think? She was . . . pretty wound up.

I said, What did she want?

Oh, she was going on and on, said Michelle. She said how she'd broke up with Darren, and she said she wanted to just leave town again for a while and she said how she wanted to make things right with Bailador and his friends—

I said, Bailador?

Yeah, some Amigo she knows. I've never met him, but Chass knew him from when she worked at that big farm, Triple Heart, I think, back in the day.

What did she have to make right?

Ah man, said Michelle, this is the part you can't tell Darren, okay? Because I don't want any trouble in my karma.

Okay . . .

Well, up until two weeks ago, Chastity was hanging out with this guy, Bailador, and some other Amigos. She'd been hanging out with them a lot since they all got back up here in March. And before you even ask, I have no idea, I swear to god, I have no idea if she was sleeping with one of them. But something bad happened, and all I know is this guy Bailador ended up pulling a knife on her and telling her to fuck off. After it happened, whatever it was, was when she got back to my place, and obviously she was real upset. She told me about the knife getting pulled, but when I tried to get more out of her, that's when we got into the fight. That's when she punched me. And now the rest you know.

Jesus Christ. So have you talked to her since she called you on Saturday?

No, said Michelle. Because, to be honest? I kind of told her to fuck off. I kind of told her to stop calling me and showing up and expecting me to help, then turning on me the minute I say one thing. I told her to get her shit straightened out, because I'm tired of being snapped at all the time. Her stuff is still at my place when she wants it, but it's on her to make amends with me. You know?

Yeah, I said.

And you can take this however you want, but maybe it's the same for you and her. Maybe it's time for her to be better to you too.

Maybe. I don't know.

She's a good person, said Michelle. Deep down inside. But she can drive everybody away. She can be her own worst enemy. Fuck. Okay, man. I'm going home. This has gotten way too heavy. Don't worry, I can show myself out. You're not wearing any clothes anyways.

EIGHT

Back in the fall, over the first couple days following the D'Amours Classic, I totally hid out. I didn't work out much, because a) I needed a rest and b) I knew the people at the gym would ask about how I'd done, and I didn't want to explain anything, I didn't want to relive it. So I hung around at home and mostly occupied my time with beer and weed and video games in the living room, sometimes with Trey, often by myself.

What had happened in the hotel, with Chastity, was on my mind constantly. Darren called once, on the Monday, and told me he was fucking sorry to hear how the show had turned out. He asked if I wanted to get together later in the week, maybe for a game of pool at Dunnigan's. For one bitter, guilty second, I almost confessed everything, right then, over the phone. Instead I just told him I might be able to hang out in a few days, nothing definite, but I was okay.

By Wednesday, my emotions got manageable again. I went for a jog in the afternoon and thought about getting back to the iron, maybe the next day. I thought about getting a tattoo. Something to symbolize moving on. Maybe one of those Chinese symbols you sometimes see. I liked the way those looked, all mystical and ancient and whatever.

What had happened with Chass already felt unreal. I knew it had gone down, but it was like a dream or a distant memory. Thinking about it turned me on and made me angry and sad all at the same time. I knew she'd stay in my life—how couldn't she?—but what had happened between us, I guessed, would only ever be a one-time thing. The worst and best mistake of my life, not to be repeated.

On the Thursday night of that week, a cold fall rain started to come down. Trey went to work at the club. I took the night off. I cracked open a beer and started up a video game.

I was not five minutes into it, getting the feel of the controls, when my phone went off against my leg. I looked down. Chastity's name was on the screen.

I answered it quick. She stayed silent for a while. I could hear background noises, enough to know that the line wasn't dead. I tried to wait her out, but I ended up breaking the silence, saying her name. She asked me what I was up to. I could hear in her voice how she was faking casualness, but I played along, told her I wasn't up to much. She asked me if I wanted to hang out. I said hanging out sounded good. I was trying to sound just as casual, but I knew I wasn't.

She picked me up in Darren's car. She was alone. This time I did ask about D. Chastity said he was busy that night. Out somewhere, she didn't know where. There was a lot Darren didn't tell her, she said, and then she added that there was a lot she didn't ask. It was just better that way.

I nodded. I didn't really want to talk about Darren. Asking had been, like, an act of duty or something, because as soon as he was on my mind, that guilt came burning back up.

We went to Dunnigan's, the same place Darren had suggested. It was a place you went for a low-key night, when you didn't want a club like the Balmoral. Dunnigan's was a smaller joint, sandwiched between a variety store and a Christian bookseller, which were both closed up for the night. A fiftyish guy, short but heavyset, was working the front door. He was the kind of guy who didn't look like he could move fast but could deal damage if he needed to. I gave him a professional nod, bouncer to bouncer, as we went in.

We played a few games of pool and shared two pitchers of beer. Chastity was distracted and moody. She was aggressive both in how she played pool and drank. I'd seen her like this before, but never with the weirdness that stood between us now.

After the second pitcher was gone, and she'd beaten me three games out of three, she said she figured she should run me home. I said okay. Meanwhile I was making myself crazy, searching for hidden meaning in everything. We returned our tray of pool balls and paid off our pitchers and left.

She wasn't drunk, but she probably shouldn't have been behind the wheel. She drove Darren's car fast, same as he usually drove it, tailgating and honking at anyone who was slowing us down. The rain washed over the windshield. She smoked, played the radio loud. In the passenger seat, I felt strange and small.

I thought she'd just let me out at home and be gone, but instead we sat in the front seats of the car for a while, listening to the radio, not saying anything. After I couldn't stand it anymore, I said her name, and right away she turned down the radio and began to talk, not looking at me. The rain on the windshield made weird shadows that moved down her face.

She said, Do you believe people can change? Because I do. It's funny to say that, to admit it, because I never used to believe it, you know, I always just believed people were stuck in their ways and would never change, and if they deal with something one way then that's probably the way they're always going to deal with it, you know, because we're all creatures of habit, so that's how we do things. I mean, look how fucking hard it is for anybody to stop smoking, right? Darren says it's rigged—smoking—so that you can't quit, like they put things in the cigarettes to make you keep smoking, but I think it's just a habit, and once you have a habit it's hard to break out of it. No matter what. Anyways. Never mind all that. Because I do think people can change, and I do think people can be better. And I think this because it's me. Because I see who I've been and I see who I want to be, and who I want to be is so much better than who I was. And I'm there. Or I'm almost there. I'm almost there. So that's what I mean. I'm proof to myself, if that makes sense. I'm how I know to keep on going. But *she* won't see it. She holds on to the past and she won't see it.

I waited for a few seconds, and then I said, You mean your mom.

She won't see who I've become, said Chastity. All she sees is what's past.

I said, This is all about Nevaeh.

Chastity didn't say. Instead she put a hand over her face. I thought she might be crying, but when she took her hand away her eyes were dry. Again the rain-shadows moved over her cheeks.

Another minute or two went by. Nothing was said. She'd turned the radio back up.

I said, I guess I'll go now.

Okay.

I said, I'm not real good at saying goodbye without it sounding weird, so . . .

Do you want to say goodbye? I mean, just yet?

No, I said. No, I don't.

Well, is anybody else home? Trey?

Not for a few hours at least. He's working.

Then let's go inside, said Chastity.

We started to open our doors, but I reached over and took hold of her wrist. I said, I want this. I really want this. I have for a long time.

I know, said Chastity. But let's not talk right now? Let's just go inside. Okay?

So I KEPT SEEING HER ON THE SLY AS THE FALL WENT ON, AS Christmas got near, as my failure at the D'Amours Classic got more in the past.

She didn't usually fuck like she had our first time, when we were liquored and coked up in the hotel room after the show. Most times she was slow and, like, thorough when we did it, working her hips beneath me, breathing in these low moans, looking me dead in the eyes all the while. She wouldn't let me say anything. She'd hold a finger to my lips or stick her tongue in my mouth if I started to speak. But everything else seemed to be left up to me. I could go fast or slow. I could pull her hair or smack her ass or go down on her or go in her mouth. I could come wherever I wanted to. It was as if she'd given all the control to me.

Except, really, I know now, she'd given me no control. Because even as I got off with her any way I wanted to, even as I did almost anything—except for talking—that came into my head, I got more and more desperate for her. From the second I finished, until whenever it was we got together again, she owned every thought I had.

I'll admit, it was a bad place for me to be in, bro, but do you think I could see that at the time? That's not exactly right. I could see it. I just couldn't seem to do anything about it. It made me think of a line from another old country song, one my dad liked, from a band called the Derailers. *When it's rolling, you can't stop a train.*

Our hook-ups were all in secret. It was always at her call, but I was constantly ready for it, and it was always in one of two places, my room at Trey's house or Darren's car, cramped into what little space there was. Once it happened three times in five days. Then it was two shitty goddamn weeks until it happened again.

Outside of our secret, there was everything else. There was my dad, Chass's family, Chass's daughter, and everyone we knew. Darren. Chastity didn't have much to say about him, other than that she didn't know what to do, and couldn't we talk about it some other time. That suited me fine. Guilt, bro. You can't stop that train, but I guess you can pretend it isn't gonna roll over you. At least for a while.

Once, in late November, I went with Darren on a collection. We went up to the north part of town, past the big-box plaza, to a little townhouse subdivision, pretty similar to the neighbourhood where I lived with Trey. A lot of the townhouses had Christmas ornaments on the doors and windows or on the little patches of lawn.

This guy we're seeing, said Darren, his name is Gary. He gets a quarter-pound of medicinal hydro every month. Sells half. I think he smokes the rest. He's kinda sick, like long-term sick. What do they call it when your body shuts down over a lot of years? *M*-something? He's got that. But usually he's pretty good about squaring up with me. He pays me on the fifteenth. This is the first time I've had to knock.

I said, So you've been fronting him?

Consignment, Ash. Fronting sounds bad.

Fronting *is* bad, isn't it?

Hey, brother, don't worry about the economics side. Anyways, it's not going to be a problem with Gary. He's chill. He's not gonna make any trouble. He doesn't have any dogs or nothing.

The townhouse Darren led us up to had a sign beside the front walk that read NU-WAY ~ THERAPY COACHING EMPOWERMENT. We didn't go to the front door. We went around to the back, onto a little board porch and to a set of patio doors. Darren, grinning in a friendly way, knocked on the glass and waved. A man with a thin grey comb-over and ponytail was standing in a narrow kitchen that we could see from the patio doors. He looked to be in the middle of making a cup of coffee or tea. A cane was leaning against the counter beside him. He was wearing fat wool socks and leather Birkenstocks, and he was looking at us with dismay and surprise and tiredness.

Darren waved again. The man picked up his cane and hobbled across the floor and let us in.

I closed the patio door behind us. The inside of the townhouse was lit by candles and mellow lamps. Pictures of oceans and mountains hung on the walls and a strong smell of incense filled the air.

Hiya, Gary, said Darren.

In kind of a half-whisper, Gary said, I've got a client in the isolation tub.

Well, let's not be real long, said Darren, not lowering his voice at all.

It's not a good time, said Gary.

It never is, said Darren.

Darren sat down on the armrest of a couch and looked at a dolphin sculpture on the end table beside him. I stood to the side, keeping my shoulders square and wide. I didn't want to look at Darren or at the little man with the cane. My thoughts were already wandering back to Chastity, to what we'd done in Darren's car two nights earlier. I thought about her tight little ass pressed against me, bare and pale in the dashboard lights. My breath caught in my throat and blood burned in my face.

I've had some investments lose some value, said Gary. And I've had some business fall through. And I've—

Knock it off, said Darren. These aren't fucking car payments.

Gary winced at Darren's voice. Then he looked scared. He was leaning on his cane and his knuckles were white. I couldn't keep thinking about Chastity anymore. I was too uncomfortable. What were we doing here, shaking down this cripple?

I have some cash, said Gary. Maybe, I don't know, fifteen hundred. Can that do for now? Please?

Go get it, said Darren.

Gary turned around and hobbled past the kitchen and disappeared toward the front of the house. For a minute I pictured the man making a break for it, limping his way out the front door, trying to get away. I didn't like the image at all.

I told you it wouldn't be a problem, said Darren. Gary's alright. One time he showed me his isolation tub. The one he was talking about when we came in. You just lie in it and there's no light or sound and I guess you float around until your mind starts playing tricks on you, and you get a bunch of insights and shit. That would be a trip, straight-up. The sessions are an hour long.

I said, Sounds pretty fucked up to me.

Gary reappeared holding a folded wad of money. He seemed to be leaning more heavily on his cane now. Maybe it was just to get sympathy. I looked around until I found a picture of a native elder clad in deerskin. It made me think of those braves on the monument in Missionary Position Park. I stared hard at it. Anything was better than looking at Gary. I heard him say, You don't have to count it.

Call it a habit, said Darren.

And you didn't have to bring the leg-breaker.

I looked away from the picture of the elder. Gary was looking at me. I said, Leg-breaker?

Yes, said Gary. I mean, what do you think I'm capable of? Look at me, for Christ's sake.

I was about to reply, to tell him that I wasn't a leg-breaker, that Gary was all wrong about me, it wasn't personal, it wasn't nothing more than a misunderstanding, and I was sorry, couldn't Gary see that, I was sorry, when Darren said, This'll do. Let's get going, brother.

I walked over to the patio door. Darren stood up from the arm-rest of the couch. Gary hung back.

I'll give you a week for the other five hundred, said Darren. And from now on, the price is twenty-two and a half.

Darren, come on. Please. That's not necessary.

That's business, said Darren. You don't like what I'm offering, you go see someone else. At least I'm not blacklisting you.

I pulled open the patio door and stepped onto the back porch. Darren followed me and on his way out of the townhouse said, Sorry to drop in on you like this, Gary.

He meant what he said too. I knew he did. That was the hell of it with Darren. I believe he saw this kind of thing as a cost of doing business, no more, no less. I don't think he thought about it in a bad-guy way, because I don't think he was a bad guy. Not then, anyways. Not before he started slinging crank on his dad's behalf. Not just slinging it locally, bro, but muling it too. But that's another issue.

Anyways, that day, before Darren dropped me off, he gave me two hundred dollars cash, ten percent of the whole amount Gary owed him. I pocketed it, picturing the man leaning on his cane, calling me a leg-breaker.

I'm going to the dentist, said Darren. But after I'm done, I'll swing back, pick you up. You can finally tell me about the weight-lifting show.

I caught sight of Darren's hand, holding an unlit dart, resting on the upholstery at the edge of the driver's seat. Beneath his hand was a dark spot in the fabric, almost invisible.

I said, I don't think I can, D. I think I'm . . . I got something on tonight, but I don't remember what it is. Maybe plans with my dad.

Hey, fair enough, said Darren. But let's go soon, okay? I feel like I never see you no more, unless we're doing business, and what fun is that.

I hear you, I said.

Darren lifted his hand from the upholstery to put the dart in his mouth. I could see the dark spot more clearly. It could have been anything, but I knew, beyond doubt, that it was the stain of my own cum, leaked from between Chastity's thighs.

I'M BAD FOR YOUR HEALTH, ASH, SAID CHASTITY.

What's that supposed to mean?

Exactly what I said. I'm bad for your health.

No you're not. At all. You're the best thing—

She put a finger against my lips, held it there for a few seconds, and then kissed me.

It was a week after me and Darren had collected from that cripple. I hadn't seen D since then.

I pulled Chastity closer. She leaned back and rested her head on my shoulder.

Trey was away for a few days, visiting some family for an early Christmas get-together, and I had the house to myself. Me and

Chastity were sitting together in the tub, each drinking a can of beer. A few more beers sat in cold water in the sink. The bathroom was dark except for a couple of candles I'd taken from the top of Trey's dresser. The idea—the candlelight, the hot bath—had been mine, a sudden one, and not one I'd ever given serious thought to or tried before. I'd put it all together quickly in the few minutes after Chastity had called to tell me she wanted to see me and was on her way over.

She'd laughed when I led her by the hand up to the bathroom. She said, Seriously, Ashley? But before I had a chance to reply, she began undressing, laughing softly.

I could've watched it over and over, the sight of her pulling off her shirt and removing her bra, unbuttoning her jeans and sliding them down her legs, and then finally stepping out of her panties. The panties were black and plain. Her socks were mismatched, one yellow, one blue.

She said it a third time, I'm bad for your health. We drink like fishes when we're together, we eat shitty food.

We kind of work it off, don't we.

I guess we do, said Chastity. Yeah.

What I didn't say was that I thought we didn't work it off enough. Over the past two weeks, I'd noticed a change in myself. The thickness of my arms and shoulders and chest stayed the same, but the definition—as perfect as it had been at the show in October—was gone. I was still eating a lot, and while I'd been at the weights again, I'd slowed down to only three or four times a week, and had dropped my cardio almost altogether. I was drinking a lot, too, way more than usual. The scales told me I was twenty pounds heavier than I'd ever been. Most of the weight was around my midsection, exactly where Chass's back was pressed in the tub. Shame darkened my mood. Weakness, such an easy and dangerous trap to fall into.

I said, I let myself go, didn't I. I gotta get things back under control.

Jesus, Ash, said Chastity. You can go easy on yourself, you know.

I thought you liked me shredded.

I do, said Chastity. But I like you as a human even better. Don't get addicted to yourself.

It's not like that. It's, I don't know, discipline.

If you need to discipline something, big man, you can focus on me instead of yourself.

Her words made my head spin. She never talked about the things we did, and she never let me talk about them either. But I stopped myself from replying. The moment was worth holding on to.

You want another beer? said Chastity.

Yeah. Please.

See what I mean about being bad for your health?

I watched her body as she climbed out of the tub. The tiles of the bathroom floor were wet and she slipped. It wasn't bad, and she easily caught herself on the vanity. She said, With my luck, Ash, I'll break my leg.

Immediately the sick man popped back into my head, saying, *You didn't have to bring the leg-breaker*. I closed my eyes. When I opened them again, Chastity was lowering herself back into the tub in front of me. When she'd settled into place between my thighs, she passed me a fresh beer.

I said, Darren.

I felt her stiffen. She said, What about him?

I don't know, I said. How long do you think he can do what he does? His, like, business. How long till it all comes crashing down?

Ashley, no offence, but I don't know much about his business and I don't want to know. It's his thing. I don't get involved with it.

I said, You really don't know anything about it, Chass? Legitimately?

She pulled away from me and said, I can leave if you want.

I moved forward, as much as the tub would allow, and pulled at her back. Water sloshed out onto the floor. I heard myself saying, No, no. Don't go. I'm sorry. I won't talk about it.

She stopped where she was, far enough forward that she was almost pushed up against the faucet. She remained there for half a minute, not looking at me. Desperate thoughts rushed through my head, but I stayed silent. I knew I had to.

Finally, she said, Darren's probably not a good subject to talk about. For you or me.

Okay, I said.

I will say this. He doesn't get me, like you do, but he's a good guy. In his heart. I know he is. Never mind his business. It's a means to an end, and in the end, he'll do right. By you, by me, by everybody. Until then, he'll do what he needs to.

I said, So what does he need to do?

I don't know, Ash. That's for him to figure out. We all come to that realization on our own.

Have you figured out what you need to do, then?

She slid back against me. She sipped her beer and sighed and said, Yeah, I've figured out what I have to do. Completely.

For a minute I thought she meant me, but as soon as the idea took shape I knew it had nothing to do with me at all. I said, Nevaeh.

Yes. I'll do anything I have to, believe me. I'll rob a fucking bank. I'll try dancing again. I'd even go back to fruit-picking with the Amigos, sunrise to sunset, like when I was a kid . . .

I said, So it's money. That's the problem.

Isn't it always? Real financial stability. That's what my mom calls it. She probably read it in a fucking magazine. Anyways, it's what I apparently have to show her before she'll even discuss anything. Real financial stability. Jesus Christ.

I said, Well, you can do it. I know you can. You set your mind to shit, Chass, and you make it happen. I've seen you do that your whole life. And if anybody gets in your way, you just knock them over.

Unless it's my mom.

Hey, remember grade ten science? What did the teacher used to say? What happens when a force you can't stop hits an object you can't move?

Disaster, motherfucker.

Disaster, I said.

Well, that's me and my mom, said Chastity. Anyways, the water is getting kind of cold. And I'm done my beer. Want to relocate?

Yes, I do.

I knocked back the rest of my own beer. We got out of the tub and dried off. I looked at myself in the mirror, patted my new belly. I said, Honestly, I have to take care of this bullshit.

What did I tell you? said Chastity. Give yourself a rest.

I can't.

She slipped alongside me, slid her hand down my thigh. I was hard within seconds. She said, Then let's go get some exercise.

As we headed through the dark hallway toward my bedroom, hand in hand, I said, What about me?

What about you what?

What is it you think I need to do? In life?

I told you, we all come to that on our own. You will too.

Okay.

But if I were to guess, said Chastity, I'd say what you need to do is keep everybody and everything together. You're the only one who can, I think.

Look, bro, I don't know for sure what Chass was doing, what she was thinking. I can't tell you why it was me she was doing this with. I mean, yes, I've been mostly with babes in my day, so it stands to reason that I attract them, not bragging or nothing. But why with Chass, given all the stakes and so forth? For starters, if she just wanted to fuck somebody who wasn't Darren, there'd be no shortage of dudes, even in Altena. And then there was her mom, my aunt Glenna, who legitimately would've lost her shit had she known. I've thought about this long and hard, and what I think is this: it was me because it had to be me. She was still with Darren, never mind all his secret business interests, because she didn't know how not to be with him anymore, and at the same time she was doing this going-straight routine in front of her mother. Yes it was for Nevaeh, but the pressure of the going-straight routine for Glenna's benefit had to be the hardest thing to swallow. So what I think is, it had to be me. I was her big secret middle-finger to the world. I don't know if I was anything more than that. I like to think so, but I don't know.

NINE

Hey, *it's Chastity*, said the message. *You know what to do.*

   I said, Chass, it's Ashley. It's Friday. Look, would you give me a call back? No big deal. I just wanted to say what's up. See how you're doing. Anyways, give me a call back, okay?

   I ended the call. Now I could only wait to see if she would call back, but I finished my breakfast and washed my dishes and changed into my workout clothes and still my phone did not go off. Like the song says, bro, waiting is the hardest part.

SHE DIDN'T CALL ME BACK THROUGH THE REST OF THE DAY, right through the time I spent at the gym, working my back and shoulders. I tried to not let it bug me, to not let it eat me the fuck up. I tried hard.

   On my way back into town, speeding down White Bike Way, I blasted past an Amigo who was pedalling a bicycle along the shoulder of the road. First the Amigo was ahead of me, and then he was behind me, briefly visible in my side mirror, and finally lost from sight. The whole encounter lasted a few seconds and no more.

But after that I started seeing other Amigos, which is to say I started noticing them. I saw them working in the fields on either side of the road. I saw at least ten of them packed into a van passing me in the opposite lane. When I got into town, I made a stop at a drugstore to pick up a new toothbrush and some other shit, deodorant and whatever, and I saw a short, bowlegged Amigo in the Bath & Body aisle, looking at all the different kinds of soaps. Not far away was a drugstore employee with a sour look on his face. He wasn't doing anything else but looking at the Amigo looking at soap. He was watching the Amigo, no doubt, like, doing surveillance on him—a lot of people thought the Amigos were thieves and shoplifters. Personally I had no idea if that was true. I had no real knowledge of the Amigos.

They came early in the spring and left late in the fall, and they hung out at their own places and had their own special church services. Most of the time, they were stuck in the greenhouses or on the farms—and thank Jesus I had never had to do any kind of farm-work bullshit, like a lot of kids around here had to do—so my path and the Amigos had never crossed.

Until now.

Now, like I said, I was *noticing* them. I didn't realize it at the time, but Michelle Levy had put them into my mind. Especially that one Amigo—what was his name? something with a *B?*—pulling a knife on Chastity. What was all that about?

The Amigo in the Bath & Body aisle at the drugstore was looking at me. His expression was straight-up friendly. A few paces behind him, the drugstore employee watched on. The Amigo looked like he was waiting for something, and I realized it was simply because I'd been staring at him. He was waiting for me to say something, like any fucking normal person would when you stare at somebody for more than a second or two.

I was embarrassed. I tried to smooth it over with a quick what's-up thrust of my chin, and before the Amigo or the drugstore employee could say anything, I pushed past them, made my way to the checkout, paid for my shit and got out of there.

And on my way out, it came to me. Bailador. That was the knife-puller's name. It popped into my head all at once, and I knew, I knew, that I'd heard it before.

THAT NIGHT I WAS POSTED TO THE BALMORAL'S FRONT door. I was paired with TJ Lemay. Between us we had a Maglite to check IDs and a Motorola walkie-talkie to talk to the rest of the crew inside. The temperature had dropped earlier in the evening and it was cold enough for jackets.

The first two hours of the night were dead, but by ten-thirty the club had picked up enough to have a small lineup. I was sipping from a takeout cup of coffee. Beside me, TJ was talking in an almost constant stream about a business idea he had. He was pausing only to check incoming patrons' IDs with the Maglite. He was saying, Because the way I figure it, Ash . . . Can I see your ID, buddy? Okay, go on in . . . The way I figure it, Ash, is it would be like an all-in-one service. Computers, stereos, you know, electronic shit, and . . . Hey, do you girls have your IDs on you? Okay, go on in, enjoy yourselves . . . Anyways, electronic shit. And what is it doctors do? Or they used to do? Like, they'd come right to your house—

I said, House calls.

Yeah, said TJ. House calls. It would be that. House calls, but for stereos and computers. I could even go with a doctor theme, like Doctor Stereo, *we make house calls* . . . Can I see your ID?

The incoming guy TJ was speaking to was this wiry kid, probably no older than seventeen, trying to look tough in an oversized hoodie and a baseball cap pulled low on his head. He had his eyes squinted almost shut. He said, It's okay, I'm twenty-two.

I still need to see your ID, said TJ.

I don't carry ID. But I'm twenty-two.

What year were you born? I said.

Seventy-nine, man, said the kid.

Wouldn't that make you twenty-four?

That's what I said, said the kid. Twenty-four.

Look, said TJ, either get out some ID or I can't let you in.

TJ and the kid argued back and forth for a minute. I stood back from it, not really interested unless it got violent. It didn't. A few seconds later, without another word, the kid turned around and skulked away, hands buried in his pockets. Maybe he would come back an hour later wearing a different hoodie and a different hat. There weren't many ways for trying to get into the club that I hadn't seen. People would say they just needed to run inside to get something they'd forgotten. People would say they knew Marcel or the DJ or Dani Knox or some other bartender. Sometimes people would try to bribe, usually with a pathetic amount of money or a dime bag of weed. Sometimes people would threaten, but almost always from ten feet away. I liked threats the best. They made me smile.

So what do you think? said TJ.

What do I think about what?

Come on, Ash. What do you think about Doctor Stereo, electronic repair house calls?

Oh, right. Well, I guess it's a pretty good idea. Do you know if it's been done by anybody else?

No, said TJ. I don't know. But I've never heard of it done by anybody else, so I'm probably the first, so don't rip it off from me, eh?

I said, I won't.

TJ turned to check the IDs of a small group of girls. They were each dressed in tiny skirts and tube tops. One of them was blue with the cold. She had her hands clasped together under her chin, and her teeth were clicking loud enough for me to hear. I shook my head as they went past me into the club.

I glanced down the street. A small crew of Amigos were in their usual place, hanging around the sidewalk bench.

Forty minutes passed. The bass beat from inside the club pushed out through the walls. The lineup at the door got longer. In the brief intervals we had, TJ asked about the incident from the night before, Brice O'Halloran getting slugged with the bottle. I told him what I'd seen, and how me and Trey had dragged the crazy patron out and thrown him to the curb. Fight gossip was always hot with us security guys.

TJ said it was crazy shit. He said a bottle could kill you, pretty easily, if it hit you in the right place. The temple or whatever. He asked me if I could imagine dying in a place like the Balmoral, which in a way was like dying *for* the Balmoral, since I'd be dying in, like, the line of duty. We both laughed in disgust at that.

I'd finished my coffee. Now I was getting cold, rocking back and forth on my feet, pushing my hands deep into my pockets. As always, I saw and spoke to a lot of people I was acquainted with. Girls I kind of knew hugged me or kissed me on the cheek. I wasn't really lusting for them, in their short skirts and tight tops, the way I sometimes did. Michelle, the night before, had tapped me dry.

And Chastity was on my mind. She still hadn't called me back.

At a quarter after eleven, TJ ducked inside to take a piss, leaving me with the Maglite. I didn't really care, that night, about checking birthdates and photographs on IDs. I just picked up each driver's licence, shone the light at it for a second, and then waved the person through.

A voice said, Hey, big boy, let me in, I'm a VIP.

I looked up. The guy standing in front of me was dressed in a hideous two-piece Sean John track suit. He had some ugly, bone-rack scag hanging on his arm.

I said, What's up, Seth.

Just a night on the town with my shorty, you know what I mean? said Seth.

I said, Sure I do.

We're VIPs, said Seth. You know what I mean?

Gone was Seth's hostility from the last couple of times I'd seen him. Now he was all friendliness. He was moving in for a hand-shake, and when I took it—what else could I do?—his hand was meaty and clammy. My skin crawled at the feel of it.

I said, There's no cover tonight, so everybody's a VIP.

Seth threw his head back and laughed. He hadn't let go of my hand yet. He leaned in close and said, How about those guys?

What guys?

Those beaner cocksuckers always hanging out down the street there. You guys never let them in, eh?

I shrugged and said, We don't not let them in, but they never try. I don't know . . .

Seth let go of my hand. He laughed again, and, passing me, dragging his bone-rack girl along, he said, Darren's right about you. You're all serious, man. You're all business. But that's okay. I respect that shit.

Then he was gone. I wiped my hands on my jeans.

A few seconds later, TJ reappeared. He said, Anything go down?

Nope, I said, handing back the Maglite.

For the next little while, the line thinned down to small, semi-frequent groups of two or three incoming people. I wasn't watching them like I should've. My eyes kept going back to the Amigos. Trey checked in over the Motorola, told us the club was almost full. He said we had capacity for another fifty customers. I doubted we would get that many. Before too long, people were going to start trickling out and heading home. If the club closed early I wouldn't be bothered. I would go straight home, make it a low-key night, forget the things I was thinking about.

TJ was going on again about his Doctor Stereo idea. I was only half listening. I heard myself say, Hey, man, can you cover me off for a few?

Sure, said TJ. You going to take a leak? Can you see if they got any coffee on behind the bar?

I said, I'm not going inside. But I'm not going real far. You need me, just shout. Just shout, my man, and I'll be there.

TJ gave me a weird look, but I was already moving. I walked down the sidewalk, actually feeling the distance between me and the Amigos getting smaller.

I was close by the time the Amigos—there were four of them—seemed to figure out that I was coming directly their way. They'd probably thought I was going to pass them by like everybody else did. They looked curious, but not bothered, not yet. None of them were big men. They were dressed almost identically in workboots and beat-up jeans and tucked-in shirts and denim jackets. Two of them were wearing old ball caps, and two were bare-headed, with their thick black hair neatly combed and side-parted. One of them was drinking a bottle of Coca-Cola.

I stopped four feet short of them. They all looked at each other. One smiled at me, and one asked the others something in Spanish. I heard words I'd heard in movies, hombre and policía. The Amigo's friends shrugged.

I said, Any of you guys speak English?

The reply was slow. Finally the guy with the bottle of Coke said, Yes. I speak it.

Okay, I said. Good. Well, look, this is maybe a weird question, but do you know an Amig— A Mexican guy named Bailador?

There was a brief pause, and then the guy with the Coke and two of the other guys looked at each other and laughed. They said the name a few times, Bailador, Bailador, and one of them did a few dance moves on the spot. I felt my ears get hot. These Amigos were laughing at me.

Except for the fourth guy, the shortest and slimmest of the group. He wasn't laughing at all.

I said, You. You know who I mean, right? Bailador?

I don't know, said the short guy, looking away. No sé, chico. No sé.

Hey, you speak English too, don't you.

Ramon speaks a little, said the Amigo with the Coke, still laughing a little, not really paying attention. Ramon always want to show off he speaks a little. He always want to talk English to the girls.

No sé, said Ramon.

I said, Bailador, is he a friend of yours?

The three other Amigos had one by one stopped laughing, each noticing that something was hanging in the air between their friend and me. They started to speak in Spanish again. Ramon waved their questions away.

I said, Tell me.

From down the street came TJ's voice, Ash, you okay?

I called back that I was fine.

Well, can you come back and give me a hand? TJ called.

I looked back to the front door of the club. A bigger lineup had formed, twenty people or so. Some of them were watching me. I yelled down to TJ that I would be back in a minute.

When I turned my attention back to the Amigos, I saw that

they were getting up from the bench and making to leave. The guy with the Coke shrugged, said, Sorry. I don't want there to be no problem, but I don't know what you ask.

Ramon was the first to walk away, head down, shoulders hunched. His buddies fell in behind him. For a few seconds all I could do was watch them go. Then one of the Spanish words I'd heard came into my head, and I said, Hey, Ramon, what if I am policía.

The Amigos all stopped walking. They turned back. Ramon looked at me, looked away, looked at me once more.

I said, What if I am policía? You understand that? What if I can make a lot of trouble for all you guys, unless you tell me who Bailador is? So what do you think, Ramon? Is your English better now?

WHAT BAILADOR MEANS IS DANCER.

I found this out the next afternoon, from Ramon, when we met up. He'd agreed to meet me under the idea that I was possibly a cop. Whether or not Ramon really believed me, I didn't care.

Ramon had told me to meet him where he worked, Triple Heart Growers Inc., one of the biggest farms in Altena. It was only later that I remembered Triple Heart was the same farm Chastity had worked on.

Anyways, not knowing what lay ahead, I'd brought Trey along with me to meet Ramon. We went in his truck. I had to at least give him some idea what we were doing, tell him a bit.

So you don't know what kind of shit Chastity's in, said Trey, driving us along the municipal road.

I said, No, I don't. But I heard this guy Bailador might've pulled a knife on her. I want to find out what's up with that.

Trey pushed out his lower lip and nodded. After a few seconds, he said, Ash, man, can I ask you something?

Yeah. Go ahead.

Well, I know she's your cousin, and you two are close, but her boyfriend is your boy, you know what I'm saying? Shouldn't he be looking out for her? How come you're not telling him any of this?

I said, How do you know I'm not?

Because you're out here to see these guys with me, dude, and not him.

I said, Stuff with Darren and Chastity is fucked up lately. Not that it isn't fucked up a lot, because it is, but lately, Trey, it's really fucked up. I don't know. So I'm doing this to look out for her. On my own, I guess. And if I have to bring Darren into it, I will, but—

It's okay, said Trey. You don't have to elaborate. I was just saying, that's all. I was just playing devil's advocate.

I said, And I brought you out here with me to have my back, like, just in case. I owe you one.

Don't even worry about that, said Trey. Hey, this your guy?

We'd arrived, as instructed, at the entrance to a dirt laneway. On both sides of the municipal road, broccoli fields stretched away in all directions. The laneway, kind of hidden by a stand of maple trees, was blocked by a crooked steel swing-gate. There was Ramon, standing beside his bike. He looked unhappy.

I said, That's him.

Trey pulled up. Ramon opened the gate. Trey drove through and stopped on the other side. Ramon closed the gate behind us and walked over to the passenger's side window. I pushed the button on the armrest and the window glass slid down. The cool air, smelling like soil, swirled into the cab of the truck. Ramon stood only a little taller than the side-view mirror.

I said, What's up.

Ramon peered at Trey, and then turned his attention back to me and said, He is police too?

I said, What do you think? Come on, let's go see Bailador.

Put your bike in the back of the truck, said Trey. You can roll with us.

Ramon moved wordlessly away from the passenger's side window and pushed his bike around to the truck bed. The second he was out of earshot, Trey fixed on me and said, What's he talking about, police?

Nothing, I said.

Ash, come on. I'm out here with you . . .

Okay, look. I didn't come right out and say it or anything, but I kind of told him I might be a cop and could get him in trouble if . . . Hey, I needed something, alright? He wasn't telling me anything. I needed something. The MAFD rule, Trey. Make A Fucking Decision. Didn't you teach me that?

Trey looked at me for a few long moments. He pushed out his lower lip again and looked as if he might say more, but then he caught sight of something in the rear-view mirror. He put down the driver's side window, leaned out facing the rear of the truck, and said, Hey, dude, you don't have to sit there. Come on up, get in the cab with us. Come on.

I looked in the rear-view mirror. Ramon was sitting on the truck bed beside his bicycle.

Come on, repeated Trey.

Ramon climbed down off the back of the truck and came up to the cab. Trey opened the driver's side door and the suicide door behind it, and gestured to the small jump seat in the back of the cab. Ramon climbed in and sat down and Trey pulled the doors closed behind him, and then put the truck back into gear.

As we drove along the narrow laneway, I could feel coolness

coming from Trey. He was usually easygoing—his size alone kept the peace for him most of the time—but I knew him well enough to know the moral code he kept. That business—me lying about us maybe being cops—was clearly not sitting well with him.

But at least he hadn't bailed. Yet.

I glanced in the rear-view mirror. Ramon was sitting on the jump seat, staring at his hands, which were clasped together between his knees. He almost looked like he was praying. Praying, or maybe thinking about pulling a knife and sticking us with it and then jacking Trey's truck. I didn't know this guy at all. I couldn't put anything past him.

Dead and buried, I thought. It had come out of nowhere. A farm field, like this one, what could you bury under it?

I said, So, Ramon, what can you tell me about him?

About who? said Ramon.

About Bailador. Who else?

A short pause, and then Ramon said, Dance. Man who dances . . .

I said, Man who dances?

Bailador. A man who dances.

What the hell are you talking about?

I think . . . I think you will see, said Ramon.

THE AMIGOS WHO WORKED FOR TRIPLE HEART LIVED IN A small horseshoe of mobile homes under a willow grove. The mobiles, set on concrete foundations, had porches made out of boards and old plywood. A couple of clotheslines were strung between them, hung with jeans and work shirts and socks and underpants. In the middle of the horseshoe were three picnic tables and a barbecue and a bunch of lawn chairs. Attached to the side of one mobile was a crooked carport where at least a dozen bicycles were stashed.

We'd arrived without Ramon knifing us. Trey crept his truck to a stop at the edge of the horseshoe. There were no signs of life around. Trey looked at me mildly, showing me it was my play now.

I said, Let's go.

I opened my door and got down from the truck, trying to push out my shoulders, make them look bigger. There were voices shouting from somewhere not far away. The air smelled like raw vegetables. Behind me, Trey and Ramon also got out of the truck. Trey went around to the truck bed and helped Ramon lift his bicycle down. Ramon walked the bicycle over to the carport and leaned it up against the others.

I said, So where's he at?

Ramon gestured for me and Trey to follow him. He led us around the back of the mobiles. I was suddenly aware. Not nervous, right? Not like I'd admit, anyways. But definitely aware, like on a busy night at the club. Sights and sounds, bro, the hair standing up on my arms and the back of my neck. You can't ever be too ready when you're going into the unknown. And the unknown was exactly where Ramon was leading us. We could come around a corner, me and Trey, and find ourselves up against it. Maybe all the Amigos, Bailador included, would be standing there with blades pulled. Switchblades and daggers and fucking machetes—don't they hack each other up with machetes in Mexico regularly? Maybe Ramon never needed a knife in the first place.

Dead and buried, with broccoli growing out of our bones.

But as we followed Ramon, what came into view was an undeveloped rectangular meadow, about three acres, all of it flattened grass. It was bordered by the mobiles on the near side, the willow grove on two sides, and the huge planted field on the remaining side. Most of the meadow was taken up by a rough soccer pitch, two rusty metal frames marking the goals at either end.

Two teams of Amigos were chasing a ball around. The players, only ten of them including the goaltenders, were dressed in shorts and jogging pants and even jeans. Some were barefoot. One team was shirtless. Three or four more Amigos watched the game from the sideline.

Far as I could see, nobody had a knife. Nobody was even looking at us.

Me and Trey and Ramon stood watching. One of the soccer players was way better than the others. He was, truth be told, goddamn incredible. He was tall and lean and barefoot. He moved easily, stopping himself to take control of the ball and then sprinting it down the pitch as if he didn't weigh anything. He moved like some kind of dancer.

I said, That's him, right?

Ramon nodded and said, Bailador, yes. You see?

Shit, said Trey. Look at that guy move.

The game lasted another ten minutes. I was unsettled, eager to get on with things, but at the same time I was fascinated by Bailador's movements on the field. I thought of Chastity watching this guy. Jealousy got into my guts and twisted them around. I looked away from the game and spat onto the grass.

When they'd finished playing, the Amigos moved to the side of the field. The skins team put on shirts and jackets. Then they all left the sidelines and started back for the mobiles, directly approaching us.

In a soft voice, Trey said, Okay, Ash. Your show. But I'm not interested in trouble. I hope you know what you're doing.

I said, I do.

I didn't know, though. I didn't have any kind of plan or idea.

The group of Amigos, fourteen in all, had closed the distance to twenty feet. Bailador was the tallest. He'd put on a windbreaker that was too big for him. As he came close, I saw that he was familiar, but I couldn't think how. All the other possibilities kept going through my mind. All the things that could happen.

The other Amigos didn't seem happy to see me or Trey. They talked quietly with each other. There were no switchblades or machetes. Yet. Honestly, what would we do if there were? I mean, honestly? Cut and run? What else could we do if it went down like that?

Bailador looked at me. He said something in Spanish to Ramon. Ramon said, Si. Bailador kind of sneered. He said, Él no es un policía.

Well, that didn't take him long to figure out, said Trey.

I didn't say anything. I kept a hard stare on Bailador, trying not to show any concern, also trying to remember where I'd seen him before. It was already driving me crazy. Beside me, Ramon shrugged and looked at the ground.

Vamos, said Bailador, shaking his head.

He led us back around to one of the picnic tables. The Amigos around him lit darts and sat down in the shitty chairs. One of the Amigos had brought out a case of Blue Light from somewhere, and then cans were making the rounds, but nothing was offered to me or Trey. All eyes were on us, me in particular.

Bailador sat down on the top of the picnic table. One of the Amigos put a dart in one of his hands and a can of beer in the other. Bailador put the cigarette in his mouth and leaned his head forward for the Amigo to give him a light.

I said, So you're the boss out here, or what?

Ramon translated. Bailador shrugged and looked out toward the road. He replied, and Ramon translated, Not a boss. Here or anywhere. The only boss is Mr. Switzer.

Mr. Switzer? I said.

He is owner of the farm, said Ramon.

It looks like you want to be the boss, I said, right to Bailador.

Ramon hesitated.

Ash, said Trey. Let's go easy with these guys.

Tell him I said that, Ramon. I don't care if he doesn't think I'm a cop. I don't care who he thinks I am.

Ramon had said only a few words when Bailador looked me full in the face and said a bunch of words in Spanish. Ramon switched to translating this. He said, We don't have much time for our selfs, and what it is you want here?

I licked my lips. I breathed in, held it, let it out slowly and said, A girl. A . . . friend of mine. Chastity Goss. You know her?

No translation was needed. The name was enough. I saw it in Bailador's eyes.

Ramon was still translating, but Bailador waved him off. He leaned back on the tabletop and smoked and looked in the direction of the road again. After a few seconds, he said a few words. One of them was sí.

He says he knows Chastity, said Ramon.

By the tone of Ramon's voice, by the way he was staring hard at the ground, he seemed to know Chastity too.

Shit, said Trey.

The only thing I was able to say was, You do know her. You do.

Sí, said Bailador.

I said, So what about the fucking knife you pulled?

Ramon blurted out something in Spanish. Bailador looked at him. They talked back and forth, Ramon getting more and more upset. Finally Bailador said something. He said it sharp too. Whatever it was, it sounded like the Spanish equal to shut up. And Ramon did shut up, but, man, he did not look pleased.

Bailador slipped off the tabletop. He put his beer can down and set his cigarette on top of it. He shook his head a little, like he was loosening up his neck. It was then that I realized the Amigos were closing around us.

Ash, said Trey.

Crees que te tengo miedo? said Bailador, straight to me.

I said, What?

I'm not afraid of you, pandillero, said Bailador.

Battle coming, was all I thought, and for the first time in a long time, long as I could remember, the idea of a battle scared the shit out of me. Knives or not—and at that point in my life I'd never been shot at either, but I'll get to that eventually—knives or not, I was scared, and I could feel myself taking a step backwards. The wrong thing to do right from the get-go.

Wait! said Trey. Wait, wait. No problemo.

Bailador looked at him. The Amigos slowed down the circle they were making.

No problemo, said Trey. Okay? We're all gonna take a step back here and me and my buddy are gonna say goodbye. Goodbye. Adiós. No problemo.

Bailador sucked a little kiss through his teeth, same way Jamaican guys sometimes do, and spat on the ground. He didn't say anything. But he wasn't making any more moves either.

Come on, Ash, said Trey.

He put his hand on my shoulder. I shook it off and stood my ground. I heard him make a hissing sound, and then I heard his boots scraping the dirt as he walked away.

I looked at Bailador. Bailador looked at me. Ramon appeared, crowding in beside his friend. He was almost hopping foot to foot. Like your friend says, said Ramon. No problem. Let's say adiós. No more trouble, okay?

Bailador kept looking at me.

In a quiet voice, Ramon said to Bailador, Necesitamos estos puestos de trabajo, okay . . . ?

After a long moment, Bailador nodded. He took his eyes away from mine.

I took a few steps backwards, slow, still conscious of all the Amigos around me. I wasn't quite sure what the hell had just happened, but I had the sense that maybe these guys had more at stake than I did. I started walking toward Trey's truck. Trey was already sitting behind the wheel. From behind me, I could feel Bailador's eyes on the back of my neck. It was then, right that second, that I remembered where I'd seen the guy before.

The hospital reception, the day I'd gone to see Darren. I'd seen Bailador . . . and come to think of it, I'd seen Ramon. Both of them, talking to the lady at the desk.

And, and, even *before* the hospital, I'd heard his name. Chastity had said it into her phone, speaking in Spanish, just as me and Darren and Seth had gotten back to Darren's car at the King's Court motel.

I stopped walking. I saw Trey cuss at me through the windshield. I turned around. Another miserable look passed over Ramon's face, but Bailador kept the hard-ass thing going pretty good.

Forget something? said Ramon.

All those Amigos, and maybe a knife and maybe not, and anyways, what had I really forgotten? What did I even know?

No, I said. I guess not. I'll get going.

It was a quiet ride back into town. I finally tried to break the silence. I said, That didn't really go down the way I thought it would.

And exactly what way did you think it would go down? said Trey.

His voice was pitched lower than normal, and it had an edge to it. I looked at him. Trey was watching the road.

I'm not sure, I said.

Trey nodded heavily, still watching the road. I looked at the surface of the dashboard in front of me. There was a small mark on the plastic, dirt or dust. I started rubbing it off with my thumb.

The next time . . . , said Trey.

Next time what?

The next time you want to do whatever it is you're doing, if it's something like this shit, you either tell me direct ahead of time or you count me out.

Trey, I—

Or, if it's real serious, Ashley, if it's real serious, you call the cops. Why are you messing around with anything like this?

I don't know. I'm just trying to help, I guess.

TEN

So, Detroit, said Darren.

I blinked. Detroit. Given everything else going on, it had pretty much slipped my mind. I said, What about Detroit?

Darren and I were at Dunnigan's. It was late afternoon, and we were midway through our fourth game of pool. We'd been playing for the full hour we'd been there, and we'd both put down a couple of beers. Darren's busted nose looked like it was healing okay. It wasn't too crooked. The bruising around his eyes had already faded.

He'd called me around lunch, had said we were long overdue for some time together, just the two of us, shooting the shit like we'd always done back in the day. If I was free that afternoon, would I come out or what?

And without any excuses I could think up quick, I'd said okay.

I took my turn on the table, missed my shot. I was losing the game and losing interest, but Darren was playing tirelessly. Something about the game's low-key, repetitive nature seemed to have gripped him. He pocketed three balls in three quick strokes.

I said, What about Detroit, D.

Yeah, brother. Detroit.

I said, We talked about it, but you didn't tell me anything.

Didn't I? I thought I did.

You were in the hospital. You were fucked up.

Right, said Darren. Right. Hey, you gonna take your turn?

I turned to take a shot on the table. Darren had already out-played me by far. I said, So tell me.

Well, there's not a lot to tell. I have to go down there, and I have to talk to some guys about business, and there's some serious cash in it. Oh, and I want you to come, because.

What, you expect trouble down there?

Not at all, Ash, said Darren. It's not like that. It's just that I always feel better having you with me. You know that. You're the only one I really trust, brother. Come on, don't make me say too much more.

I didn't reply right away. I took my shot, pocketing the ball I was aiming for. I lined up another shot and missed.

So what do you say? said Darren. You in?

I said, You know I don't usually want the details. But tell me one thing.

What is it?

You're not trying to take anything across, right?

What? said Darren, laughing.

Hey, bro, you said there was money in it. You're not planning to mule anything across the fucking border, are you?

Darren had to pause to get his concentration back. He took his turn and for the first time really missed, like, wide across the felt, way off. He laughed a little more, shook his head and said, No, no, Christ, it's nothing like that, Ash. Nothing that crazy. It's just busi-ness. We'll tell everybody we're going to see a Tigers game. And then when we get there, we're just gonna have a meeting with some people. That's it, that's all. Legitimately.

A SHORT WHILE LATER I MANAGED TO GET DARREN AWAY
from the pool table. We sat down, had another round of beers and
a platter of nachos, vegetarian for Darren. I thought about the
body I needed to be building. For a second I felt this intense blast
of self-hatred. Beer and nachos. I made up my mind to go twice
as hard in the gym the next day. And I would cut out the shit, I
would, the closer I got to the next show.

Meanwhile, Darren was talking fast and kind of crazy, mostly
about his straight job at the electronics store at the mall. I listened,
looking at him. I realized again how thin he looked. There were
a small number of sore-looking spots on his face, little scabs and
rough patches, some on his jaw and cheek and two on his eyebrow. As he talked, he kept scratching his forearms and the backs
of his hands.

I said, D, you okay?

Am I okay? said Darren.

Yeah. You're all over the place.

Ha, sorry, brother. I got a lot on my mind. You know how I am. My
mouth can't ever keep up with my head. Hey, how's your old man?
When I was at work the other day, I saw him. I saw him and his . . .

Partner, I said, biting into a nacho. His partner, Greg. And
he's good.

Good, said Darren. I like your old man. He's never given me
that look, you know?

What look?

The knucklehead look. Same one I used to get from just about
every teacher I ever had.

You and me both, I said.

That's true. Oh well. Fuck them. Where are they now?

Darren got quiet then, concentrating on whatever was itching his forearms. The whole time we'd been together at Dunnigan's I hadn't asked the obvious question, but it had been there, burning away in the back of my mind. I hadn't asked because I hadn't, like, known how. There'd been Darren's fixation with the pool, and then Darren's ramblings about work, and only now was there a pause. It probably wouldn't last. So I took a sip of beer and said, Hey, bro, how's Chass?

What? said Darren. What? Oh, she's fine. I think.

You think?

I don't know. I told you things aren't great, didn't I? That we needed some time apart? Didn't I tell you that?

I said, Yeah, you mentioned it. I just wondered if it happened. I haven't really been talking to her much.

No, said Darren. That doesn't surprise me. You know how she gets.

I do. So are you two apart right now?

Yeah, we are.

And where is she?

Jesus, Ash, said Darren. What's with the third degree? We're apart right now, and it's fucked. It's fucked up a lot of things . . . She's at her mother's place.

At her mother's, I said.

Or at Michelle's. Or . . . I don't know . . . She's back in London, trying to strip again. Look. I don't want to talk about Chastity right now. It just messes me up.

Fair enough, I said.

Darren scratched at the sore spot on his eyebrow. He said, I'm sorry. I'm on edge.

I noticed.

I've got a lot of things on my mind. A lot of stresses. I need to get well, it's no big deal.

What do you mean, get well?

Nothing, said Darren. Listen, you want to get out of here, blow off some steam? Come on, I'll drive.

LARS FABRICATION WAS TWENTY MINUTES OUT OF TOWN ON White Bike Way, a good distance past my gym. The complex's three buildings had been shut up and abandoned for the last five years. The cinder-block walls were covered in graffiti. Empty bottles and cans and cold firepits and little piles of trash littered the property. A number of large signs said that the place, all twenty thousand square feet of it, was for sale. Some smaller signs said that trespassers would be prosecuted. Past the complex was a huge empty field, zoned for townhouses but not yet developed. The sun, sinking low, was sending long, lonely rays across the field and between the empty buildings.

It felt creepy for me to be there. This was where my dad had been outed.

I was standing on a flat pad of asphalt, Darren beside me. Behind us was the wall of the complex's largest building. Forty feet in front of us was a low, grassy mound running along the edge of the property.

Still think it's a fake? said Darren, grinning around a dart.

I said, I don't know.

Well, man, up and pull the trigger and find out.

In my hands was Darren's little pistol, the one he'd stuck in Junior's face at the motel. The pistol was not exactly heavy, but it had a certain weight to it. A seriousness. Two minutes before, Darren had showed me how to cock it, how to rack the slide and see the twinkle of brass as the round was chambered and how then to thumb the safety on and off. It had made that same badass movie sound effect. Just like in the Nam, motherfucker. I had never fired a gun in my life.

Fifteen feet in front of us, with the grassy mound as a backstop, an empty washer fluid jug sat on top of a wooden cable spool. I had the feeling Darren had been out here before, to this very spot, doing what I was about to do.

He said, Come on, let's see it.

I squeezed my left eye shut and with my right eye looked down the pistol's sights at the jug. A small part of me still believed this was just an Airsoft gun. I'd shot lots of those, and they were no big deal at all. Might leave a welt on you, sure, or worst-case scenario, put out your eye, but that shit is a lot different than a bullet hole.

I tightened my finger on the trigger. The shot came as a surprise. It cracked out, flat but way louder than I'd expected, with a hard echo against the building. The recoil snapped against my wrists. The casing tinked out onto the asphalt.

Jesus, I said.

Boom! said Darren. That's the way, motherfucker, that's the way. Of course, you didn't hit anything.

I hadn't even looked yet, but when I did I saw that the washer fluid jug was exactly where it had been before I'd fired at it. I said, I missed.

Yeah, but no big deal. Still a rush, eh?

Totally, I said.

Okay, said Darren. Let me see—

I took aim at the jug and fired again, and then twice more, finding the trigger-pull easy. When I'd stopped shooting, my aim was six inches higher than where I'd started it, and still the jug hadn't moved. My ears were ringing and there was a pins-and-needles sensation in my hands and wrists.

Okay, Ash, said Darren, softly. Let me have it back.

I thumbed on the safety and handed Darren the pistol, grip first, the way I'd seen it done in the movies.

Alright, I said. I'm convinced.

I told you, said Darren. It's not real big at all, either, not a nine-mil or a four-five or anything like that. It's just a .25. A pocket rocket, bro. But up close, you know? If I ever have to make a point, like I did with Junior, it works fine.

Pocket rocket. We give stupid-ass nicknames to shit, don't we, maybe to take away from what they really are, what they really do. I wondered again, like I had back at the motel, who Darren might've become. Good guy? Bad guy? Fucking dangerous guy?

I said, Where did you get it?

Oh, from a guy. A buddy of Seth's. Four hundred bucks cash, which also got me two hundred bullets for it, hollow-points, which will fuck you up. I've gone through, I don't know . . . fifty bullets maybe? . . . just practising, and here, let me show you, brother . . .

Darren aimed the pistol, one-handed, and fired. I saw the jug turn on the spool. Darren fired again and the jug fell onto the ground. The empty casings rolled at our feet.

Practice pays off, said Darren.

The slide was already locked back. Darren took the short magazine out from the bottom of the grip and inspected it. As far as I could tell, it was empty. Darren let the slide forward and put the magazine back in and dry-fired the pistol and put it into the back of his jeans. Then he bent over and began picking up the casings. He put them in his pocket. I guess he wasn't keen to leave any evidence around.

I went over to the washer fluid jug and picked it up. There was one pair of holes, entry and exit, dead centre near the bottom. The entry was very small. I couldn't fit my fingertip into it. The exit was a little bigger, jagged-edged. Toward the top of the jug a long furrow had been torn out of the plastic along the side. The bullet had grazed it there, I guessed, and the damage looked bad. I thought about what that would be like on flesh and veins and bones. I dropped the jug back onto the spool and said, Should we get out of here now?

I guess, said Darren. We don't have to rush back to the car, if that's what you mean. There's nobody out here.

I said, Alright. Hey, one thing. And again, I don't usually want the details, but, uh, why?

Why what? said Darren.

Why'd you buy the piece?

Right away, saying the word piece made me feel stupid, like what the fuck was I trying to play at, for real?

I should've got one a long time ago, I think, said Darren. Just in case. You gotta be security-minded, you know? God forbid I ever have to use it, Ash, but if I need it, I have it, and that's what matters.

As he spoke, he looked off in the direction of the sunset. That certain light made him look good, made his eyes glow and coloured his skin, enough to hide the paleness and the sores.

I almost asked him, then, when he'd decided to take business in a more serious direction, when he'd started selling crank to people like Junior, when he'd started selling crank at all, and why, and how much of it was his dad's idea, and would Darren be okay, and, once more, where was Chastity.

I opened my mouth, said his name, and he looked at me, and I said, I . . . I've gotta take a piss.

Don't let me stop you, brother.

I pissed against a chained-up steel door fifty feet down the side of the building. The light was turning blue, fading fast. With it came the cold. My piss was steaming a little. As I stood there, I listened for sirens, wondering if every cop in town had been alerted to the gunshots out at the old Lars Fabrication complex. But there was nothing.

My dad came to mind. My dad, working here as a younger man, a machinist, both smart and powerfully built, and then meeting a company accountant named Greg. Despite how much I hated these thoughts, I wondered how it had started. Did my dad and Greg both know, from the minute they saw each other? Was their first time out here, maybe in a clearing in the bush behind the complex? Or was it in the washroom, where the hidden cameras eventually caught them?

I gritted my teeth, tried to shake the images out of my head. I finished pissing and zipped up my fly.

I turned around, and then turned back and kicked the steel door and spat on it and said, Fuck you, fuck you, fuck you. I didn't know who I was cursing at. Nobody. Everybody.

Darren's car was still parked around the front of the building, where we'd left it when we arrived, but I found it locked and dark. Darren was nowhere to be seen.

I said his name. I looked around. I said his name again, got no reply. Then I caught sight of a long, human-shaped shadow, leaning against the shadow of one of the complex's smaller buildings, thirty yards away. The shadows were almost gone with the last of the sunlight. A minute or two later and I wouldn't have noticed it at all.

I made my way over, turned the corner.

He was squatting with his back against the smaller building's wall. He glanced up at me. He was holding a glass pipe to his mouth, rotating it with his fingers, and with his other hand circling his lighter under the bowl at the end of the pipe. The bowl was glowing. Darren snapped off his lighter. He inhaled and held it and then released a thick cloud of ghost-white smoke. The last of the smoke he formed into a perfect O. The smell wasn't weed or tobacco. It was almost odourless, except for something faint that made me think of floor cleaner.

Then he was looking at me again. He held the pipe and the lighter up and said, You want to get well with me, brother?

I shook my head.

Ah, I thought not, said Darren. It's okay. Help me up.

I reached down and hauled Darren to his feet. He turned the pipe upside down and tapped out the bowl. He slipped the pipe and lighter into his pocket and started back in the direction of the car. I followed, not saying anything. Halfway to the car, Darren stopped and shadowboxed the air for a few moments. Then he carried on, moving lightly.

Before we got into the car, he went around to the trunk and opened it. He took the pistol out of the back of his jeans, wrapped it in a bandana, and tucked it away behind one of the speaker boxes. All the while he was beaming at me. He said, Come on, I'll take you home.

Darren drove fast on the way back to town. He turned his stereo way up. I watched out the window into the gathering dark. I saw the lit-up windows of my gym blur by, and a short distance past that, I caught a brief glimpse of the white bicycle chained to the post.

Feels good, doesn't it? said Darren.

What feels good?

This whole thing, Ash. This whole goddamn life.

WE GOT TO TREY'S DRIVEWAY WITHOUT CRASHING, WHICH I found kind of amazing.

Here you are, sir, said Darren.

Thanks, bro. I'll talk to you soon.

It was fucking good to get some time in with you, Ash. I mean it. You're one of the most important parts of my life. You know that, right?

I do, I said, not looking at my friend.

I started to get out of the car, but Darren reached over and grabbed my wrist and said my name.

I said, What is it?

I'm serious about Detroit. It's a big opportunity. There's nobody else I want with me. There's nobody else I can trust. Will you help me out?

I remained halfway out of my seat. I could feel Darren's fingers tight around my wrist. The seconds felt like hours. There was fear of what I didn't know but what I was starting to think was possible, but there was the guilt too. More than anything, that guilt, burning like bad food in my gut. I couldn't look at him, but I breathed in and out slowly, and I said, Yeah, bro. Of course I'll help you.

ELEVEN

On the 23rd of April, the scales told me I was 225 pounds. The mirror told me that my body was powerful all over, that I was starting to succeed again. I looked thick and strong and jacked. The mirror made me believe that I was almost ready enough for whatever the future held. The mirror made me believe I was strong enough to take on all the fucked-up things that were happening in the present.

I slapped my own face, hard, and reminded myself of the weakness, the weakness that was always waiting to take over, the weakness hiding in my own heart. I couldn't ever stop battling the weakness.

Then I swallowed my gear and got ready for the gym.

CHASTITY'S FAMILY HAD MOVED TO CHATHAM, AN HOUR away from Altena, when me and Darren and Chastity were all eighteen and finishing up high school. At the time, Chastity hadn't relocated with her family. Instead she'd moved in with her boyfriend, Adam, the painkiller guy. Six months later, popping pills, she'd gotten pregnant. And all the rest of what followed was what I already told you.

I sat on my bike across the street from the house where Chastity's family still lived. The front yard and the house were pretty well-maintained. Red brick, white trim, new shingles on the roof, a satellite dish, a detached two-car garage. On the driveway in front of the garage was a trailer with a big new-model ATV strapped to it.

I manoeuvred into the driveway behind the trailer. I dropped my kickstand and turned off the engine and took off my helmet. The day was another nice one, but the ride from Altena, after my workout, had chilled me. I flexed my fingers and toes.

Up close, I got a better look at the ATV—500cc, not more than a month out of the dealership. Something about it bothered me.

I could hear voices coming from the backyard. One was unmistakably my aunt Glenna's. Another voice was soft and high-pitched. A little kid's voice. Nevaeh.

I didn't go toward the backyard, and for almost a full minute I didn't even approach the front door. I'd been out here a handful of times over the years. The last time I remembered was a barbecue for Chass's birthday during one of the times she and her mom were getting along. But that was two years ago. I hadn't seen these people since then.

These people, blood ties, family, same as Chastity.

I'd called her again that day, and again I didn't get anything but her voice-mail message. By now I knew the message almost by heart. I knew the tones of her speech, I knew all the little pops and hisses of background noise between words. Although I hadn't left another message for a couple days now, I'd begun listening to the recording from beginning to end, every time I called. I don't know why. Listening for some clue, I guess. Some sign.

I'd also called ahead, here, to Aunt Glenna's house, but the line had just rung and rung with nobody answering. After a dozen rings I'd hung up, knowing already that I was going to get on my bike and come all the way out.

I finally went up to the front door and pushed the buzzer. I expected Glenna to answer. I'd even steadied myself for it. But when the door opened it wasn't Glenna standing there. Instead it was this longtime girlfriend of hers, Rosemary something-or-other. She had a hard face but was kind of attractive, I guess, and she was nice enough. She was the kind of lady who wore a lot of rings and low-cut leopard-print shirts, you know? She'd grabbed my thigh a few times over the years.

She looked surprised. We hadn't seen each other in a long time. Then she said my name, happily, and leaned out of the doorway. She hugged me and kissed me square on the mouth and said, What are you doing way the hell out here?

I said, I was just seeing a buddy in Chatham. I thought I'd stop by. I don't see Aunt Glenna real often.

She'll be glad, Ashley, said Rosemary. Come on. We're in the backyard. Don't bother about your boots.

I came in and set my helmet down beside the door. I almost asked Rosemary if Chastity was there, but I stopped myself. If I'd ever in my life needed to play things cool, now was the time. I couldn't do this the same way I'd tried to do with the Amigos.

Rosemary led me through the narrow vestibule into the house. It was the same as I remembered. Bright, tacky decorations, a smell of cigarette smoke, but neatly kept. The same as my dad kept his own house. Neatness ran in the family. To the left was the living room. There was a new TV on a stand in the corner. A small collection of colourful kids' toys was scattered on the floor.

To the right was the kitchen. First I heard a familiar male voice in a one-sided conversation. Then I could see him. Glenna's husband, Chastity's father, Stepan Goss, sitting at the kitchen table, talking to no one. He was thinner than I remembered. Sick-thin. His eyes were red and bleary. He had a glass of clear, strong-smelling booze on the table in front of him, and he was finger-pointing to emphasize what he was saying. He said, And wasn't that a goddamn shame.

My uncle Stepan had worked for a long time as a farm equipment mechanic. Seven years ago he'd had a bad motorcycle accident, enough to leave him in a coma for a few weeks. He'd survived it, but he'd lost his job and his driver's licence. Since then, whenever he drank, which was often, he would talk to himself, like he was doing now. Chastity used to laugh or make jokes about her old man blathering away to nobody, but it made me sad to see him again. I'd always liked him, in spite of what had happened between the families.

I said, Hello, Uncle Step.

He didn't even look at me. Instead he rapped his knuckles on the table, sat back, and said, And nobody could've saw that coming, could they.

Rosemary went around Stepan to the fridge. She opened it and got herself a wine cooler. She said, Something to drink, Ashley? A beer?

Not just now, thanks.

Rosemary led me from the kitchen, through the dining room, to the screen door at the back of the house. Up ahead, maybe Chastity was sitting there, smoking a dart, having an afternoon drink. I had no idea. I did know, though, that Glenna would be out there. I felt a mixture of little-boy fear and hatred, both at her and at myself for being afraid in the first place.

Through the screen door I could see the deck. There were

chairs, a wooden table, a barbecue and a big hot tub. Sitting cross-legged on the deck boards near the hot tub was Nevaeh. The little girl was playing with a couple of toy trucks, crashing them into each other. She'd grown so much since I'd seen her last that I almost didn't recognize her. For some reason seeing the kid made me feel a little, like, emotional. I couldn't tell you why.

Rosemary slid the screen door open and stepped outside. I could hear her saying, . . . a real surprise, your nephew . . .

And I could hear Glenna's hard, smoke-cracked voice saying, What? Are you joking?

I stepped out onto the deck. Glenna, dart in one hand, wine cooler in the other, was halfway out of a chair, looking at me doubtfully. And Chastity wasn't anywhere to be seen.

Aunt Glenna, I said.

Holy hell, said Glenna, flatly. How are you?

She hugged me, showed her cheeks for me to kiss, European-style or something. My dad was six years older than her, but the two of them had real similar features. I'd never taken much notice before. Even stronger was the resemblance between Glenna and Chastity, from the face, through the slim figure, the expressions and gestures. She told me to sit, asked me what Rosemary had already asked me—did I want a drink. This time I said yes. I needed something, I realized. Something to hold on to. I kind of had the shakes again. I hoped they weren't visible.

Nevy, honey, said Glenna. Go on and get a beer for Ashley. You remember Ashley, don't you?

Nevaeh looked up from her toy trucks at me. There was something in her face. What's that thing you sometimes hear people say? Old soul or whatever? Jesus, yeah, I'd never thought of that before as an actual thing, but that little girl, she had it, an old soul. I could see it in her face.

She said, Hello, Ashley.

I said, Hey, Nevaeh.

Go on, get Ashley a beer, said Glenna. You know where they're at, in the fridge. If Papa's still in the kitchen and he's talking to himself like a crazy person, just don't pay him any mind. He won't bug you. Go on.

The little girl got up and walked into the house. Rosemary closed the screen door behind her.

I thought back to when the kid was born. It wasn't a happy thing, like births are supposed to be. Chastity was, like, just a kid herself, basically, and she had that deadbeat boyfriend, and they both had the problems with the pills. The baby came out way before she was supposed to, weighing nothing at all, and the docs weren't sure she was even going to live.

I remember me and Darren seeing Chastity in the hospital when she was finally able to have visitors. She looked like a corpse, bro. Her skin was the colour of paper. The baby was somewhere else altogether. Chass told us, Nevaeh, right? It's Heaven spelled in reverse. Then she told us, My mom is trying to get custody, because . . . because of everything. Then she started crying, hard. Me and Darren both sat down on either side of her hospital bed and each of us held her hands while she bawled her eyes out. She kept saying she was sorry, over and over. It was one of the few times I'd seen her lose it like that. Maybe the only time, to be honest.

I wasn't able to think of anything clever to say, so I said, She's growing up.

Yes, she is, said Glenna. She's doing good at school too. Sharp as a knife. Ha. Better than you kids ever did.

You kids. Chastity and me and Darren. Before I could reply, Glenna added, I'm just making fun, Ashley. You know that. Don't tell me you got oversensitive since the last time I seen you.

I said, It's all good, Aunt Glenna.

Good man, good man, said Glenna. Anyways, holy hell but you were almost the last person I expected to have out here today. Not the last-last—that would be your dad—but close to it. Not that I'm not happy to see you. But it is a surprise, isn't it?

I said I agreed, it was a surprise. And I told Glenna what I'd told Rosemary, that I'd just been visiting a buddy in Chatham and decided to swing by. Glenna nodded at the explanation.

Nevaeh returned with a beer. I noticed that it was already opened. Had the little girl done that? I took it from her and said, Thanks, Nevaeh.

With that same old-soul seriousness, she said, You're welcome.

Then she went back to her toy trucks.

So, said Glenna. You're here for a visit. Let's visit. Tell me everything.

I told her I was still working at the club and that I was starting to train for another bodybuilding show in August. Glenna nodded in a friendly way. We managed to make more small talk for ten or fifteen minutes. Long enough for me to drink most of the beer. She asked me about my sister, and she even asked about my mom, but she didn't say a word about my dad.

For a long time, I couldn't understand why Glenna had turned on my dad like she had, but Chastity had eventually explained it to me. She said it wasn't exactly because my dad had turned out queer, as Glenna put it, but because he'd pretended for so many years to be something else, something normal or whatever. So when the truth broke, it, like, shamed everybody around him. It was probably that shock, according to Glenna, that had killed their sick father, my grandfather, even though he'd been fighting liver cancer for two years longer than the doctors had expected. In Glenna's words, through Chastity, if my dad wanted to live that kind of life, why was he doing it here, where he continued to shame everybody who'd been connected to him? Why couldn't he have just moved away somewhere?

In some ways the explanation seemed a bit reasonable, but I had my doubts. Sometimes hate was hate, and sometimes hate was strongest where there'd been love before. Like between family or friends.

Still, the present conversation wasn't as bad as it could've been. Glenna was sharp and funny and charming when she wanted to be. Lighting up another dart, she said, So I hear from the kids that Donnie Braemer is back in town.

Donnie Braemer? said Rosemary. Oh jeez. I grew up with him. He was T-R-O-U-B-B-L-E. Always.

One *B*, love, said Glenna.

He had that beautiful thick hair, said Rosemary. Always. I was never real attracted to redheads, but around when we were sixteen or seventeen? Donnie? Nevy, honey, cover your ears . . .

Nevaeh gave Rosemary a doubtful look. Rosemary cackled.

I said, Yeah. DB's back. He's fixing up the house on Free Street. Darren's mom's old place.

Trying to beg her back? said Glenna.

I guess so.

Barb was always uppity, said Glenna. Rosie, you remember Barb Collins, don't you? She was always uppity, but I can't blame her one bit for finally giving Don the boot. Always putting up with him coming and going, and gone for months on end. I wouldn't have lasted near as long as Barb did before I'd've run him out the door. She made the right choice. If he manages to beg her back now, well, she's as dumb as she is uppity. Don Braemer is a man you can't trust as far as you can throw him.

In a quiet voice, I said, Darren turned out alright.

I felt the problem of it, how quick I was to defend him, no matter what I'd done behind his back. I'd spoken up without even thinking.

I like Darren, said Nevaeh. He's funny.

He gives you candies and junk food, said Glenna. That's why you like him.

No, said Nevaeh. It's because he's nice. And he's always nice to Auntie Chasty too, even when she gets mad at him.

I shifted in my chair, uncomfortable. I saw Glenna's mouth get a little tight.

How about you, Ashley? said Rosemary. You look like you still pump a lot of iron.

I said, I try to keep after it.

Girls like a guy with big pipes, said Rosemary. I always did.

Just think, Ashley, said Glenna. If you had Donnie Braemer's nice red hair to go with your big pipes, Rosie here might be interested.

Who says I'm not? said Rosemary, cackling again. Who says I won't show you a thing or two? Nevy, cover up your ears again. Ha ha. I'm only kidding, Ashley. Unfortunately I think I'd eat up a young thing like you way too fast.

Aunt Rosie always says she'll eat people up, said Nevaeh. That's murder.

See? said Glenna. Sharp as a knife.

I forced a smile and sipped the dregs of my beer and said, Do you see them much? Darren and Chastity?

What makes you think I don't see them all the time? said Glenna.

I don't know. I just—

Darren doesn't visit us anymore, said Nevaeh. But Chasty does . . . Except she hasn't been here in a while. When's she coming to visit again, Nana?

That's enough about that, Nevaeh, said Glenna.

I said, Sorry. I didn't mean to get into your business.

Are you sure about that? said Glenna.

I blinked.

Glenna was smiling but the smile was thin, and the lids around her green eyes had narrowed. She said, There's always something going on with you kids. The three of yous. Always.

I said, I don't get what you mean. Anyways—

What's your friend's name?

My friend's name?

The one here in Chatham, said Glenna. The one you were supposably visiting today.

I hesitated for just a second. It was all Glenna needed. She sat back, lifted her eyebrows. She took a drink of her wine cooler and a drag of her smoke. I broke eye contact with her. I looked out over the backyard, my mouth dry.

Isn't this weather on the up and up, or what? said Rosemary.

The truth is I don't know when's the last time I seen you by yourself, said Glenna. You never came around here without Chass. You never came around just for a visit, even though I don't have a problem with you. But that's besides the point. You kids are always up to something. You always have been. Should I be surprised that it's only gotten worse with time?

I said, Aunt Glenna, I only came around to catch up and ask you a couple things.

Still smiling, Glenna said, I'll tell you, if Stepan was young, hell, even Stepan ten years ago, we'd have a very different state of affairs.

I said, Chass has been here a lot lately. Hasn't she. Way more than she . . . than for a long time. I know she has. You guys are fixing things up or whatever you're doing, but she's been here a lot.

Everybody on the deck was listening now. I could sense it. Even Nevaeh was paying attention.

She sure has, said Glenna. Imagine that. A person in this family looks at something they did wrong in the past and finally says sorry and starts to do right by it. To put things back together. It's been hard as hell for her, too, being bullheaded the way she is, but I'm real proud of her.

I said, You want to have this talk in front of the kid?

What talk is that?

This one we're having.

Why, I don't have a problem at all with the talk we're having, said Glenna. I'm telling things like they are and that's all.

I said, Well, look. I only want to know where she's at. I came, honestly, to see if she was here. I even tried to call ahead, but, whatever, I ended up coming straight out to see for myself.

She's not here, said Glenna. I don't know where she is. Sorry to let you down.

I said, But she's been here. And she's been giving you money too.

I beg your pardon?

I said, Yeah, that's what you mean by making it right. She's been giving you money. A lot of it. I mean, I saw that four-wheeler in the driveway. Brand new. And the TV in the living room. That's making it right, eh?

That is none of your goddamn business, Ashley.

I said, Chastity's money. And it's for—

Auntie Chasty's gone away to be a dancer again, said Nevaeh.

Glenna's attention flashed down to the little girl. She said, What?

Oh, nothing, nothing, said Rosemary. She's not saying anything. Kids. Ha.

What did you say, Nevaeh? said Glenna.

That's what Auntie Rosie told me, said Nevaeh. Auntie Chasty's gone away to be a dancer again. Like before.

I don't know that, said Rosemary. I was only making a joke. I have no idea what she's up to.

That's a hell of a joke, said Glenna.

Rosemary shot a mean look at the kid, who was not even looking at her, and then Rosemary's face got scared. She started to backpedal, in one breath kind of pleading, in the next trying to make light of it.

Glenna's expression was clouding over by the second. She said, You know real well that's all effing nonsense. That was a mean little rumour. But it's joking around about rumours that makes them spread out to everybody.

Rosemary said, Oh, sweetie—

And you say those rumours to a kid, no less? To this kid?

Glenna was rising from her chair. Her voice was peaking. It bothered me to hear it. Rosemary looked straight-up terrified. Nevaeh kept playing with her trucks.

I didn't mean nothing by it, said Rosemary.

Well, pay attention, said Glenna. Because I'm about to tell you exactly what's what.

I got up, accidently knocking my empty beer bottle off the armrest of my chair. It clunked onto the deck and rolled away. Glenna and Rosemary both paused to look at it, and then at me.

I walked past them, opened the patio door and went into the house. I was most of the way to the kitchen before I heard Glenna's voice trail after me, Where in the hell is he going?

I didn't stop to see if she would follow.

In the kitchen, Stepan was still at the table, drinking the clear booze and rambling to himself. As I passed him, Stepan said, Say, is that you, Ashley?

I looked at the man. Stepan was watching me with curiosity in his eyes. From outside, out of sight, Glenna's voice was rising again. I couldn't make out the words but the tone was clear.

Ashley, said Stepan.

Uncle Step, I said.

Good to see you, young fella.

Good to see you too.

You ought to come by more often.

I glanced toward the back. Glenna's voice was still raging. I said, Yeah, I should. Hey, Uncle Step, have you seen Chastity lately? Like, has she been here?

Chastity? What? Sure I've seen her. I was talking to her not five seconds ago. Then she went to the can.

Stepan gestured at a bathroom off the front vestibule. I looked. The bathroom door was standing open. There was nobody in there.

By the way, when are we gonna see your dad again? said Stepan. I feel like I haven't seen that bastard in a couple months.

I said, I . . . I'll tell him you said hey.

Stepan nodded. He turned his attention to the other side of the table and rambled on, That's the way it goes, isn't it? Isn't that what I always say? Too much cash-money makes an asshole out of anyone. Every time.

I collected my helmet from beside the front door and went outside and closed the door behind me. Glenna's voice continued from behind the house, quieter now only on account of the distance. I stepped down the walk and onto the driveway. The big new ATV sat on the trailer. I thought, briefly, of damaging it somehow. Cutting the cables or pouring sugar into the gas tank. But I knew it for the petty gesture it was.

And that's how I saw myself and my little-boy fear. I was leaving Glenna's house almost on the run. I was afraid of her, I was afraid of her buggy husband. I was afraid of DB and the Amigos and everything else. Most of all I was afraid of how my mind kept taking me back to these thoughts I couldn't shake, thoughts about Chastity being laid out in a ditch or a forest or a field somewhere.

TWELVE

On Saturday I rode out to my dad's to help move some furniture. My dad and Greg were getting a new living room set. Their old stuff, still in good condition, was going to Lori and Ben.

Greg opened the door when I arrived. He offered a handshake and said, Hi, Ash. Come on in. We really appreciate you helping out like this.

I said, No problem.

My dad was in the living room, holding a measuring tape to the end of the couch. He gave me a hug when I came in.

This'll suck, said my dad.

Yeah?

Yeah. This goddamn couch has a pullout bed in it. It weighs about three hundred pounds.

I said, At least you're honest about it.

That's the code, said my dad. When you ask a guy to help you move, you have to be straight with him about everything.

Ha, said Greg. Straight.

I just looked at him. Greg's face coloured. My dad cleared his throat and suggested we get started.

The couch was as heavy as my dad had said it would be. We couldn't fit it out the front door so we had to take it out the patio doors at the back of the kitchen. From there it was a longer trek to the garage, where the furniture would be stored until Ben and some friends could come to get it. With the couch and with the other things, Greg tried to help where he could, but he wasn't all that strong. I carried a coffee table with him and we had to make a couple rest stops along the way.

I'm serious, said Greg. I'm going to get you to train me up in the gym. This is ridiculous.

It took an hour to get everything moved into the garage, and by the time we were finished we were all sweating.

The three of us stood in the garage for a while, each having a beer, even Greg.

How's your bike running? said my dad.

Awesome, I said. No issues.

Big weekend plans?

No, but on Monday I'm going to Detroit with Darren.

As soon as I'd said it, I wished I hadn't.

Oh? said my dad.

I said, Yeah. He's got tickets to a Tigers game . . .

On the other hand, I thought, Darren had promised me we weren't going to do anything more than talk to some people. There wasn't supposed to be any troublesome shit whatsoever. The Tigers game wasn't true, but I didn't have anything else to hide. So why did I feel weird about the whole thing?

That'll be fun, said my dad. Is your cousin going too?

I don't think so. Her and Darren are . . . I don't think we'll see her, put it that way.

Fair enough. None of my business.

Say, Ashley, said Greg, have you given any thought to what we talked about?

I said, I don't know. What did we talk about?

My friend's company. He's been waiting to hear from you.

I said, What? Oh, you mean that janitor job?

Greg's expression quirked a little.

Son, said my dad.

I think they prefer to call it custodial services, said Greg.

I shook my head, chuckling. I said, Thanks, Greg, but no offence, I think I'll pass on the custodial services. Somebody else can clean toilets.

Okay, said Greg. Suit yourself. Mike, I'm going in to start supper.

Greg started out of the garage. Then he stopped and turned around and came back and said, Ashley, what exactly were you laughing about a minute ago?

I said, What?

You were laughing when you said you weren't interested in my friend's offer. I'm just curious what was funny about it.

Greg, said my dad.

No, said Greg. No, I want to know what was funny. Ashley can tell me, can't he? What was funny?

I shrugged, said, I don't know. Me as a janitor or a custodial service guy or whatever.

Yeah? said Greg. And what's funny about that? Are you getting the same benefits at the nightclub?

Greg makes a good point, said my dad.

I said, It's none of Greg's business what I'm getting at the club. I like working there. I don't want to clean out friggin' toilets. Jesus Christ. Why do you even care, Greg? You're not my dad.

Greg's mouth moved but he didn't say anything.

You're out of line, son, said my dad.

I looked at my dad and then at Greg and then back at my dad. A moment passed. I said, I don't care. It is not Greg's business. And even if it was, he's what, trying to set me up with work as a janitor? What the hell? That's an insult.

Whoa, said my dad. And when did you get this goddamn chip on your shoulder?

Forget the whole thing, said Greg. I shouldn't have even brought it up.

You owe Greg an apology, said my dad.

I said, The hell I do. I told him I wasn't interested. He was the one who made it into a big deal.

It's fine, Mike, said Greg. Never mind.

I don't know what's gotten into you, son, said my dad. But I do know you owe Greg an apology.

You heard him, Dad. He said never mind. So never fucking mind, okay?

Before I knew it, my dad's face was six inches away from my own, and his eyes were staring straight into mine. I felt sweat pouring out of my skin. It took every ounce of my will not to step backwards.

In a soft voice, he said, Do you think I haven't learned some lessons about respect, living the life I've had?

Dad, I—

I'm not going to tell you again.

I did take a step backwards. My ears were burning and my vision was blurred around the edges. I inhaled and exhaled a few times and said, I'm sorry, Greg.

It's fine, Ashley. It's nothing.

Those old words flashed through my head again. Faggot, queer, cocksucker.

Now I think you should head back home, said my dad. You've got your job to get to, right?

Yeah, Dad. I do.

Whatever this attitude is, son, I won't have it here again. You understand me?

A FEW MINUTES LATER I WAS MOUNTING MY BIKE IN THE driveway outside my dad's garage. I was by myself. As I strapped on my helmet I wondered what the fuck had just happened. My whole face was burning, and I knew I was close to tears. I'd only ever seen my father like that once before. I was eighteen at the time. It had scared me then, and it scared me now. I turned on my bike and put it into gear and gave it some gas and navigated slowly out of the driveway, not trusting myself to open it up like I wanted to. When I turned and looked, I saw my dad standing outside the garage, arms crossed, watching me go. Neither of us waved.

AT WORK THAT NIGHT, I WAS CRANKY, STILL BURNING FROM what had happened at my dad's place. I was glad that the club wasn't real busy, even though it was a Saturday. The DJ was spinning a hard house mix, but even at midnight the dance floor was only two-thirds full. The lack of people made the music lonelier, somehow.

The only concern was this birthday group, half a dozen guys from the college, all of them seniors. They were big boys, too, and three of them were wearing matching OCAA rugby jerseys with numbers on the backs. The birthday boy was wearing a cheap plastic tiara. He and his friends were all taking up room on the dance floor, cheering a lot, hitting on whatever girls came close.

It was the kind of group all the other bouncers and me had seen countless times before. Dealing with them could go either way.

For most of the night, I patrolled the area near the bar. Dani Knox kept me supplied with coffee or water, whatever I needed. She didn't mention anything about the night she'd been at our place, last weekend, when Brice had brought out the crank. That little bag with the laughing cartoon elf on it.

I looked out at the dance floor and hated everyone I saw.

A little after closing time there was some trouble near the front door. I was coming up from a check of the washroom—deserted, no vomit—when I saw it. A small crowd, mostly those birthday party college guys in their rugby jerseys, arguing with Trey and TJ.

Trey was talking to one of the guys, a solid-looking boy with thick eyebrows. Trey was saying, We had to escort your friend out of here. I'm sorry you don't see why we had to do that.

No, said the solid-looking boy. No. I don't see that. Alls I see is you insulted him.

I'm sorry that's how you see it, said Trey. But next time you see your boy, maybe ask him why.

One of the other party guys tugged at his friend and said, Come on. Let's get out of here. Drop it.

No, said the solid-looking boy. It's bullshit. These guys.

I said, Is there a problem here?

Oh, said the solid-looking boy, and now there's three of them. Fucking bouncers.

There's no problem, said Trey. These dudes are just on their way out.

The birthday boy, still in the tiara, started pulling the solid-looking boy toward the doors, telling him to forget it. The solid-looking boy went a few paces and then yanked free of his friend and walked back to Trey. He said, Hey, I got something for you, dark meat.

The boy spit on Trey's shirt.

Before anything else could happen, I lunged forward and grabbed the boy by his rugby jersey and hauled him off his feet and hip-swept him to the floor. Then I was on him, laying punches to his face.

I heard my name being called just before TJ and Trey pulled me free.

Friends of the solid-looking boy picked him up off the carpet. His face was bloody. He looked dazed, and he was swaying on his feet. TJ told him and his friends to get the fuck out of the club. They went, dragging the boy with them. That was how their big night out ended.

A small crowd had formed. One of them was Marcel, who'd emerged from his office. He was looking right at me.

I DON'T KNOW WHAT THE HELL THAT WAS, SAID TREY.

I said, It is what it is.

What does that even mean, when you say that?

The two of us were just getting home, going in the front door.

I said, That asshole spit on you. Spit, Trey. He could've slapped you in the mouth and it wouldn't be the same disrespect.

I know that, said Trey. Jesus. I know that. But still. Marcel saw it, dude. He saw everything you did. That might be bad news.

I said, Come on. Marcel needs me. I'm, like, a veteran, and summer's coming up.

Before we'd left work, there'd been an incident report to fill out, up in Marcel's office. Trey and TJ and I had all been in there, but mostly the questions had been directed my way. Were you threatened, Ashley? Did this guy physically threaten you at some point, or what? Tell me you were threatened, tell me you thought you had to defend yourself.

It doesn't have to be a battle, said Trey.

I said, What doesn't?

Your *life*, dude. It doesn't have to be this battle.

You don't even know. No offence, Trey, but you don't.

Trey didn't say anything else. He changed his shirt and spent some time in the downstairs bathroom washing his face. Then he rolled a joint and we smoked it and drank a few beers and started playing a video game. Trey lasted ten minutes before he passed out.

I stayed at the game for twenty more minutes before the screen started to blur. I got up and turned off the console and headed upstairs. My fist was sore. I ran cold water over it in the bathroom sink. I'd already forgotten that solid-looking boy's face, even as I clearly remembered what hitting him felt like. It had felt good. He'd had it coming. Marcel and everyone else could go to hell if they wanted to question that.

I was on my way to my bedroom when I felt my phone vibrate. It was Chastity. I was sure of it. I took my phone out of my pocket.

It was my dad.

I didn't wake you, son, did I?

I said, No. I'm not in bed yet. What are you doing up?

I've been watching TV. I couldn't sleep. I'm bugged by what happened earlier tonight. I acted exactly the way I hate to act. That's on me. I'm sorry. I don't want you to ever see me like that.

It took me a few seconds to find my voice. I said, It's okay, Dad.

On the other hand, son, I never really saw you like that before. Not since you were in high school.

I said, I didn't mean to be like anything.

I sat down on the mattress in my dark bedroom and listened to him say, If you've got a problem, Ashley, if you're having issues with your friends or work or whatever, we can fix it. You know that, right? You come to me, tell me what it is, and we can fix it.

I was quiet for a little while. I looked at the deep shadows around me. My hand was still hurting. I said, It's all good, Dad. Really. There's nothing going on I can't take care of.

It always makes me a little nervous when you say that.

It shouldn't. I learned how to handle shit from you.

Well, the offer stands. Anyways, I'm glad we talked, and I'm glad you got home safe for the night. I'm gonna head back to bed. But, one more thing, okay?

I said, Okay.

You know what Greg means to me, right? How big a part of my life he is?

I said, I know.

Well, he's no bigger a part of my life than you or your sister. I don't know if I'm making any sense, but do me a favour and think about that.

I WANT YOU TO UNDERSTAND SOMETHING, BRO. I LOVE MY dad. Even with the complications, like my mixed feelings about Greg, like the argument in the garage, what my dad and I have is good. He's one of the most important parts of my life, and letting him down kills me.

But it wasn't always like this. In high school, in the worst of my battling days, I kind of hated him.

My dad hadn't come out on purpose. Lars Fabrication brought him out when they put the cameras in the washroom and caught him and Greg. There were lawsuits, and in the end, both my dad and Greg got some money. Not a lot, because Lars was in trouble anyway, and ended up being bought out by a bunch of Japanese or Chinese guys and then shut down a few years later.

When I was thirteen, my dad moved out of our house, but he didn't leave town, like a lot of people thought he would. He rented an apartment—alone, not with Greg just then. Me and my sister didn't see much of the old man for a while. Maybe once a month, always back at our house. That was the way it went until I was fifteen, and then I didn't want to see my dad at all. I couldn't stand the idea of it. I was willing to battle anybody who said the disrespectful words, the Chris Hagars and Raj Kumars and Brian Kozaks and the countless others, but as far as my own relationship with my dad went, I guess I wasn't any better than anybody else.

Later, I came to know those were hard years for him. First off there was all the hate and disrespect. Then there was the family, both close and extended, breaking apart, people like Glenna disowning him. At the same time Greg moved away for a while. My dad had to pick up what work he could, here and there, just so he could send money back to his kids. I don't know if my dad ever had to fight, one guy or a group of guys or something—like you hear about on the news, groups of guys going out at night to stomp gay people—but if it ever had happened, my dad never talked about it. Even so, I'm sure he had at least been threatened, and had had to look over his shoulder. He was drinking a lot in those years, and my sister told me he thought about killing himself.

It makes me fucking sick to think about that.

Anyways, things started to change when my dad got the auto-shop instructor job out at the college. I was turning seventeen when that happened, and that was during the time I was barely speaking to him. That was also around the time when I fought Brian Kozak in our high school weight room, which made the VP accuse me of being a bully. As it turned out, the VP had already called my dad to discuss things, even before he got me into his office to give me another lecture.

I remember that day clearly. By the time my meeting with the VP finished, there was only ten minutes left in the period. No sense going back to class. I went down the empty corridors. As I passed through the foyer, I saw my dad's blue Ford Ranger at the curb in front of the school. Right up until that moment I had just been pissed off at the VP and pissed off that Brian Kozak had snitched on me and pissed off at everything in general. But as soon as I saw my dad's ride outside, all the being pissed off went away. I felt almost nothing at all, maybe a little cold, a little scared.

I went outside. It was January, freezing. The sun was already setting. I walked to the Ranger. I could see my dad behind the wheel. I hadn't seen him since Christmas Day, and then only for a couple of hours, at a diner downtown.

I got into the cab. As soon as I'd closed the door, my dad put the Ranger into gear and started driving.

I said, All my stuff's still in my locker. I don't even have my coat. I'll bring you back.

My dad didn't say anything else while he drove. He was looking better, though, even since Christmas. He looked like he was eating again. A few years later I found out he'd cut way back on his drinking and he'd started exercising again. Most important, Greg had moved back to town and back into his life.

We didn't drive very far. My dad parked on the edge of Missionary Position Park. The grass was covered with snow. The monument was just this big white shape. There was no one around. My dad sat with the engine idling and his hands on his thighs, looking out through the windshield.

I said, Dad, look—

He hit me then. Bang. A hard open-handed cuff to the side of my head. I had barely realized it happened before he did it a second time and then a third. Then he was looking at me, and he was so angry he was pale. I'd never seen him like that. The side of my head was throbbing. I was scared too. All the hardness I'd thought I had, the badass I thought I was, was gone in that one second. I was a little kid again.

What do you think you're doing? said my dad.

I started talking fast: You have no idea, do you. I'm standing up for you, for fuck sake. The things people say about you. How can I let that shit go?

You think I don't know about it? You think I don't know what people say? I live here too, son.

It's bullshit.

It is what it is, said my dad. And you don't fix anything by mucking up your own life over it. It's real clear to me, son, that I haven't been doing my job. That's about to change.

I said, What do you mean?

Your mom and I still have you and your sister to worry about, and everything else has to take a back seat to that.

I said, Well, good job you've done so far—

My dad hit me again, the same open-handed whack to the head. Tears filled my eyes.

Then I could see there were tears in his eyes too. He said, Don't make me do that again. Everything you're pissed off about, son, you have a right to be. But we're tackling those things now. Man to man. I won't put up with anything less. That includes backtalk. Do you understand?

Yes. I do.

Good, he said. Because things are going to change now.

He talked about a lot of things after that. My battles, my grades, my friends. He said I was on my way to making sure I'd never go further than Altena, never go to college. I asked him what was so bad, how was it anyone's business, if I didn't want to go further than town or go to college. My dad said that was fine, but he'd be damned if I didn't at least have the option. He said from then on he was going to be back in my life, whether I liked it or not. He told me I could keep living with my mom for the time being, but if I got in any real trouble one more time, I was coming to live with him, no questions asked.

Do you understand?

I said, I do.

And do you believe me when I say I'm serious, son?

Yes.

Then there's only one more thing I need to ask you, he said.

What is it?

Are you ashamed of me?

I said, What?

Be honest.

Thirty seconds passed.

No, Dad, I finally managed to say. I don't . . .

It was all I could say, because I got choked up again, just like somebody had their hands around my throat. I knew if I said anything else I'd lose it. I'd start crying like a baby, and god I hated crying. Crying was the biggest sign of weakness I knew, and for the first time, I knew I had to show my dad—the queer, the fag, the homo, the big shame—that I, too, was a man.

AFTER THAT, I STARTED SEEING HIM MORE REGULARLY. A couple times a week my dad would take me to the gym at the college and we'd hit the weights together. Every Thursday night we'd go to Dunnigan's. We'd eat pizza and watch the hockey game, and I would have a Coke and Dad would have a pint of beer.

I was afraid, at first, of what people might think or say when they saw us together. I wondered how many more battles this was going to lead to. But then a funny thing happened. This super-fine uptown girl named Rachel McCann, who went to my school but was way too good to hang out with any of the skids like me, was a waitress at Dunnigan's. She worked there most Thursdays, and usually ended up serving me and my dad.

One time, when Dad had gone to the washroom, Rachel came by the table. She started talking to me about school and this and that, as if we'd been friends for a long time. I just nodded and went along with it. I didn't know if Rachel knew about my dad, until she said it was progressive, seeing me and him together. That was her word, progressive. Ha. Anyways, talking at Dunnigan's led to me and her going on some dates and fooling around a few times.

But even without being progressive enough to hang with the uptown girls, those nights out with my dad got easier and easier, until I didn't even notice them. I just had my old man back again. I finished grade twelve, and managed to get my shit together enough to pull a C+ average. I didn't go to college, but it was okay, because I was starting at the Balmoral and earning some legit cash—never mind the odd job I did with Darren.

At least staying in Altena was my choice. My dad had been right about that.

THIRTEEN

O n the 28th of April, there was a setback, despite the gains I'd been making. The scales told me I was back up to 239 pounds. I felt it too. I'd skipped my workouts not one but two days in a row, having felt burned out and tired, having given in to my weaker self. In the mirror there was the body of a strong man, but for all its standing there in front of me I could not see it.

Instead, what I saw was two things at the same time. One was a fat shapeless lump. The other was a cowering little boy. I felt shitty. I felt the temptation to give up, to give it all up, to turn my back on everything.

I slapped myself in the face. I slapped myself twice more, hard. Weakness. Then I geared.

I SPENT THE EARLY AFTERNOON AT THE GYM, DOING A LONG, hard workout, trying to break through the dark clouds in my mind. What had happened over the weekend—my fight with my dad and Greg, my battle with the stupid college kid at the club—was still bringing me down. And Chastity. Since I'd gone to see her mother and not found her there, my thoughts had started to take a bad turn. A dead-murdered-buried kind of turn. I didn't like thinking that kind of stuff, but there wasn't much in the way of distraction. In an hour's time, I would have the Detroit trip with Darren.

I showered and changed into jeans. I put on my hoodie and overtop of it a light windbreaker. Then I went out and stood in front of the gym, bag in hand, waiting.

The weather was okay, warming up. Across White Bike Way was the unchanging sight of the fields and the greenhouses. Way out between the fallows were some men working near a tractor. They were too far away for me to see if they were Amigos, but I guessed they probably were.

At two-thirty, Darren's car pulled up. I opened the back door and threw my bag in and then I got in the passenger seat.

Good morning, my brother, said Darren.

Morning?

Ha. I got up an hour ago. You ready?

Sure. Let's go.

Darren was wearing one of his polo shirts. He was also wearing a new-looking ball cap, navy blue, with a flat brim and a D for Detroit in white on the crown. Under the hat, Darren didn't look well, worse even than when I'd last seen him just a few days ago. His skin was very pale. He had more blemishes and sores. There were dark circles around his eyes.

We just have to make a quick stop, said Darren, pulling onto White Bike Way.

He drove us into the south part of town, down to the house on Free Street, and parked out front. He told me he would only be a minute and asked if I wouldn't mind chilling in the car until he got back.

I watched him walk up the driveway and push open the plywood gate and disappear around back.

I waited. One minute and then two and then five. Darren had left the radio on, loud. I turned it down. I took my phone out of my pocket and scrolled through the contacts and looked at Chastity's name and phone number and fought the urge to call her again.

There was a thumping on the window beside me. It came out of nowhere. I almost shit myself. My head whipped around and there was DB. He had a tight, pissed-off look on his face. I pushed the button to bring the window down.

Hey, DB.

Yeah, Ashley. What's going on?

What's going on? Is that a trick question?

I saw DB's eyes get narrow. Narrower than they already were. But in my defence I meant the question honestly. Behind him, up at the top of the driveway, I could see Darren and Seth both. They looked like they were arguing, but I couldn't hear them. I saw Seth go back into the house.

So you've got yourself a little trip lined up, do you? said DB.

I'm just along for the ride, I said.

DB straightened up. He looked like he was going to say something else. A vein in his forehead was standing out. Finally what he came back with was, You just want to mind your p's and q's, you get me?

He turned around. I watched him walk back up the driveway and talk to, or at, Darren. DB kept jabbing his finger into his son's chest and then looking past him, down at the car, at me, again. Darren's arms were moving in big circles.

Slowly I unbuckled my seat belt. I put my hand on the door handle and pulled it halfway. But when I looked again I saw

Darren walking toward the car. DB stayed at the top of the drive-way, watching, arms crossed.

Darren got back behind the wheel and put the car into gear and pulled away from the house. For once he was driving slowly.

I did my seat belt back up and said, What was that?

Nothing, brother.

He didn't know I was coming, did he.

I suppose I forgot to tell him.

You forgot to tell him.

DB's problem with it isn't you, so don't worry about that. His problem is, if I needed to take someone, he says, why wasn't I taking Seth? I guess he worries I don't include him enough, some-thing like that. It's apparently not good for Seth's self-esteem.

Well, why aren't you taking Seth?

Darren gave me a look. He said, Since when are you and DB smoking the same shit? Seth's my brother, yeah, like, my biological brother, but come on. I don't even like going to the grocery store with him if I can avoid it.

As he finished saying this, Darren laughed. The sound was high and cracked. Almost a little panicked.

I looked back. DB was still standing at the top of the driveway, watching us go. It made me think of my own dad, standing in the driveway outside of his garage, just a few nights before. It wasn't a good feeling.

THE DRIVE TO WINDSOR, AND THEN ACROSS THE BRIDGE INTO Detroit, would take us a little more than an hour. Once we got out of Altena and onto the highway, I found myself relaxing, despite all the ongoing shit and the weird thoughts. I was even feeling okay in Darren's company. We were driving somewhere, doing something—probably something stupid—but I could let myself believe it didn't matter, that only the journey and the present had any importance.

I'm trying to think of the last road trip we took, said Darren.

I don't know, I said. A couple years ago, I feel like.

You know what? It was when we all went up to Grand Bend, you and me and Chass and Michelle and that guy she was with, what was his name? Ted?

I don't remember.

It was Ted, said Darren. And remember we're all sitting around the fire, and we hit some blow, so we're all talking our heads off, and this guy Ted, he gets talking about politics or some shit like that, and he says he doesn't think gay people should, like, have the right to marry, or to even live in normal society or whatever, and you say, all casual, how about if I knock you the fuck out in your chair? Remember that, brother? How about if I knock you the fuck out in your chair.

I said, Jesus. Ha. Did I say that?

You did, said Darren. You absolutely did. He had no idea about your dad or anything. He just ran his mouth until you said that, and then he shut up so fast I swear I heard his teeth click together. And everyone gets, like, silent for a minute, until Chass busts up laughing. You remember?

I laughed. I did remember, but Darren's telling added a good extra feeling to it.

You and Michelle, brother, said Darren. You should've, you know, with her. Official, I mean, not just creeping around from time to time. You always should've. You still could.

I said, I think about her sometimes. But I don't know. Every time we try it, me and Michelle, it doesn't work. It's like there's something stopping us . . . I can't explain it, D.

I looked out the window. We were passing Tilbury. I could see the water tower standing over the town on the south side of the highway. Someone had managed to climb up and paint a huge weed leaf on the side.

You can't commit, said Darren. That's the thing. You can't commit with her. You like your freedom too much. That's alright.

Yes, I guess I do.

Raising his voice, Darren sang the chorus of "Travellin' Man" again.

A cold feeling passed through me. I didn't say anything.

Jesus, said Darren, cracking his window and lighting up a dart. Ever since DB's been back, we've been listening to his country music. Full time. That shit makes me lose my mind.

I said, How's it going at your mom's old place, anyways?

The renovation? Slow, slow. It's DB and Seth, right? How fast is it gonna go?

Is it all?

All what? said Darren.

All DB's got going?

Ha. No. It's not all. Like I told you, he kinda has to keep a low profile right now. Just the way business goes. You remember that time when we were kids, we dropped off the bag for him?

I looked at him, surprised. Darren had never talked about that day.

I said, Sure, I remember.

I mean, it was messed up a little, wasn't it, said Darren. I know it was. And he knew it was too. We were, like, too young to be legit runners back then, but . . .

But what?

Ah, but nothing. He'll retire one of these days. Settle down. Quit being the Travellin' Man . . .

Darren shook his head. He turned up the radio. The house beats got loud. We'd passed Tilbury and were moving through endless farm country.

For some reason I was thinking about the night of my nineteenth birthday. I'd been over at Darren's new place. The two of us were pre-drinking before we went to a strip club to meet some other friends. Darren had just moved into the two-bedroom apartment where he would live for the next several years, eventually with Chastity. I hadn't seen the place before that night. It was bigger and fancier than I'd thought it would be. There were tiled floors and new appliances, including a dishwasher. Darren had bought himself a rear-projection TV with satellite and a surround-sound stereo system and a laser-disc player.

I hadn't asked and Darren hadn't told me anything, even back then. But before we headed out to the bar, Darren led the way into the apartment's second bedroom, where he'd set up a small office.

First, he gave me a birthday gift, this good-looking stainless steel Guess watch. I still have that watch, even though the band doesn't fit around my wrist anymore. After he gave me the watch, he took a metal strongbox out of the back of the bedroom closet. He put the strongbox on his desk and thumbed in the combination and opened it up. Inside the box, I saw a small digital scale, the kind you use in a kitchen, and a brick of what I guessed was coke, maybe half a kee, tightly wrapped in plastic.

Darren brought out a Swiss Army knife. I wondered if it was the one his dad had given him when we were kids. D carefully unpacked a corner of the brick and shaved off a small bump with the tip of his knife. He lifted it up to his nose and snorted it. Then he shaved off another small bump and offered it to me.

I hesitated. I'd never done coke before. But it was also my nineteenth birthday. Who could tell me what to do anymore, what was right, what was wrong? I took the knife and pushed my left nostril closed, the way I'd seen Darren do it, and snorted the bump.

I remember turning my face to the ceiling, already feeling invincible. Snot was dripping down the back of my sinuses. I said, Jesus fucking Christ.

I know, said Darren. I know. Happy birthday, brother.

Happy birthday, brother.

And back in the present, in the car on the way to Detroit, he said, Hey. You with me here?

Sorry, D. Yeah, I'm with you.

WE STOPPED AT A BIG GAS STATION OUTSIDE OF WINDSOR. Darren got out to fill the tank. I could see a café on the other side of the parking lot.

I said, I'm going to get some food, D. You hungry?

No, said Darren. Maybe just a bottle of water.

In the last twenty minutes, Darren had become paler. Kind of pissy, too, giving me short, snappy replies to anything I said, smoking dart after dart, driving too fast. Gone was the happy guy he'd been for the first forty minutes of the drive.

I went into the café. I bought a cup of coffee and a bottle of water and a chicken salad sandwich and a bag of peanuts. I came out and crossed the parking lot back to Darren's car. Darren wasn't in it. I found the passenger door unlocked. I put my food on the seat and walked up to the gas station, looked through the front window but didn't see Darren.

I followed some signs around to the back of the building, knowing already what I would find. I was right. Darren wasn't in the men's room, but he was walking up from a shallow, trash-strewn ditch fifty feet away. He was walking with a light step and he was snapping his fingers in time to a beat that could be nowhere else but inside his head. Maybe it was that country song again. He was smiling now too. He clapped me on the arm and called me brother and walked me back around to the car.

WE WERE ANOTHER HALF HOUR DRIVING THROUGH WINDSOR. Darren was energized again, talking almost non-stop. I could barely get a word in edgewise. He talked about his job at the electronics store. He talked about his mom. He talked about wanting to get a dog. He talked about going on a trip, somewhere tropical, sometime soon, which he'd talked about many times before but had never actually done. I ate my sandwich and drank my coffee.

We turned off the highway and made our way to Huron Church Road, heading north for the bridge. We passed through an ugly little industrial area, where I saw a strip club called Cheetah's. The windows were all blacked out. The marquee said, LIVE GIRLZ XXX. I couldn't help but wonder if she was in there, or maybe someplace like this.

It made me realize, for all Darren's endless talk, that Chastity's name had not come up once. In its way it was like my time with her, back in the fall, when Darren's was the name that never came up.

A short while later we were on the bridge itself. Traffic was slow, squeezed down by roadwork to one northbound lane. There wasn't anything to see of the river, or the freighters on it, which would at least have been a distraction. The cars and trucks crept along.

With the slowed-down pace, Darren's rambling slacked off to nothing. He rolled down his window and had another dart. I started to feel edgy.

We came down the bridge on the north side and made our way

into the wide lineup for the customs station. Here the traffic was slowest yet, almost at a full stop.

I felt sweat break out under my clothes. I said, D.

Fuck, said Darren. This is slow. It never used to be like this, did it. I came through here, like, two years ago to do some shopping. This whole thing, the bridge and all this shit, was ten minutes, tops. But that was before all the 9/11 stuff. Different world back then.

I said, D.

What?

Tell me. Tell me there's no dope in this car.

What? said Darren. Are you serious? I thought we talked about that.

Tell me, man. Promise me.

Holy Christ, Ashley.

I said, What about back there, at the gas station?

Oh, come on. That was just a taste, just enough to feel well. I didn't even bring a pipe or nothing. Here. Look.

Darren made a big show of pulling the linings of both hip pockets out of his jeans. The fabric hung loose, free of anything but lint.

Up ahead, an attendant in a reflective vest was waving us into one of the individual lanes. There were two cars in front of us. I was trying to see what might be past the customs station. Dogs, border cops with assault rifles, anything.

Ashley, said Darren. Look at me.

I looked at him. Darren's eyes were hard and bright.

I swear to you, said Darren, you search this car inside and out, you tear it apart, down to the last fucking bolt, and you will not find one gram of dope in it. I swear to you.

When did it go like this, D?

When did what go like what?

Everything, bro. You never used to operate like this.

Darren didn't reply and I couldn't think of anything else to say. Anyways, it was too late. We were next. Darren was already pulling up to the booth. A sign fixed to the wall said Do Not Proceed Until Directed To. A short distance past this, a surveillance camera mounted on a concrete pylon was pointed straight into the car.

Darren turned off his stereo and rolled down his window and said, How's it going today?

He was speaking to the customs agent, a brown-skinned man in a dark uniform. Hanging in the booth behind the man was a framed poster showing the World Trade Center towers with the smoke pouring out of them and a caption that read *Never Forget*.

The customs agent was speaking, but from where I was sitting, I found it hard to make out the man's words.

Just for the evening, said Darren. We're going to see the Tigers game, although they're not off to a real good start this year, are they? . . . What's that? Yeah, coming back tonight. Both of us have to work tomorrow. It'll be a long day. Ha.

There was a dog, I saw. Thirty yards away, at the secondary screening station. The dog was a big shepherd on the end of a leash, held by a border cop. The cop wasn't carrying an assault rifle, but he was wearing a Kevlar vest and he had a pistol on his hip. The dog was sniffing around an SUV that had been pulled over.

The customs agent said something and Darren said okay and then took his wallet out of his pocket to show his driver's licence. As the agent looked at it, Darren reached over to the glovebox to get out his ownership and insurance. To me he said, He'll want to see your ID too, brother.

The agent gave Darren his licence back. I leaned across the

seat and held my driver's licence up. The agent took it and looked at it and looked at me. The agent said something.

I said, Pardon?

What I asked is if you're a big baseball fan, said the agent.

I said, Oh, yeah. For sure.

I wasn't. I didn't follow baseball at all. I didn't even know who'd won the World Series last year. If the agent started asking for specifics, we were fucked. I realized Darren probably didn't even have tickets for the game, to prove we were going to it. The sweat was running down my back and pooling in my crotch.

The agent handed me my driver's licence. He said, Enjoy yourselves. Don't drink and drive if you're coming back this way tonight.

Seconds later we were driving out of the customs station. Passing the dog and the border cop and the SUV they'd pulled over. We came up to a small toll house and Darren rolled his window down again and leaned out and paid the toll, and then we were on I-75.

Darren reached into the map pocket on his door and dug around and came out with a crumpled piece of paper. Doing this caused him to swerve a little. Somebody honked at him. He said, Yeah yeah, fuck you too. Here, Ash, have a look at this, will you?

He handed the piece of paper over. I uncrumpled it. I was looking at a page torn from a road-map book. It was showing somewhere on the outskirts of Detroit.

The place we're looking for is on there, said Darren. DB put a circle around it, with marker, because he apparently thinks I'm simple-minded. Anyways, see it?

Yeah. I see it.

Darren turned the stereo back up. He grinned at me and said, You know, you had me worried back there, brother.

I had you worried?

Sure you did. All this time, all these years, I thought you were an Altena OG, cold as ice. You had me worried back there.

I just—

You just what, Ash?

I said, I don't know. Maybe I'm not cut out for this, after all. I don't know . . .

Darren was quiet for a while. Then, gently, he said, I can let you out somewhere up ahead if you want. I have to keep going, but there are buses that'll take you home. I can give you some cash if you're short.

I held the map page in both hands. The image of it blurred until I blinked my eyes. I said, No. Never mind, D. I just got tense is all. Keep going.

THE DIRECTIONS TOOK US TO A RUNDOWN LITTLE SHOPPING mall in Dearborn. At one end of the mall, accessible from the parking lot, was a plain-looking restaurant called Model-T's. A sign in the window said FINE FAMILY DINING!! Darren parked against a hedge, a short distance from the front of the restaurant.

He said, This is it.

I said, This? Model-T's? This place looks like a dive.

Yeah, it does, doesn't it.

This whole mall, D. Shit.

I hear you, said Darren. Ah, I fucking hate Detroit. Anyways, we're early. Come on, let's stretch our legs.

We went into the mall and walked around. There wasn't much to see. A number of the stores were shuttered. The only interesting thing was that many of the other shoppers and storekeepers looked like Muslims. Men with beards and funny little knitted caps. Women with their faces showing but scarves tied around their heads. There was a word for those scarves, I knew. Something foreign.

We found a dark arcade on the far side of the mall. Some of the classic games were in there, so we got change from a wall-mounted machine and wasted an hour. I mainly played Street Fighter. It was different than I remembered. Easier. Not as fun. The buttons and the joystick left a greasy feeling on my hands.

At six o'clock we headed back to Model-T's. The inside of the restaurant was decorated with a huge assortment of Ford memorabilia. Pictures of vehicles—Mustangs, Fairlanes, vintage F-250s—pictures of the assembly plant over the years, pictures of Henry Ford himself. The dining room was half full, mostly more Muslims. They seemed an odd fit, somehow, against all the Ford stuff on the walls.

A teenaged waiter led us to a booth and gave us menus. As we sat down, I said, Do we have time to get food?

Probably, said Darren. You get some if you want. I'm okay.

You haven't eaten a thing all day.

I'm not hungry.

I said, Alright. Suit yourself. If the waiter comes by, order me the steak salad. No fries or fat-ass shit, okay?

Okay, said Darren.

I got up from the table and walked away from the booth. Past the restaurant's front door was a short corridor marked RESTROOMS. Inside the corridor was a little nook with a couple of pay phones in it. There were two big phone books attached to the wall by metal cables. I made my way down to the men's room and went in and took a leak.

On my way out I found myself stopping next to the pay phones. I held off for a while, standing there, staring at the number pad, before I did anything. Then I picked up the receiver and pressed zero. I talked to the operator, made a collect call. There were a few seconds of silence before the connection was made. It didn't even ring before I could hear the message, her voice, *Hey, it's Chastity*, and then the operator cut the call off and asked me if I wanted to try another number.

I put the receiver back on the cradle and stood there a little longer, thinking my thoughts. I did not want to be in this shitty restaurant outside of a shitty American city, about to eat shitty food.

When I came out of the corridor, back into the dining room, I stopped in my tracks. I could see Darren in the booth, and across from Darren were the backs of two heads. Darren was talking to them, whoever they were. He was trying to frown, trying to look hard, but his eyes were shifting around a lot. Then his eyes met mine and he held the gaze for a long second and then he looked back at the people in front of him.

In that moment my blood went cold. I didn't move. Darren's eyes were on mine again. I might've imagined it, the tiny, tiny shake of Darren's head, the slight dip of his chin. But I did not imagine Darren's eyes looking into mine.

The eyes that said, Go. Go, brother. This isn't for you.

That was enough to get me moving. I did go. I turned ninety degrees and headed straight out the front door. There was a man standing outside, not far from the door, smoking a dart. He was fat but also big and solid, taller than me by six inches, and he was wearing a jean jacket and workboots and a pair of cheap sunglasses. He looked right at me and then looked past me, back at the restaurant's front window. Maybe he was nobody at all. Not involved. I didn't believe that, though. Right then I believed everybody near and far was in on it, whatever it was.

I passed the man, my hands in my pockets. I heard myself whistling. When had I started doing that? I realized it was

"Travellin' Man." It was out of tune. There was cold sweat all over the inside of my shirt. I walked faster. By the time I was fifty feet across the parking lot, I was almost jogging.

I got out to the edge of the lot and stopped. Across the road was a low-rise office building, closing down for the evening. There were lights on in the fourth-floor windows, and I could see a janitor working a vacuum cleaner. The janitor was brown-skinned. He looked like an Amigo. I stared at him for a while. In my mind I kept seeing Darren. Two images of him at the same time. One, smoking his crank out at Lars Fabrication, and two, in the restaurant a few minutes ago, looking at me over the shoulders of the two strangers, telling me with his eyes that I was free, I could go. Under my clothes, the sweat dried out and got itchy.

Darren's car was right where we'd parked it, forty or fifty yards from the front of the restaurant. From the parking spot, I could see that the big man with the cheap sunglasses was still out front, smoking his dart, keeping an eye open for something. If he was trying to be anonymous, he was doing a bad job of it, but I didn't think the fat man knew which one was Darren's car because he wasn't looking this way.

The passenger's side door was again unlocked. I looked at the interior, the console and the steering wheel and the gearshift. The seats. The butts in the ashtray. I bent down and pulled the trunk release. I closed the door behind me and went back around to the trunk and lifted it and pushed Darren's junk around, his old clothes and sneakers, until I could reach behind the right speaker box. Dope aside, I didn't know if we'd crossed the border with what I was looking for now. Darren had told me repeatedly the car was clean, that we weren't muling anything, but I had had my doubts all along, and had them now more than ever. Behind the right speaker box all I felt were wires.

Then I saw them at the front door of the restaurant. Darren and two men. They were too far away to see much of their faces. They were talking to the fat man. My mouth went dry.

All four of them started walking. There I stood, frozen all over. I didn't think anybody'd noticed me yet, but there was still plenty of daylight and it wouldn't take them long. Seconds at most. Before I gave it any thought, I rolled into the trunk and pulled it closed overtop of me. The blackness was complete. I was on my side and my back was curled and my knees were against my chin. Outright panic wasn't far off. I whispered, Oh fuck oh fuck oh fuck.

It felt like years before I heard the doors opening, more than one, and felt the suspension shift. Voices spoke, neither of them Darren's. I couldn't make out the words. Then there was music, the loudest music I'd ever heard. House, the same as Darren and I had been listening to for most of the trip. It ripped into my head. The bass was shaking my bones apart. I had my fist in my mouth and was biting down on my fingers, otherwise I would've been screaming.

The music cut out only a second or two later. It must have started when they turned on the ignition, and they turned the stereo off almost right away. My ears were ringing. I could hear laughter up front. There was more muffled talking. Darren's voice still wasn't part of it.

The car was running. I could feel the vibrations of the engine, and then I felt motion. Reverse first, a hard brake, and then forward gear. The upshifting was slower and more relaxed than when Darren was driving.

With each passing second, I wanted out of there more. Real bad. I was sweating again. Shaking. I could feel the trunk pressing in on me.

I stretched my feet out as far as I could, just to get them moving. I stretched my arms out over my head, moved my hands around, flexed my fingers. My right hand bumped against the other speaker box, the one on the left. I walked my fingertips along the plywood, around the corner, to the tangle of wires at the back.

And there it was. The feel of the cotton bandana, the hard metal underneath. We'd crossed the border with it after all.

I DIDN'T EXACTLY FALL ASLEEP IN THE TRUNK, BUT THERE was, like, blackness and a loss of consciousness and kind of a dream that I was somewhere else. Home at my dad's place. Later, when I had time to think about it, I figured I'd passed out. I'd been breathing hard, hyperventilating, squeezing the pocket rocket with both hands. Then everything had gone away for a while. Everything had faded out.

I came to with a shudder. The car wasn't running anymore, and there were no sounds, no strangers' voices. I had a splitting headache. When I tried to shift my body, my hamstrings cramped up hard. I kicked them out as best I could, breathing hard, almost hard enough to pass out again. When the cramp finally released, I moaned. I felt like I might throw up.

It took me a while to feel around for the interior trunk release. I was shit-scared, and the tight blackness of the trunk was almost better than whatever was outside it.

I pulled the release. The lid lifted and light came in. There were fluorescent tubes overhead, one of them flickering, attached to the underside of steel roof trusses. The air was cold and smelled like machine oil. I lay on my back, staring straight up. My hands were shaking enough that it took me three tries to pull back the slide on the pocket rocket, the way Darren had showed me when we'd shot it out at Lars Fabrication. That had been only the week before. The passage of time didn't feel real.

I led with the pistol over the edge of the trunk. I was in a big shed or a garage, with a concrete floor and steel-framed walls. Not far from the car I saw a red metal tool chest. I spotted an impact wrench, and a few feet away from that was a portable MIG welding set. Taped to one of the steel wall-studs was a swimsuit calendar. In the other direction was a wide metal roll-down door and a man-door set in the wall.

I got myself out of the trunk. My right leg cramped again and I went down on one knee, pounding my fist against my thigh. It loosened, but the muscle was trembling like a cable. I stood up slowly.

The garage was similar to my dad's. Half again as big. Darren's car had been driven onto the runway of a four-post lift, but it wasn't raised. Past the lift, a Fat Bob Harley with blue trim was standing on its kickstand. The bike was partly disassembled, and its filter and pipes were carefully laid out on a piece of newspaper beside it.

I limped over to the bike. A Michigan plate lay next to the rear tire.

Then I heard a door open and close behind me. A scrape of boots on concrete. I turned around. The big fat man I'd seen outside the restaurant was just now coming in through the man-door. The cheap sunglasses were pushed up on his forehead. He was seeing the open trunk and then he was seeing me and seeing the pistol I was pointing at him.

Oh, said the man. Oh. You got to be kidding me.

KINNY, SAID THE FAT MAN. WE GOT AN ISSUE.

Kinkaid—Mr. Kinkaid, the guy we'd given the bag of money to a fucking decade ago—looked up from the Formica table where he was sitting. There was a small TV on the table. The baseball game was showing, the very one Darren and me had told customs we were coming to see. The sound was turned down almost too low to hear. Kinkaid pulled his attention away from the game. He saw the fat man, and behind the fat man, he saw me, prodding the fat man forward. Kinkaid was older now and thinner. He was shorter than I remembered. His moustache was all white. But the sham-rock tattoo on his neck was bright and sharp. Maybe he'd had it touched up. He had one arm on the tabletop, and in his hand was a small black plastic tube of some kind.

Looking at me, he narrowed his eyes. He lifted the black tube from the tabletop and pressed it against his throat. When he spoke, his voice sounded robotic and flat and not at all human. The voice said, Well then, what's this about?

The back office was full of cigarette smoke and beat-up fur-niture. I was standing in the doorway, so I couldn't see the whole room. All I could see was the fat man in front of me, and past him, Kinkaid at the table. It was strange to see Kinkaid again. It both-ered me, and it made me more scared than I was already. I said, Where's my buddy?

Who's your buddy? said Kinkaid.

Darren Braemer. Where is he?

From out of my line of sight, I heard Darren's voice. Ash?

Go on, I said to the fat man. Sit down. Get out of my way.

I poked the fat man's back with the pocket rocket. The fat man walked forward into the office. I followed. The fat man did not so much as look at me. He waddled over to a mini-fridge in the corner and opened it and took out a can of pop, then closed the fridge and leaned against it and had a drink.

Sitting in an old swivel chair beside the mini-fridge was Darren, smoking a dart. He was the palest I had ever seen him. He looked at me with bloodshot eyes and said, What the hell, brother?

He isn't your brother, said Kinkaid.

I turned the pocket rocket to Kinkaid. I said, Stay there, asshole. For real.

Kinkaid smiled and shook his head, but he didn't get up. He had both legs extended out in front of him, under the table, one boot over the other.

I said, Darren.

What are you doing here? said Darren.

I came in your car.

What, in the fucking trunk? Jesus. You did, didn't you?

Kinkaid, still smiling, was watching us. The fat man wasn't. All he was doing was drinking from his can of pop and examining his fingernails. I had this crazy urge to shoot the fat man in his face.

I didn't need you, said Darren. You should've just went, brother, like you wanted. Straight-up. I knew it the minute I saw them. I didn't need you anymore. It's all just business.

Trying to keep the edge out of my voice, I said, What is it? What business? Your dad's?

This whole time, said Kinkaid, I been thinking, where've I seen you before. I think I know now.

Kinkaid's toneless robot voice was fucking me up. So was the smoke in the air and the too-bright lights overhead. And so was Darren, sitting there, looking sick. I could see the little sight shaking at the front of the pistol. I said to Kinkaid, You don't know anything.

You were DB's other little helper that time, said Kinkaid. I know you were.

I said, Shut up. Shut up, or . . .

Kinkaid was ten or twelve full seconds in replying. In that time, the air in the room got heavier. I could feel Darren staring at me.

Even the fat man was paying attention now. Then Kinkaid smiled again. He said, Or what. What are you planning to do, chief.

The pistol in my hands didn't weigh much, so why did I think I was going to drop it? I gripped it tighter and tried to hold the sight on Kinkaid's chest. The sight kept weaving back and forth. Sweat went into my eyes.

Ashley, said Darren.

What are you going to do? said Kinkaid.

I blinked the sweat out of my eyes. I took in some air and held it, and I said, Look, I just want to help my buddy. I want to get us out of here. That's all. I don't know about your business and I don't care.

That's reasonable, said Kinkaid. We can talk about all that. Or are you going to shoot me?

He was right. Totally. I didn't say anything, but I lowered the pocket rocket and took my left hand off it.

The pistol wasn't quite at my waist when the fat man sprang off the mini-fridge. I had never seen anybody move that fast, let alone a huge tub of guts like him. I didn't even have a chance to react, to block or dodge or lift the pistol back up or anything. The fat man plowed into me like a cannonball, and the next thing I knew I was on the concrete floor of the body shop, outside the office doorway. I was trying to cover my head with my arms and cover my belly with my knees. The fat man's boots came in, one after the other. I thought I was going to die. I thought I was going to be stomped to death, right there. My dad would probably never find out how I'd disappeared.

I heard Kinkaid's robot voice. The fat man's boots stopped coming in. I looked through my fingers. I could see Kinkaid and Darren both watching me, crowded shoulder-to-shoulder in the office doorway. A foot or two in front of my face was the pocket rocket. I saw the fat man's hand reach down and pick it up. He had fingers like sausages, with black lines of dirt around the fingernails.

I heard the fat man say, Your call, Kinny.

No, said Kinkaid. Let him up. It's his lucky day.

Kinkaid moved back and took his seat at the table again. Darren stayed in the doorway.

I was shaking. There were at least six points of throbbing pain on my body. One was on my shoulder. One was on my shin. There was a graze or scrape on the top of my head. The rest were on my torso. I maybe had a busted rib.

The fat man took a handful of my hair and pulled me into a sitting position. He pushed the muzzle of the pocket rocket against my cheek. He said, Next time, you stupid cunt, if you're going to be serious about pointing a weapon at somebody, at least make sure you got the safety off, even if it is a little play-toy like this.

He dug the sight into my cheek, hard, and then he let me go. I sat there on the floor and watched the fat man walk past Darren, back into the office. Kinkaid was fixed on the baseball game again, as if nothing had happened.

WE WERE WAITING FOR SOMETHING, BUT FOR WHAT I DIDN'T yet know. I was wordlessly offered a seat at the table where Kinkaid was sitting. Darren went back to the chair beside the mini-fridge. The fat man continued to drink his can of pop. There was a light shine of sweat on his forehead, but that was the only thing that showed the effort he'd just put out, kicking my ass. I didn't know what he'd done with the pistol.

Darren lit a fresh dart with the butt of the one he'd been smoking. He looked like a corpse. Even from where I was sitting, I could see his hands shaking.

The sounds of the baseball game chattered from the TV. The commentator said, The umpire is calling it safe.

Kinkaid hissed through his teeth and rapped his knuckles on the tabletop.

I hate this game, said the fat man.

Kinkaid glanced at him but didn't reply.

Just then a new voice said, It's all— Hey, who the fuck is this?

Another man was standing in the office doorway. He was tall and skinny, with long grey hair pulled back in a ponytail. He was wearing dirty jeans and a blue undershirt. There were latex gloves on his hands. The gloves made me think of condoms. This guy was frowning at me.

Kinkaid put his speaking thing to his throat and said, This, Steve, is the leg-breaker DB sent. He was just a little late getting here. Surprised us.

I hate surprises, said the fat man.

So I see, said Steve. He's not a problem?

No, said Kinkaid. Never mind him. What's the score?

The score is it's all there, said Steve. One pound, Kinny.

Darren exhaled loudly. I looked over at him. Darren was leaning his head against the wall behind him and he'd closed his eyes. He rubbed the back of his hand across his eyebrows and said, I told you guys.

It's good, said Steve. Not great but better than we need. And it isn't cut with no fucking Epsom salts or any of that shit, either, so there's that.

Kinkaid nodded. The fat man reached down and grabbed the top of Darren's head. His hand looked like it could easily crush Darren's skull. He said, You all did okay, boyo.

I told you, said Darren. I told you guys.

I said, So can we go now?

The big boy talks, said Steve, and at the same time the fat man told me to shut my goddamn mouth.

But I was looking at Kinkaid, and Kinkaid was looking back at me.

No sense sticking around here any longer than you have to, is that it? said Kinkaid in his robot voice.

I said, Something like that.

You understand what'll happen to you if you talk about what you seen here.

Like I said, I just came here for my friend. I don't know what your business is.

You're alright, big boy, said Kinkaid. Take DB Junior there and get going. We got nothing else to square away tonight.

Hold on, said Darren. I mean, aren't you forgetting something?

What would that be? said Kinkaid.

What? said Darren. How about the fucking money?

There was a screechy edge in his voice. He was sitting forward on his chair and his bloodshot eyes were bugging out of his head. The fat man was watching him closely.

That's fifteen thousand dollars right there, said Darren.

Kinkaid wrinkled his brow and took a toothpick out of his pocket and worked at something in his teeth.

Come on, man, said Darren, voice cracking. Fifteen thousand.

He started to get out of his seat, but the fat man moved with that same creepy speed. He didn't hit Darren, like he'd hit me, but he did put his hands on Darren's shoulders and push him back down into the chair.

Don't do that again, said the fat man.

Fifteen thousand goddamn dollars, whispered Darren.

Kinkaid put his tube against his throat. He said, How exactly do you think this works? What do you think you do for us? Tell me.

Whole . . . wholesale, said Darren. And, you know, cheffing it up. Fucking manufacture. On the other side of the border.

And transport, said Kinkaid.

Yes, and transport. Jesus.

The manufacture and transport are right, said Kinkaid. The wholesale isn't. At least not for a long time yet.

What the hell do you mean? said Darren.

This isn't buy and sell, kid. This is payment against a debt.

I looked over at Darren and saw that he'd become even paler. All at once it seemed like somebody had let the air out of him. He slumped down in his chair and said, I don't get it. I straight-up don't understand.

Your dad, said Kinkaid. He doesn't tell you much, does he?

YOU KNOW WHAT, BRO? WE GOT OUT OF THERE ALIVE. I'LL admit, I had had my doubts. Steve and Kinkaid walked us to Darren's car. Steve had the keys. I slowed everybody down because I was limping and hurting and stiff. It took me ten whole seconds to get into the passenger seat. Nobody said anything. Darren wasn't looking at me.

The roll-down door lifted. The fat man was on the other side. Past him was a gravel parking lot and a chain-link fence. It looked like a wasteland, a nowhere place. The sky overhead was dark. I had no idea what time it was.

Before Darren could close his door, Kinkaid bent down and said in his robot voice, Triple that sample. Every second week. And there are better ways to move it.

In a tired voice, Darren said, We have to get it across.

That's your problem, said Kinkaid.

For all the weird tonelessness of his voice, he didn't sound unkind. He pushed Darren's door shut and stood back.

Darren started the car. He popped it into gear and stalled right away. He sighed, restarted the car and got it moving. We drove out of the body shop and as we were coming to the edge of the gravel parking lot, Darren braked hard. He rolled down his window. The fat man was leaning down by the driver's side, looking across Darren and right at me.

He said, Next time you want to pretend you're some kind of stickup man, you might want to bring something a little more serious than this.

The fat man tossed two things across the narrow space. They landed on my leg, narrowly missing my balls. The pocket rocket with the action locked open and its slender magazine. All the bullets had been taken out.

I stared at it stupidly until Darren reached over and collected the pistol and the magazine both and pushed them under his seat. He rolled his window back up. Outside the car, the fat man was already walking away.

Let's go home, said Darren.

Way later, when I had a clear head, I wondered why the fat man gave us the gun back. I think it was a final little poke, a little fuck-you for us—for me—having tried to play it serious. Like he was telling us he knew we weren't gonna use it.

Of course, it did end up getting used after all, at the end of this whole shit-show. Funny how that worked out.

It was eleven o'clock when Darren drove us down off the bridge and back onto the Canadian side. We came up to the customs station. I was hunched down in my hoodie. Darren had given me his cap to wear so that I could hide the purple welt on my forehead.

The Canadian customs agent gave our IDs a quick look and asked us what we'd been doing in Detroit. Darren told him we'd been there for the baseball game. The customs agent just nodded and sent us on our way.

The gun was still in the car, now under Darren's seat. We'd gotten away with it again. I was too tired and hollowed out to care.

In Windsor we stopped at a fast-food drive-thru. Darren ordered himself a large fries and a milkshake. The voice on the other end of the intercom asked us if we wanted anything else. Darren looked at me, eyebrows raised. I shook my head. Darren shrugged. Then, just as he was starting to tell the voice we were finished ordering, I leaned across him and ordered everything he had ordered, plus a double cheeseburger. A minute later we pulled up to the window. Darren paid.

When we got back on the highway, we both ate hungrily, not saying anything. I put down my cheeseburger and fries and milkshake fast enough to make my gut hurt. I crushed the wrappings and cartons into the paper bag the meal had come in and rolled down the window and tossed the garbage out onto the shoulder of the road.

That was the quietest ride of my life. Neither of us talked at all. Darren didn't even play the stereo. As he drove, I nodded in and out of consciousness.

It was well past midnight by the time I realized we were driving on familiar streets in Altena. Everything looked shut down and deserted, the way it always looked late on a weeknight.

Darren took me to Trey's place. He parked the car in the driveway but did not turn off the ignition. This reminded me of the second time I'd hooked up with Chastity, the way we'd sat in the car, right there, in Trey's driveway, while it poured rain outside. It wasn't raining tonight. It was clear and there were stars overhead, a bit washed out by the lights of town.

I wondered what Darren knew. The bad thoughts were coming back into my head.

Darren laid his hands flat on the steering wheel and flexed his fingers. I heard him inhale and hold it and then exhale slowly. He said, I don't feel all that great, to tell you the truth. I feel like ass.

I said, Me too. Fast food does it to me every time.

I'll get well when I get home, said Darren. No problem.

I hit him then. I leaned across the seats and hit Darren hard on the side of the head. An open-handed blow. Exactly the same way my dad had hit me, all those years ago. Darren jolted. He lifted his hands to shield himself but by then I had already hit him twice more. When I sat back in my seat, my eyes were burning.

I said, You don't need to get well. You need to get clean, you fucking idiot. You need to get clean. Look at you.

Brother, said Darren. Listen—

It was all in your gut, wasn't it. A pound of crank in your fucking stomach. Do you know how straight-up white-trash dirty that is?

I was managing to keep my voice level, quiet even, but I was crying. I hadn't cried in a long time, not even when Chastity called things off.

I thought I wanted you there, said Darren. You're the only one I ever trusted, brother, and I was scared. I was scared. I thought I wanted you there. But things are different now. You're right about what you said, how this isn't for you. I figured that out today. When we were at the restaurant, and you went to the can, and they came in, and for all they knew I was alone, because I was supposed to be alone, it was supposed to just be me, and I thought how different everything is now, and how it's not for you, Ashley. So I tried to let you go. To just go, brother. And I thought you did. I watched you walk out that door, and you know what? I was relieved. I had a clear conscience for the first time in as long as I can remember.

I said, But I didn't go.

I know, said Darren. You didn't go.

And nothing worked out the way you thought it would.

I know that.

I said, You did it for free. You risked your own ass, and mine, for nothing. How's your conscience now, Darren?

It is what it is, said Darren. We're back here now, and it's over, and I'm gonna go home and get well and think about it tomorrow. Right now, all I know is, this isn't for you. You're too good for it.

I sniffed and wiped the tears off my face. I said, Don't tell me that bullshit. I'm not too good for anything. All this, it's not for you either. You're not some bad guy, not really. You're not really some dangerous motherfucker.

Stop it, said Darren. You're rambling. And you don't know what you're talking about.

And it's not even your business, is it. This is all DB.

Darren's head moved sharply. He said, Don't bring my dad into this. I never talk about your dad, so don't talk about mine.

It's true. I know it is. This is all him.

Fuck you, said Darren. Don't you say one more word about him. You have no idea. You have no goddamn idea about anything.

I know you need to get clean, Darren. I know that.

Get out of my car.

I unbuckled my seat belt and opened the door and put one foot on the driveway. Then I looked at him again. He was trying to light a dart. His lighter was only sparking.

I said, She's not at her mom's place. I know because I went. So where the fuck is she, Darren?

Darren kept at the lighter for a few more tries and then gave up. He said, She's . . . I have no idea where she is.

I said, And what happened with the Amigos? Why did one of them pull a knife on her?

Darren shook his head and looked away. I thought he might not reply, but after a couple of seconds he said, That wasn't anything. A goddamn mix-up is all. Nobody got hurt, and it didn't go anywhere and it doesn't mean a fucking thing.

Are you lying to me?

No, said Darren. I'm not lying to you. I've never lied to you about anything. I've never hidden anything from you—

Unless it was a pound of dope in your stomach.

—that you didn't want to know about. Now, all of a sudden, you want to know everything. And you want to get all high and mighty about it too. Jesus.

Where is she, Darren?

I told you, I have no idea.

I got out of the car. Before I closed the door, I said, I swear to god, Darren. If she's hurt . . .

Then what? said Darren. What'll you do, knucklehead? Why don't you go help somebody that really wants it? Leave the serious business to serious people.

I slammed the car door shut. Darren reversed hard and peeled away up the street. I watched him go, and then I sat down on the driveway. I was crying again. I slapped myself across the face.

I tried to say weakness, but the word wouldn't come out.

FOURTEEN

The voice on the phone was Greg's. He was saying, I woke you up, didn't I? I'm sorry, Ashley. I didn't mean to do that. I sat up on my mattress, blinking, holding the phone to the side of my head. The light coming in the window looked like mid-morning. I rubbed at my face and winced when I touched the sore spot on my forehead. It came back to me clearly, the memory of the fat man's kicks.

I squeezed my eyes shut and tried to pay attention to the phone call. I said, No, it's okay. What's going on, Greg?

Well, for starters, the other night . . .

I said, Don't worry about that. We can talk about it another time. Okay.

Is there anything else?

Yeah, said Greg. Remember a while back I asked you if you'd show me a thing or two in the gym, help me get my butt in shape?

I said, I remember.

Well, I have an unexpected day off today, and I figured no time like the present. But now I think I caught you at a bad time, maybe. Getting out of bed for one thing, and I really have no idea what you might have on for the day, so I'm sorry, because I'm sure it's a major inconvenience to ask.

I said, No, no, it's not an inconvenience . . . Ah, look, you know where Champ Fitness is? How about I meet you there in, like, an hour.

I GOT TO THE GYM AT ELEVEN O'CLOCK. THERE WERE SIX OR seven other people working out. I recognized a few, but not enough to greet them with anything more than a nod.

Greg was wearing new running shoes and out-of-style sweatpants with tight, elasticized cuffs and a high waistband. His body was skinny, his shoulders narrow. When we met up outside the change room, he offered me a handshake.

Thanks for doing this, Ash. Like I said on the phone, no time like the present.

I said, It's cool. I would have been coming out here anyways.

My first feeling was gratitude that Greg hadn't tried to hug me. I didn't want to feel that way, and I didn't want to wonder if anyone else in the gym knew who—faggot queer fag—Greg was. But I did wonder. I couldn't stop myself.

Greg was eyeing the purple bruise on my forehead.

I said, It's nothing. I slipped in the shower, like a retard. Hit my head on the wall. Come on, you got a water bottle?

I started Greg off on a treadmill, ten minutes of jogging to warm up. Greg sometimes ran with my dad, so at least he wasn't starting out completely new.

I got on the treadmill beside Greg's and jogged myself out for a short stretch. My body was tight and slow. The spots where I'd taken the kicks were hurting, even now. I thought I should get my rib X-rayed.

We finished jogging. I led Greg over to the bench press and said, Do you know about the holy trinity?

Greg smiled and said, I was raised Catholic. Irony of ironies.

I said, Oh, well, I don't know about that, but in the gym the holy trinity is the bench press, the dead lift and the squat.

That makes sense.

I'm no trainer or nothing, but I figure if you spend two weeks just getting the holy trinity down, plus some, you know, jogging and ab work, you'll be ready to move on to the other stuff.

Okay, said Greg.

He'd already broken a sweat. He got down on the bench. I started him off with the bar by itself, and when Greg had no problem with it, I added forty pounds. Greg huffed as he lifted. Deep colour flooded his face and a vein stood out in his forehead. He managed to do nine clean reps.

I said, Ninety-second rest. Then you go again. Do as many as you can. Slow and steady. Make sure you touch it to your chest every time or else you're cheating. We do three sets. Always in threes.

Greg did eight reps for his second set. He finished his third set with five. I stripped the plates off the bar and led Greg over to the squat rack. I demonstrated the exercise, using just the bar. My hurt rib screamed at me, but I did my best not to let on. I told Greg how to keep his posture throughout the motions. Then I loaded the bar up with fifty pounds and wrapped a towel around it where it would sit on Greg's shoulders. I said, Okay, let's see it.

Greg stepped into the cage and took up the bar and started his squats. Slow and steady, like I'd shown him. He was breathing heavy now, and that same deep colour came into his face. He'd started to sweat through his clothes.

I said, It's all about the holy trinity. Dad showed me this stuff when I was a kid. I don't know if you know this or not, but back in the day, when dad was in college, he could squat five hundred pounds.

I didn't know that, hissed Greg, mid-squat. I knew he was a beast, but . . .

A beast, I thought, suddenly uncomfortable. Those old thoughts, those old how-do-they-do-it curiosities, flashed into my mind, as unwanted as ever.

Greg did three sets of the squats. After he finished the third and replaced the bar, he got a cramp in his leg. He walked around in a circle, stepping the cramp out. I asked him if he was okay to continue. He nodded that he was.

I led him to a spacious corner of the gym. I got a bar and showed Greg how to do a dead lift. I loaded forty pounds onto the bar, same as what Greg had benched. I said, Alright, last exercise, then we'll do some abs and finish up. Three sets. Rep it out.

Greg struggled with the dead lift way more than he had with the squats or the bench press. He couldn't seem to get his form down. For the first set he managed only five reps. When he finished and set the bar down, he grinned a strained grin and said, Impressive, eh?

I said, Don't sweat it.

I stripped twenty pounds off the bar. Greg did his second set, better this time, exhaling loudly. I glanced around, wondering who might be watching us. Then I decided not to care. Greg was trying. What the hell else could he do? Trying was all that mattered. Trying was always the first, and maybe the hardest, step in fighting the weakness.

He needed more than ninety seconds before he did the third set. He managed three reps and then let go of the bar. The plates clanged together. He said, Sorry.

I said, I do that all the time. It means you finished hard. Okay, good work. Let's go hit up our abs.

Ash . . . , said Greg.

Yeah?

The deep colour in Greg's face had disappeared. His skin was white. He said, Ash . . . I think I'm going to throw up.

THIRTY-FIVE MINUTES LATER THE TWO OF US WERE AT A table in the all-day breakfast joint next to the gym. I was having an omelette with bacon and home fries and a cup of coffee. Greg was having toast and tea. It was all he could manage. At least some colour had come back into his face.

He said, How was that for a start?

I said, Could've been way worse. Whenever I miss anything more than two weeks, the exact same thing happens to me when I get back at it.

Have you started training up for your next show?

Not as much as I should. The first of next month, that's when I'll start. That's when I'll lay down the law.

I think it's pretty admirable, said Greg. Training like that takes the kind of discipline I've never had. Your dad and I wanted to see your show in October. Did you know that?

No, I said. I thought you guys were busy.

We were. My mother's eightieth birthday, a hard one to skip. But we wanted to be there for you. We should have told you that. Next time. Fair enough?

Sure.

I could feel Greg's eyes on my bruise again.

Listen, said Greg. About the other night—

I said, Don't worry about it. It's whatever. History.

No, no. Listen. I'm sorry, alright? It isn't my place. I've just done that for as long as I can remember. Managed things, or tried to manage things. You're good at weightlifting and self-discipline and whatnot, I'm good at being a manager. Hell, they pay me to do that at work. But it doesn't always fly in my personal life. You're just . . . important to me, Ashley. It's hard not to think of you as family. I'm sorry if that makes you feel weird, because I know it's been a tough road for you.

I said, It's . . . It's been harder for you guys. You and Dad. I know Altena is, like, one of those places where people love to talk and judge.

You know what? said Greg. That's every place.

I said, Well, nobody talks and judges around me, not if they know what's good for them.

I thought Greg might say he didn't like to hear that, the same as my dad would say, but instead Greg said, I appreciate that, Ashley. You don't know what it means to have you on our side.

The words flashed through my mind again. Queer faggot cocksucker. A little piece of potato stuck in my throat. I coughed it out and chased it with coffee. Then I said, I'm sorry about the other night too.

From now on I won't try to manage your business, said Greg. Anyhow, what else is new with you? Lots going on?

This and that. The usual stuff.

You see a lot of your friends? Darren and Chastity?

Before I could stop myself, I said, I don't see them much, no.

Oh, said Greg. Sorry to bring it—

Things got fuck— messed up with us, with the three of us. I don't want to get into the details, but it's not good. Put it this way. We three aren't talking to each other. That's basically where we're at.

Was there a catalyst for all of this?

I said, A what?

A catalyst, said Greg. Something that led to where you guys are. Maybe a falling-out or a fight.

I said, You could say that. It was, like, a bunch of decisions and actions all leading us in a certain direction. A chain reaction, you know? And we didn't know it at the time, and I still don't know why it all happened like it did. And now I don't know what to do about it. That probably doesn't make any sense.

It sounds complicated, said Greg. I don't need to know the specifics, because I'm sure they're quite personal. But I can tell you this. If you're in a situation where you don't know what to do, doing nothing is the worst thing.

The MAFD rule, right?

I don't know that, said Greg.

Make A Fucking Decision. MAFD.

Greg laughed, said, Yeah. Make a fucking decision. Sometimes you have to shake the tree and see what falls out.

I've been trying that, I guess.

Well, maybe it's time to shake the tree a little harder, no? Put those muscles to work?

I said, Maybe it is.

GREG PICKED UP THE BILL FOR OUR LATE BREAKFAST. AFTER we left the restaurant, he thanked me again for the workout demonstration and asked if we could do it again soon. I said we could, no problem.

I walked Greg over to his little Toyota. Before getting in, Greg offered me a handshake. I took his hand. Then I hugged him. I did it quick, with no warning, and in full view of the gym's front windows. I resisted the urge to look in through the windows, to stare right into the faces of anybody who might be staring back. Fuck them, I thought. Fuck them all.

I said, Talk soon.

You bet, said Greg.

After he was gone, I went back into the gym. Nobody seemed to be paying me any attention. For a little while, waiting for my food to settle, I shot the breeze with the girl at the front desk. Maybe she'd seen me with Greg. Maybe she'd thought to herself how *progressive* I was, you know?

Then I did my own workout. I pushed through the soreness and stiffness of where I'd been kicked. I tried to avoid my ribs. My workout was long and hard and good. I'd needed it.

I TOOK MY TIME RIDING ALONG WHITE BIKE WAY BACK into town. The afternoon was warm and clear. I slowed down to pass an Amigo pedalling a beat-up bicycle. I tipped a little wave to the Amigo. He nodded and waved back.

In town I stopped at the Canadian Tire gas bar on Bannock Avenue to fill up my bike. I was just taking up the nozzle when a big hardtop Eldorado glided to a stop on the opposite side of the pumps. It took me a few seconds to realize I was seeing DB's car.

The passenger's side window was down. Seth was sitting there, trying to mean-mug at me. DB was in the driver's seat. He leaned across the interior, toward the open window, and grinning, he said, Funny running into you like this.

I said, It's a gas station.

We seen you out at your gym, said Seth.

We wanted to give you something, said DB. But you were with an older gentleman, showing him some tips and tricks, so we figured we'd leave you all to it. I suppose this is as good a place as any.

I glanced around. Bannock Avenue was quiet. The only other person at the gas bar was a little old man, standing with his back to us, filling up a station wagon.

I said, You want to give me something?

DB nodded to Seth. Seth, shaking his head, not making eye contact with me, held out a blank letter-sized envelope.

I took it. It had the weight and thickness of cash, but I didn't open it. I held the envelope in my hand and said, What's this for?

Your troubles, said DB. You been going out of your way. And I hear there was a little misunderstanding between my associates and my number-two son. He was lucky to have you there with him.

Even if it does look like you took a beat-down, said Seth, mean-mugging at me again.

Shut up, Seth, said DB. Anyhow, I think you'll find there's a fair deal in there. You haven't gone unnoticed, Ashley.

I remembered my gas tank was still filling, just in time to release the trigger and take out the nozzle and hang it back on the pump. I still had the envelope in my other hand. I said, I don't want your guys' money. You can have it back. Whatever you think I do, or did, or whatever, I don't do that anymore.

That's all yours, said DB. Call it a payout if it makes you feel better. Fair is fair. There's something I like about you. You got a real man's quality. I'm glad your dad didn't have too much of an influence on you.

See you around, said Seth.

DB put the Eldorado into gear and pulled away from the pumps. His car disappeared down the street. I stood unmoving for several moments.

Finally I opened the envelope. I managed a bitter little laugh at what I saw. Then I balled it all up and tossed it in the garbage can, the envelope and the two thousand dollars of Monopoly money it contained.

FIFTEEN

Michelle Levy lived in the ground-floor apartment of a three-storey house a few blocks north of downtown. She wasn't there when I showed up, even though she'd said she would be when I called her. I stood on her porch and knocked on the door, waited, knocked again. She had a couple of Muskoka chairs, one bright pink, the other bright yellow. I sat down in the pink chair.

Five or ten minutes passed. I was about to call her again when I saw her up the street, dressed in tight-fitting exercise clothes, jogging in the direction of her place. Leading her was her dog, a grey and white pit bull named Libra. They both slowed to a stop when they got into the front yard.

I stood up. The dog saw me and barked. Michelle gave me an offhand wave. Then she bent over and let Libra off her leash. The dog bounded up the front steps, barking. To someone who didn't know her, she would have been terrifying coming on the run like that. But she stopped dead a foot in front of me, sniffed a circle around my legs and then offered her head to be petted.

Michelle came up the steps next. She said, Hello, Rosco.

I made to hug her but she ducked me, said she was sweaty. She seemed cool. I thought I'd just imagined it in her voice on the phone, but now I knew for sure. She unlocked the front door and opened it and gestured for me to go inside.

I have to say, said Michelle, you look like you got the shit kicked out of you.

I said, It was nothing.

I probably don't want to know anyways.

Yeah, probably not.

Jesus Christ, she said, shaking her head.

WE WERE IN HER LIVING ROOM. LIBRA HAD GONE TO SLEEP on a mat in the corner. Michelle had the TV on with the volume turned low. An afternoon talk show was playing, some busted-up American family throwing insults at each other. From time to time they got into fights that were quickly broken up by the show's bouncers. Watching gave me a certain guilty pleasure.

Around the living room, Michelle's decorations were bright, nice to look at, but the space was messy and disorganized. Dog hair was stuck to everything. I was sitting on the couch. Michelle was sitting cross-legged on a large easy chair. Before we sat down, she'd thrown some bananas and kiwi fruit and yogourt into her blender and made us a couple of smoothies. I liked the taste okay but the greenish colour put me off. I could only sip mine, and even then not while looking at it.

I didn't quite know how to say what I'd come to ask. I took a moment to look at Michelle, how she was sitting. We'd made out on that easy chair once, I remembered. A year or two before. She'd given me a handjob that time.

She returned my look, as if sensing what was on my mind. Darren was right, I thought. It could've worked with me and Michelle. She had her shit together and would have straightened me out in a hurry.

But she wasn't Chastity.

Michelle looked away and said, I thought I might've heard from you before today.

Ah, yeah. It's been a busy time, you know what I mean?

If you called me up because you thought you might get laid, forget it. I'm on my period.

I said, It's not that.

You've pretty much never called me out of the blue, Rosco. So I'm almost afraid to ask what's up.

It's kind of weird, I don't know.

If you say Chastity . . .

I said, Well. I'm going to.

Goddammit, said Michelle. What the hell is it with you? She's your relative. You know that, right?

Listen, have you heard from her? Like, since the last time I talked to you?

Michelle made a sound of disgust, shook her head, turned back to the TV. The talk show host said, You're a prisoner in your own home, is that true?

What do you think you're doing, Ashley, really? said Michelle. This isn't a mystery movie. This is real life. You can't roll like this.

Have you heard from her?

No. I haven't.

So, are you worried about her?

Shit, said Michelle, and she said it with enough force that Libra woke up and looked at her. Yes. I am worried about her. And no I'm not, because when it comes to her it's pointless. Wherever she is, she's probably fine, she's probably just ducking everybody for a while, because that is what she does. You know this.

I said, I'm worried about her too. And this time, I don't know. This time it's different. Like this time I think it's legit trouble.

Business shit, said Michelle. Am I right?

Yeah. Business shit. I won't lie to you about that.

So what do you want with me?

Well, you said she was crashing here for a while, right?

Yes, said Michelle. She was.

I want to look at her stuff.

That's creepy, Ashley, said Michelle. I am telling you, honestly, that's creepy. You know that, right?

I didn't reply. I frowned, scratched at a loose thread on the armrest of the couch.

Michelle rubbed her eyes and said, Man, you're like my dog with a fuckin' steak bone, aren't you?

THE EXTRA ROOM IN MICHELLE'S APARTMENT WAS NOT QUITE big enough to be a bedroom. It was the right size for a small home office, but it was where Chastity had been staying. There was a closet, a desk, a swivel chair, a drying rack and a loveseat, which Michelle said Chastity had been sleeping on. The air smelled like Chastity's perfume, White Diamonds. It made my head spin.

Her stuff is in the closet, said Michelle. Like I told you, I haven't touched any of it. It's here, but it's up to her to make amends and come back for it. I don't think that's unfair.

I opened the closet. There were half a dozen shelves in it. I saw shoes and clothes I recognized as Chastity's. The clothes were all neatly folded, in contrast to the messiness of the rest of Michelle's place. I picked up a hoodie and unfolded it and turned it in my hands and resisted the urge to sniff it. It said *Volcom* across the chest. I put it back, but I was unable to match the neat way it had been folded and stowed.

Do you know what you're looking for? said Michelle.

No.

Fair enough. Just . . . don't start going through her underwear, okay? This is all weird enough as it is.

I didn't find anything interesting in the closet, and after a little while I stood back, rubbing my hands together.

There you go, said Michelle.

I said, Yeah.

Well then. I don't want to hurry you, but I have to get cleaned up and head to work—

I turned from the closet and started pulling open the desk drawers. The first drawer was empty except for a pencil.

Okay, said Michelle. Apparently we're still at this.

In the second drawer I found some of Chastity's things. Some CDs and hair elastics. A tube of lipstick. An old-fashioned metal cigarette tin that said *Sweet Caporal* on it. I was sure these things were Chastity's because I'd seen the tin before. Beside the tin was a small stack of photographs, the kind you could get developed at the mall or the drugstore.

I picked them up. The first half dozen showed Nevaeh, mostly in close-up. I recognized the deck at my aunt Glenna's place in the background of a couple of the pictures. There was a playground in another. The little girl, sitting on a swing, was giving the camera a serious face. Old soul. I continued to look through the pictures. I saw people I knew, but most were of Chastity and Michelle, laughing or trying to look goofy. Then I came to an old picture. It showed me and Darren and Chass on our last day of grade twelve, standing outside the school, all three of us giving the middle finger to the camera. When I set this picture down, I put it to the side rather than returning it to the stack.

I found Darren in only one more picture. He was driving his car, smiling, looking like he was thinking about something. His face was fuller in the picture than it was now. His hair was longer. The scenery outside the driver's side window was a frozen blur of greys and greens.

Maybe this is enough now, said Michelle. What do you think?

I came to the last three pictures. They were all of me, posing on the stage at the D'Amours Classic in the fall. I saw my body, my tan, my tiny shorts, my oiled muscles.

Come on, Ash, said Michelle.

I put the stack of photographs back in the drawer. I picked up the Sweet Caporal tin. I opened it with my thumb. Looking up at me were four cartoon elves on four plastic baggies of crank. There was a blue lighter and a glass stem with burnt patches on it.

I looked over at Michelle. Her eyes, fixed on the tin in my hand, were hot. Her lips moved. She took a breath. She started to say something, and then she burst into tears.

SHE SPENT TIME CRYING IN THE LIVING ROOM, COLLAPSED on the couch, hugging a cushion to her chest. Then she got angry again. She put the pillow on the couch beside her and punched it with both hands. Libra watched her, whining. I stayed across the room, leaning against the wall.

I knew, said Michelle. I fucking knew.

I said, You did?

She glared at me. She said, How about you get me a glass of water.

I went into the kitchen and poured tap water into a glass and carried it back to her. I found her sitting on the couch, head down, not moving except for the rise and fall of her shoulders. Libra was by her side. I held the glass out at arm's length, not wanting to get too close. After a few seconds she took it.

Look, let's be clear, said Michelle. I don't know what you're trying to prove, Ashley, but let me tell you something. This is not an interview or a what-do-you-call it, interrogation, or anything like that. You're not whatever you think you are.

I don't think—

Just shut up. Shut up, okay? I say I knew but that isn't quite right. Like, yes, I know now. I know now, but I didn't then. Or I did, and I was only tricking myself, or . . . Jesus . . . I just have to talk this out. If you want to listen to me, you can. That's up to you. But this is not some kind of confession, and, like I said, you're not whatever you think you are. Get me?

I said, Yes. I do.

Then sit down.

I took a few backwards steps and lowered myself into the easy chair, the same one Michelle had been sitting in earlier, the one she'd once given me a handjob in. I noticed the TV was still on, the volume still turned low. The talk show was over. Now it was a sitcom. I couldn't see much of it. The screen was washed out by the afternoon sunshine from the front window. I heard a one-liner, Dirt is my enemy, followed by canned laughter.

I knew Chass was into something, said Michelle. I didn't want to think it was this. I'm not one to judge. Get high all you want, right, but do it natural, do it organic. Do what grows in nature. This other shit, you know? Some dirtbag makes it in a shack or a basement somewhere, with drain cleaner and batteries and god knows what else, and you want to smoke that? You want to put that up your nose? Jesus Christ . . .

I said, But Chass was hitting it.

She'd been so sketched-out, man, said Michelle. This was when she was living here, but it was before that too. The last couple months. For a while I figured it was stuff with Darren or all those Amigos she was hanging out with. One or the other was calling her, like, all the time. The middle of the night. I'd hear her on her cell phone. She'd either be saying Darren's name, or she'd be talking in Spanish. There were those three of them I think I told you about. Bailador and Ramon and another one. Cesar.

I said, You want to know something? I went to see them. The Amigos. After you told me about them pulling a knife on her.

Why doesn't that surprise me?

That guy Bailador? It's a, like, nickname. It means dancer. They call him that because he's this amazing soccer player. He moves like crazy, Michelle. I saw him. I talked to him. Him and Ramon. It wasn't a good scene, though. I thought shit was gonna go down—like me and Trey versus a dozen angry Mexicans, way out in the sticks. Anyways, I didn't really find anything out.

Michelle shook her head. She said, Listen to you.

Listen to me what?

I'll say it one more time. You're not whatever you think you are.

What's that supposed to mean?

Nothing. Look. Get me another glass of water, will you?

I did. I gave it to her and I sat back down and watched her drink the water in long, deep swallows. She emptied the glass and wiped her mouth on her sleeve. She leaned down and scratched behind Libra's ear. Libra, who'd dozed off, opened one eye and closed it again.

I talk about Darren and the Amigos, said Michelle. But you want to know Chass's biggest issue? It was, and, like, no surprise here, her mom. I mean, a grand a month. That's more than I pay in rent for this place.

I said, A grand a month?

Chass was giving that to her mom. For Nevaeh. Her mom wouldn't let her see her otherwise. But here's the thing. My cousin Rae? She's got a kid, Nevaeh's age. Rae gets two-fifty a month from her ex. It's not a lot, I know, but it's not nothing. And on top of that it's all legit, through the courts, figured out by a lawyer or whatever. So with Chass we're talking a whole grand, a thousand bucks, more than my rent, going to Glenna each month? I mean, she told Chastity it was mostly going into a college fund for Nevy, but with Glenna, who knows?

I said, I hear that.

What I can tell you, Ashley, what I can tell you, you don't make enough money to afford that, not to mention everything else in your life, working thirty hours a week at a fuckin' tanning salon, and that's not counting after you get let go.

I said, Wait, what? She got let go? I didn't know about that.

Yeah, said Michelle. She got in a fight with Deb, the manager. Some blowout a month ago, god knows over what. Told Deb to go fuck herself. Chastity has a short fuse, Ashley. You know that. But she's always been pretty smart about work stuff, about who to try it with and who to let it go with. She was always good at playing her advantages. But, like I said, she loses it at work, gets her ass fired, and when it comes to her that's weird enough, but the weirder part is, she was still giving her mom that cash, that grand a month . . .

A moment passed before I realized that Michelle had stopped speaking. She was staring at a midpoint in the room, maybe the carpet or the bottom of the easy chair. Her eyes were red.

Chass wasn't just hitting it, said Michelle. She was selling it too. Wasn't she. She was doing business.

I couldn't think of anything to say. I wished I'd gotten myself a glass of water. I heard another one-liner from the TV, quiet but clear, You don't really want me to wash your skivvies, do ya?, and another low-pitched ripple of canned laughter.

I knew, said Michelle. For fuck sake. I knew. I was tricking myself. I was letting us fight about all the old bullshit. I was letting her go at me, letting myself pretend I was some kind of a victim, done wrong by my best friend. And then . . . then I kicked her out. And when she called me I told her to fuck off. And all along I knew. Didn't I.

I said, I knew too.

Michelle's red eyes blinked at me a bunch of times. She looked exhausted. She leaned her head back and stared at the ceiling. Her dog was sleeping at her feet. She said, One thing, and this is just a guess, but Darren has no idea you're here, does he?

No, he doesn't.

As soon as I'd finished admitting that, I felt a prickly sweat break out between my shoulder blades. I scratched at the spot.

Can you leave me alone now, Ashley? said Michelle.

I WAS BACK OUTSIDE, ABOUT TO GET ON MY BIKE, WHEN I heard Michelle call my name. I looked up. She was holding her front door open. Libra's face was peering out from between her thigh and the door frame.

Something to think about, Ashley, said Michelle.

I said, What is it?

Calling the cops, man. Seriously.

I'll think about it.

I mean, if you don't, maybe I will. For everybody's good. Like I told you, you're not what you think you are.

I said, So what exactly am I, Michelle?

You know that already, said Michelle. You're a caveman. Don't take it the wrong way, because it's okay. It's an okay thing to be. Everything else aside. I kind of love that about you. So just . . . do what's right, okay?

SIXTEEN

After I got home from Michelle's, me and Trey played video games for a while. We didn't talk much. Trey hadn't asked me about the mark on my forehead. At two o'clock Trey left to visit his mother. He said he'd be going straight to work and would see me there.

I kept at the video games for a little longer. I was thinking about what had happened at Michelle's place. It all meant something or it meant nothing. The dead-murdered-buried thoughts went through my mind. I had them a lot now. I could shake them off here and there, but they always came back. But then I got thinking about the Chastity of the past, up to and including the Chastity of the fall and winter. The Chastity who'd gone with me to the show, taken pictures of me when I'd been at my fittest. The Chastity who'd told me what fools the judges had been, the Chastity who'd made me feel like a god.

I jerked off in the shower before work, thinking of her, thinking of one of the times we'd fucked in Darren's car, her small round ass pressed against my hips.

After, when I was dressing, all the bitterness and hurt came back. Why should I care what had happened to her? I tried to remember telling her she was on her own. I tried to hold on to that feeling.

I got to the Balmoral at eight o'clock, and as soon as I stepped into the main room and saw my co-workers I knew something was wrong. Trey was nowhere to be seen, but the rest of them, Dani Knox and the other bartenders and Brice and TJ, they were all acting weird. They wouldn't make eye contact with me, and they only spoke in short sentences. I tried to get some information out of TJ, but all he'd say was he didn't know.

As I was stashing my helmet and coat in the staff room, Trey appeared in the doorway. He was frowning. He looked like he'd been coming from the direction of the office.

I said, Hey, bro. What's going on with everybody? They're all acting like someone died.

Ash, said Trey. Listen—

Then Trey glanced behind him and stopped speaking. He shook his head, bumped the door frame with his fist and headed back into the main room.

Right away the space Trey had left was filled by Marcel. He stood there, all five feet of him, looking at me. A few seconds passed. Finally Marcel said, Alright, well, let's go have a word.

MARCEL SAT ON HIS DESK, NOT BEHIND IT, SMOKING AND talking and gesturing with his hands. He was saying a lot of things. He was asking about the marks on my face and then just as quick saying he didn't want to know. Then he was talking about how rough I'd got with that college kid on the weekend, and in front of lots of eyeballs, no less, and since when did I think that was part of my job description.

I found it hard to listen to him. My attention was caught up with the crooked Bob Marley poster on the wall behind the desk. *One Love.*

Then Marcel was saying he didn't need me to work that night, and he didn't need me to work on Saturday night either.

On the poster behind Marcel, Bob Marley's dreadlocks looked a little like tarantula legs. I had never thought of that before. Tarantula legs, thick and hairy, dozens and dozens of them. Hadn't old Bob died of cancer? Darren would know. Darren was a big fan. Sometimes when I was in the car with him, D played that one song— the one with the acoustic guitar, the one that told you to emancipate yourself—over and over on the car stereo. Darren would smoke a joint to the song, offer the joint to me, call me brother.

Matter of fact, said Marcel, I don't need you to come in for the next while at all.

So you're firing me?

No, said Marcel. I'm not firing you. But I'm cutting you back until the crap clears. Because that's you, lately. You're a liability, seems like. You're a shit-bringer. And trust me, none of us need that.

I said, I don't even know what to say, Marcel. I've been dealing with some things, okay?

Marcel stood up from the desk and walked around behind it and stubbed his dart into an empty pop can. He said, I'm not firing you because if you can get your life sorted out, if you can stop being the shit-bringer, I can still use you here. Especially come the summer. You been doing this for a long time, and you usually got your head screwed on tight. But.

But what?

But this, said Marcel. I'm not normally an advice-giver and I bet anything you're not the kind of guy who listens. So for what it's worth, here it is. Look for something, Ashley.

What do you mean, look for something?

I mean look for something. Like a steady job.

I said, This is a steady job. Isn't it?

This? said Marcel. This is where you get to still be the biggest dog in the yard, like you were in high school, and get paid for it. But really? This? This has an expiry date. And it passes before you know it. I don't believe in much of that self-help bullshit, but maybe if you're away from here for a while, you'll at least think about what I'm saying. Maybe there's that much.

I LEFT THE CLUB NOT TWENTY MINUTES AFTER I'D ARRIVED, smelling like cigarette smoke. Friday night stretched away in front of me, the first one I'd had to myself in a long time.

My co-workers had all kept their distance as I made my way out. I guess they'd known already. That much was obvious. The only one who'd come up to me was Trey. He said he thought it was all bullshit and Marcel should've called me instead of letting me come in to work. He said he didn't know how they were gonna manage that night, short one hand.

I shrugged and said, It is what it is.

Now I stood on the sidewalk out front. I had my bike helmet under my arm. My riding jacket was back on but the evening was almost too warm for it. It was only fifteen or twenty minutes after sundown and the sky was a rich, deep blue. Under other circumstances I would've felt pretty good. It could've been the kind of night for possibilities and new starts. Spending time with my dad, maybe, my dad and Greg both. Or calling on Michelle and taking her on a proper date. It could've been a night for putting all the Chastity and Darren bullshit behind me.

I looked over. Some distance to my left was the two-by-six rail of the Balmoral's lower patio. I'd been leaning against the rail, on New Year's Eve, when Chastity ended things. She'd said, Stop it. Please. We can't do this here.

But we had done it there. I'd been standing at almost the exact same spot when I took the call from her a few weeks ago. When I told her she was on her own.

Behind me the club was just opening up. In a few minutes, Brice or TJ or Trey would come outside to work the front door. Maybe they would ask me where I was going to go that night, what I was going to do with myself.

I'd be gone, I decided, before they could ask. My first thought was to go to the gym, but I just didn't have the energy to do a full-on workout. My second thought was to go home, get high, play video games. Then I looked over at the sidewalk bench where the Amigos would gather before the night was out, and I had an idea.

THE FIRST THING I NOTICED INSIDE VILLAGERS WAS THE music. There was a kind of stomping, country beat. On top of the beat was an accordion. And on top of that were the vocals, two or three men's voices, singing in Spanish. The tone was both sad and happy.

I stood just past the vestibule, looking around. The place was crowded but the lighting was muted. I could see I was one of the few locals there. The bartender was a white guy, older, with thick biceps and broad shoulders. I kind of knew him from the gym, but I couldn't remember his name. Around the bar there were a few white women, all of them patrons, most of them fat. They were each hanging around or hanging off the Amigos, who made up the rest of the clientele.

I went up to the bar carrying my bike helmet by my side. The bartender eyed me with some curiosity and said, You lost, big guy?

I said, No, just checking out a new scene, I guess.

Fair enough, but I won't tolerate it if you're here to make any trouble with the pickers.

I'm not, I said.

Okay. So what'll she be?

You got Keith's?

I do, said the bartender. Your name is Alex, am I right?

Close enough. It's Ashley.

Right, Ashley, said the bartender. You keepin' at the iron these days?

You know it, bro.

Good to hear.

The bartender opened up a bottle of Keith's. I put a five on the bar. My fingers were tapping in time to the funny music.

The bartender, as he took my money, said, Norteño.

I said, What?

The music, said the bartender. It's called norteño. These pickers all eat it up. Since I put it on the juke, my liquor sales have tripled. I suppose it reminds them of being home.

I said, Hey, you think you could tell me about a couple of these guys?

What do you want to know?

I took a look around the bar. My eyes had adjusted to the dark shadows and coloured lights. Ramon and Bailador were both standing at the jukebox, Ramon in jeans and a jean jacket, Bailador in baggy khakis and a shiny black soccer jersey. I'd seen them and already looked past before I realized it. I snapped my attention back, made sure they were who I thought they were. Who I wanted them to be. They hadn't seen me yet.

I turned back to the bartender and said, You know what, bro? Never mind.

I approached the jukebox. Ramon noticed me first. The little Amigo stood up straighter. He'd been grinning, but now his expression turned blank. He prodded Bailador's ribs and said something and Bailador looked at me. Then he looked past me, too, and I knew he was trying to see who I might've come in with.

I said, I'm alone. Tell him, will you?

Before Ramon could translate, Bailador nodded. His face stayed blank. His dark eyes were locked directly on mine. I didn't think he was afraid of much.

Around us, the norteño music jangled along.

We don't want trouble, said Ramon.

I said, Me neither. Listen. This isn't easy for me to say, but . . . I'm sorry for how I met you guys. I was an asshole about it, okay? I owe you some respect.

I put out my right hand.

Ramon spoke close to Bailador's ear. Bailador said a couple words, not taking his eyes off me. Ramon spoke some more. At last, Bailador nodded, just a slight tip of his chin. He reached out and shook my hand. His grip was rough and strong.

Ramon shook my hand next. He said, Okay. It's good. But you did not come here for this only, did you.

I'D TAKEN ONE OF CHASTITY'S PHOTOGRAPHS, THE ONE OF Darren and Chastity and me giving the middle finger on our last day of high school, from the desk at Michelle's place. At the time I didn't really know why. Maybe because it was the last image I knew of our lives before everything had become serious—just before Darren's business started to make real money, just before

Chastity found out she was pregnant, just before my own first shift at the club.

The photograph had been in my jacket pocket ever since, folded in half and already dog-eared. Now I laid it on the table-top. I was sitting in a booth at the back of Villagers. Bailador and Ramon were across from me. I'd properly introduced myself to them and then bought a round of drinks. A rum and Coke for Ramon. Another beer for me. And for Bailador, a glass of the best rye Villagers had behind the bar. It was a pick I hadn't expected. But by now I had no idea what to expect.

I gave the Amigos a short version of my life and the lives of Chastity and Darren. How long we'd known each other and had been close friends. I almost said like family but the words stopped in my throat. Ramon translated and Bailador nodded. Neither asked me any questions. They remained cool and detached. I couldn't blame them. I ended by saying I was a bouncer at the Balmoral. I said, I'm not police, or policía. I never was.

We know this, said Ramon.

I said, Yeah, I figured. But what I am is worried, okay? About my friend.

Your friend, said Ramon.

I tapped Chastity's face in the photograph and said, You guys know her, right? I mean, I know you do. I know you do.

Ramon looked at Bailador. Bailador kept his face blank. Ramon turned back to me and said, Yes. We know her.

You know her a long time?

Not me, said Ramon. I have only three years here. But Bailo and Cesar—

Bailador said something in Spanish. Ramon nodded and went quiet. He was troubled, I thought. Something was bothering him.

I turned to Bailador and said, How many years have you been coming up here?

Ramon started to translate but Bailador held up his hand and in slow, careful English said, Now I have twelve year here.

Always at the same farm?

Sí. Three . . . Corazon.

Triple Heart, said Ramon.

I said, Yeah. And Chastity, she worked there when she was a kid. It was her first job, bro. She was there for a bunch of summers in a row, then again a couple years ago.

Bailador nodded.

Yes, said Ramon, frowning at his drink again. She had work at Triple Heart.

I said, She was a picker too. It didn't take her long to hate it. Same as every other local up here . . . But she's known you guys a long time, hasn't she?

Maybe Bailador understood and maybe he didn't, but Ramon translated, maybe just to have something to do. When he was done speaking, Bailador nodded again, said, Sí.

I said, I don't know if you guys know this, but I saw you at the hospital. A couple weeks ago. I figured it out at the farm. I saw you both at the hospital. On a Sunday morning. I'd bet everything I own you were there visiting your friend. Cesar, right?

For a minute neither Amigo spoke. Then Ramon started to say something, but pretty quick Bailador cut him off. Callarse, said Bailador. No.

Bailo don't want to talk about that, said Ramon.

I said, Okay. So . . . maybe another round?

I leaned out of the booth and caught the bartender's attention and drew a circle with my hand. The bartender nodded.

Across from me, Bailador and Ramon were talking quietly in

Spanish. Bailador's blank expression had finally given way to a slight frown. There was worry in his voice. Ramon kept glancing at me.

Then I heard two words stand out from their conversation. Drogas and narcos. Both words were traded back and forth a few times. Bailador shook his head.

I said, Drogas.

The Amigos both stopped talking and looked at me.

I said, I know what that word means. So, what, weed? Marijuana?

No reply. The bartender arrived with the drinks and put them down on the table and went away again.

I said, Cocaine?

No reply.

I said, Or something else? Like, methamphetamine . . . ?

I didn't remember ever saying that word before. Methamphetamine. It sounded scientific and serious, too big for my mouth. The Amigos still didn't reply, but something passed over Ramon's face.

I said, Ramon. Is that it?

I don't know, said Ramon. I don't think I know this word.

Tell me.

I don't know, said Ramon.

He looked like he wasn't sure. Beside him, Bailador had gone blank again.

Then I had an idea. At the edge of the table was a small basket of condiments, including the salt and pepper shakers. I picked out the salt shaker and unscrewed the cap and poured a spoonful of it onto the tabletop. The two Amigos watched me. I reached over and took the straw out of Ramon's glass. Then I bent over the little mound of salt and held the straw between my lips. Like a pipe. I pretended to flick a lighter and take a haul and exhale it slowly.

Maybe it looked ridiculous, but I was too into it to care. When I leaned back and looked at them, I saw they knew exactly what I was trying to say.

Tacha, said Ramon.

I said, Keeps you up all day and all night, right? Maybe two, three days straight?

Yes. Make you crazy.

I leaned back against the booth wall. Things were coming to me real quick. I thought, Chain reaction. My mind was doing that right now. I tried to drink my beer but I found I had no taste for it. I said, You guys work long days at the farm, right?

Ramon nodded.

Like, what, ten hours?

Ten hours, yes, said Ramon. Sometime more. Today we have only eleven hours, but yesterday and day before we have fourteen hours. Before the morning, before the sun is up, until after the sun is gone away we work.

I said, Right. Long-ass days that people around here wouldn't put up with. But never mind that. You guys do that, what, six days a week?

Yes.

I tapped the little mound of salt I'd poured onto the table, and I said, So would this shit maybe make it easier to work all those hours, six days in a row?

Ramon looked at Bailador. Neither of them answered. I didn't need them to. My hands were shaking and my foot was drumming under the table. I forced down a mouthful of beer. Overhead, the norteño music on the juke cut out and stayed off for half a minute. The bar's mixed sounds of conversation and laughter filled the space. Then the norteño started up again, a snare drum and a crazy-sounding accordion and a wailing singer.

I said, Chastity. She was selling to you guys, wasn't she.

Ramon looked at Bailador. Bailador nodded.

Yes, said Ramon. She was selling the tacha.

Bailador spat out a bunch of words in Spanish. He sounded angry. Ramon asked him something. I thought I heard the word idea.

What're you guys saying? I said.

Bailador looked at me and talked some more in Spanish. This time I heard this word, estúpidos.

I said, Estúpidos what? Who's estúpidos?

Nothing, said Ramon. It is not anything. Bailo is just very tired with this.

Bailador sighed and shook his head. He did look tired. He picked up his glass and drank down the last of his second rye.

He wanted me to tell you about the others, said Ramon.

What others?

In the beginning, the first number of times Chastity come out to us with the tacha, she come with some others.

Who? I said, guessing already.

One, a fat boy, said Ramon. His hair, canelo, red. And the other boy, his brother we think. Red hair too. His body is not fat. Very not fat.

Bailador stabbed his finger on Darren's face in the old photograph. He was looking at me again. The anger in his eyes was plain. I didn't know if it was directed at me or at Darren.

The very not fat one, said Ramon. Here in this picture. He and the fat boy come with Chastity. Two, three times they come.

I said, You ever have a problem with them?

No, said Bailador flatly. No problem.

No problem, said Ramon.

I said, And after a while it was just Chastity, coming by herself?

Yes, said Ramon.

But something ended up going wrong, didn't it.

Neither Amigo said anything, but Ramon nodded.

I swept the little mound of salt off the tabletop and said, Something went wrong. Maybe it was your boy Cesar, I don't know. Maybe he OD'd on that shit. I've heard of that happening. You can blow out your heart. Is that what happened to Cesar?

I looked at them.

Bailo don't want to talk about that, said Ramon.

I said, Either way, whatever happened, you pulled a knife on her, right? Told her to fuck off and stay away. This was, like, two and a half weeks ago.

They stayed quiet, both of them watching me. I didn't ever remember a time in my life when I'd figured out so much from what wasn't said.

I said, Let me ask you this, and it's the last thing, but it's the most important, okay? I swear, I'll just ask you this and then I'll pay for our drinks and I'll leave. But this is the most important.

Ramon translated. Bailador tipped his chin.

I said, Have you seen her since?

No, said both Amigos.

I nodded. I'd known, but I needed to hear it.

Is she in trouble now? said Ramon.

I don't know.

What you going to do? said Ramon.

I said, I don't know that either. I'm just trying to make things right, I guess. For her and for everybody else. I'm not trying to fuck anything up. Goddamn. Look, I'm sorry about whatever happened to you guys, to your boy Cesar. You're all a long way from home.

HEY, PANDILLERO.

I was midway across the parking lot outside of Villagers. I stopped and looked back. Bailador was coming down the front steps. Ramon was not with him.

As Bailador came closer, I felt real alone. Both Villagers, behind Bailador, and the Dynasty, across the street, seemed far away.

I said, What's up?

Bailador got closer. Just then I felt my phone vibrating in my pocket. I ignored it.

Bailador stopped a few feet away. He said, I try to talk to you, okay? But my English is not good, like Ramon.

I said, So I'm guessing you understood most of what I was talking about, even without Ramon.

Most, yes. So. My name is Luis, not Bailo or Bailador. That is other name. Name for friends.

My phone stopped vibrating. I said, Bailador means dancer.

Sí, yes. Dancer. Bailador.

Because of the way you play soccer. Football.

Yes. When I had twenty years, I play in Cuidad Juárez for the segunda division.

What is that, the pros?

It is not the top, said Bailador. Not the . . . NHL. It is the one below the top. I play segunda two years, but I break my leg on motocicleta. And I have to go back to Saucillo, where I come from. In Saucillo we are farmers. Ramon and me and los otros. Todos. So we come here to work. It is more money.

I said, And you have twelve years here.

Yes.

So you used to be in the pros, the segunda or whatever, and then you became a farmer again, and started coming up here with all the rest of the Mexicans.

Yes, said Bailador.

I said, No offence, but why are you telling me this?

A little grin pulled at the corner of Bailador's mouth. He said, For two year, I live in Cuidad Juárez. You know this place?

No.

It is okay. Big city. I live there, I have nice time. Best of my life. Muchos amigos, muchas novias, best time of my life. But also in Juárez there are many narcos. They deal the drogas into the United States. You see? And they are bad. They are very bad.

My phone started vibrating again. I wanted to take it—by now it was a pretty mean habit—but I wanted to hear what he had to say, so I ignored it again. I said, Drug dealers are usually pretty bad. They have to be.

You do not know, my friend, said Bailador. There was a new boy in my football club. He had problems with the narcos. He owe money. He do not pay, because he think he is a tipo duro. Then the narcos get him, this tipo duro, take him away from his bed in the night, make him not appear. One day we go to club to do the practice. In the morning. And we find him at the goal. His head is cut off from his body. His body is all burned up. He has only eighteen years old. And what he owe is seven hundreds pesos. Fifty dollars. No more. You see?

I swallowed. I said, I see.

I say this because I think your friends, Chastity and the other boys, I think they are not the same as the narcos. I think they do not cut off the head and burn up the body. I do not know how to say what I mean . . .

I said, You think they're all talk.

Yes. Not real narcos. So when there was trouble with the tacha—

When your boy Cesar ended up in the hospital.

Sí. When there was that trouble, enough is enough. For me. So I pulled out the knife. I say to Chastity, I will kill you for this, and I will kill your friends.

I said, And? And were you all talk, Luis?

Bailador grinned, said, No or yes, who here will know? It is enough for your friends if they think I am the pandillero.

I said, I wouldn't underestimate them. I don't even know what they're capable of anymore.

We were friends of Chastity, Bailador said, his voice softer now. All the years here. We teach her to speak Spanish. And, I think, she is chica fuerta, strong. Fuerta y inteligente. One time she show me pictures of her daughter. So. I do not want to pull out the knife or say what I say. Es lo que hay.

I said, Did your boy Cesar die?

No, said Bailador. But it is not long before he was sent back to Saucillo. Lose all the work here. All the money. And in Saucillo he is still sick, and there is no work for him. He have a wife, cuatro niños . . .

Is he your brother?

He is my mejor amigo de la infancia. My best of friend. He is the same as my brother. Now I think I should have stopped the tacha in the beginning, but I do not.

I said, I'm sorry.

Bailador just shrugged and said, If you want to tell the policía, the real policía, it is for you. But now I think you okay, pandillero. Don't make troubles for yourself.

He put out his hand. I shook it. Then he turned around and went back inside Villagers.

I walked slowly toward my bike. I knew I shouldn't be riding, three beers down, but I was going to anyway. Home wasn't so far. Home and whatever was to happen next.

As I put on my helmet, I felt my phone vibrate in my pocket for the third time. I took it out. The screen told me the caller was unknown. I thumbed it on, said hello.

Darren's voice said, Ashley, I tried you a few times.

A long moment passed before I said, What's up?

Listen, brother. Listen. I've been thinking about a lot of things. And I know. I know how fucked up everything is. I have to get it all sorted out. I know that. But it's gonna take time, you know? It can't . . . like it can't happen overnight. It's gonna take time. But then it'll be better. Trust me. It'll be better. And, hey, listen. I know my old man, and my brother, I know they came to talk to you. I wanted to tell you, it doesn't mean anything, okay? Straight-up. DB's just stressed is all. He's worried. He's only doing what he knows how to do. That's all. Okay?

I held the phone away from my head. I looked at the glowing screen. I heard Darren's voice starting to say Okay? again, but before the word was finished, I hung up on him.

SEVENTEEN

think I told you it ended with me and Chass on New Year's Eve. At the fucking club, my place of work, no less.

I remember saying, It can work. It can. For sure. I mean, it's not gonna be easy, and people will talk, sure, but you know what? Fuck them, because, it can work, you know, it means something—

I remember Chastity saying, Ashley. Stop it. Please. We can't do this here . . .

By here she'd meant the lower patio. Coloured lights were strung along the railing and the posts. The Balmoral's New Year's Eve event had a higher cover charge, twenty-five bucks, which got you into the club, as well as a glass of cheap sparkling white wine and a bright cardboard hat with *Happy 2003!!!* printed across it. The patrons were dressed in what they thought passed for classy formal wear. The bartender girls were all wearing short black cocktail skirts and spike heels. Me and the other bouncers were wearing white dress shirts and bow ties. My bow tie was a clip-on, and it kept canting over to a crooked angle. It made me feel ridiculous.

The lower patio had three fat propane heaters spaced across it to keep the smokers warm. Still, me and Chastity were both wearing winter coats. She had her hood up. She was leaning on the railing, smoking a dart. I was trying to look like I was working, standing with my back to the railing, holding my walkie-talkie in one gloved hand, pretending to keep an eye on the eight or nine patrons huddled close to the heaters. But my attention was all on her.

It was an hour and a half into the first day of the new year. Music pounded from inside the club. The place was at capacity. New Year's Eve was always busy like this, and it was the one night a year that last call wasn't until three o'clock. The pay would be good, almost twice what I'd make on a regular night. I wasn't thinking about any of that.

At that point, the last time I'd slept with her was on the fifteenth of December. The last time I'd heard from her was a few days before Christmas. It wasn't unusual for us not to see each other for a while, and for the phone not to ring for days on end, but this time had been different. The silence had dragged on for longer, long enough to bring up all my darkest doubts.

I guess I knew, bro, at the time, that things were fucked up, were probably even coming to an end. But how many times do you know what's what, like, what's actually what, but you still keep going on whatever crash course you're on?

On Boxing Day I'd broken, called her, got her voice mail, left a message, did not hear back. I'd called her twice after that, getting nothing but voice mail. By then I'd stopped leaving the messages. Funny how I would find myself in the exact same position, doing the exact same thing, four months later.

Then she'd showed up at the club for the New Year's party. She'd come with Michelle Levy and Darren and a few of their other friends, all of them dressed up for the occasion. To his credit, Darren had better taste than most of the other patrons. He was wearing an actual suit, tailored to his slim build, and I had to say he looked sharp in it.

I was working the door when my friends came in. That was at eleven o'clock. I'd had no idea they were coming. Seeing them, seeing Chastity, the surprise I felt was not pleasant. They'd come up the stairs, Darren leading, smelling like darts and cologne. He'd hugged me and said, Didn't mean to catch you off guard, brother, but it was Michelle's idea to come here tonight. We figured if you couldn't join us for the festivities, we'd at least be where you're at.

Michelle had hugged me next, holding it a little too long.

And then Chastity, giving me a quick embrace, not meeting my eyes, gone before I could say anything other than hello.

Through the night I'd stayed away from them as much as I could, sticking to patrols around the darker parts of the club. It wasn't easy to completely avoid them, and when the DJ started counting down to midnight, Michelle found me and pulled me to the hightop table where Chastity and Darren were drinking their sparkling white wine.

The DJ announced the stroke of midnight. Bright spotlights came up. Everybody cheered. Michelle kissed me before I knew what was happening. I had my eyes open, and two feet away I could see Darren and Chastity locked together, her fingers on his cheek, his hands in her hair, both their mouths working. When all the kissing quit, Darren grabbed me and hugged me again and said into my ear, I love you, brother. Happy New Year. This one'll be the best yet, I know it.

By that point, Chastity had already slipped away.

I avoided them again until twenty after one, when I saw her going out by herself onto the lower patio. I followed. I had to do something.

And so that's how we got to where we were, Chass smoking in her pulled-up hood, me pretending to work, both of us pretty cold.

I've had to dodge things for a while, that's all, said Chastity.

I said, You don't have to dodge me. You know that.

She didn't reply.

I said, You do know that, right? Or are you saying you do have to dodge me?

Ash . . .

I said, No, Chass, fucking tell me. Why do you think you have to dodge me?

Are you really asking me that? Do you really have no idea?

Well, look, it's Darren. I mean I get that. I do. And we're just gonna have to tell him. We've been putting it off too long, I agree. We're gonna have to tell him. Fuck. Let's do it first thing tomorrow.

Darren is the tiniest part of it, said Chastity.

Okay, so there's the other issue. You and me. What we are. But we're not . . . goddamn brother and sister . . .

She took a last drag of her smoke and pitched the butt over the rail. She said, I don't care about that at all. I never did.

I said, So what is it?

Come on, Ashley. Think.

Don't talk to me like I'm stupid. Don't do that.

I remember how I was forcing my voice to stay quiet. I wanted to scream at her and everyone on the patio.

She looked at me. She was exhaling through her nose. I'd known her long enough to know when her temper was about to flare. She held up her finger and said, One reason, Ashley.

What?

One reason is all she needs.

I felt a gut punch. I leaned back on the rail. I heard chatter on my walkie-talkie, something going on, but I ignored it. I said, Glenna.

One reason is all she needs, said Chastity. And everything I've done up till now, all the credibility I've gained, the fucking financial responsibility . . . all that shit is gone. I wouldn't even get the chance to kiss my little girl goodbye, and I'd never be allowed to see her again.

I said, Come on. Can it be that extreme?

In a soft voice, Chastity said, If you don't want me to talk to you like you're stupid, don't say stupid things. You know her as well as I do. If she found out what I've been doing with you—and never mind what we are, man, because you're Mike's son—it'll be all over. So listen. I'm the one to blame, Ashley. For all of this. Because I knew all along the risk I was taking, and I did it anyways. I was an idiot and I was self-serving and short-sighted. She calls me that. About a lot of things. And you know what? She's not wrong when she calls me that. Whatever it was between you and me, that's the proof.

I said, Chastity.

There's nothing I want more in the world than making things right with Nevaeh. Making things right for her. I can't fuck this up by doing what I always do, don't you see? I can't fuck this up by being me.

She lit another dart, her hands shaking. She was still exhaling slowly through her nostrils, but her eyes were also shining. The mascara below her left eye was just starting to run.

I said, I understand.

No you don't. There's not a man on earth who can understand this.

Just then Trey showed up on the patio, coming to me at a fast pace. He said, Ash, you listening to your radio or what? We need you, dude, right now.

I said, Can it wait?

Ah man, we got some girl in the back. She's all frigged up on E or K, I don't know. Hyperventilating and all that shit. I need you to help me sort her out without us having to bring the paramedics through the front door. Come on.

I said, You can do it.

Ashley, said Trey. What the fuck? I need you. Come on.

For chrissake, said Chastity. Go, Ashley. This is your job.

I pushed myself off the rail, feeling torn-up and shitty. I started to follow Trey, but then I stopped and turned back to Chastity and said, We can make things right, Chass, I know we can. I can help you.

Finally her anger got the better of her. She pitched her second dart to the ground beside my boot and said, Listen to me, you goddamn fucking knucklehead. I don't need your help. Now or ever. Stay out of it.

I remember how I couldn't speak. How I could feel the eyes of everybody on the patio. I walked a few steps backwards, Trey now pulling me by the jacket. Chastity turned back to the rail, her face disappearing inside her hood. That was how it ended for us. That was the last I saw of her for a long time.

EIGHTEEN

Y ou remember that creepy rat-faced motherfucker from out West? He was, what, a pig farmer or something like that? And do you remember how all those girls went missing and then turned up on his property and nobody—I mean, like the cops—nobody'd done nothing about it for the longest time, mainly because they were mostly hookers and junkies? Anyways, all this shit with Chastity going AWOL was happening not long after the time they finally picked that rat-faced motherfucker up and charged his ass. I mention it because I see now how truly easy it is for someone to go AWOL, like really AWOL, missing, gone, out of sight, out of mind. The shit out West proved it was even easier if the person wasn't a square, wasn't a respectable member of the community. Let's face it, Chastity was pretty close to fitting that exact same description, you know? Point is, should I've made the connection sooner? Should I've done something more official-like? I can't say. I guess you be the judge on that one.

THE ALTENA COP SHOP WAS IN THIS SMALL MODERN BUILD-
ing on Bicentennial, six or seven blocks up from the Balmoral.
The morning sunlight flashed on the windows. The cruisers were
parked around back somewhere, out of sight from the street. I'd
been in the building once on a class trip in grade five. Us kids had
all stared at the four empty holding cells in the back.

I parked my bike in a municipal lot across from the police
department. I crossed the street and went in through the front
doors. In a way I was pushing myself through every motion. If I
stopped or paused, I'd quit.

The lobby had a tiled floor, a small waiting area to the left of
the front doors, and portraits of the Queen and the prime minister
hanging on one wall. The air smelled like coffee.

Ten feet away was a front desk, where a cop in a Kevlar vest
sat reading a thick binder and eating a Mars bar. I approached and
stopped at the counter.

The cop looked up and said, Can I help you, sir?

I said, I want to talk to one of you guys.

Okay, said the cop. You got an issue of some kind?

I might. I don't know. Maybe I just want some advice.

Okay, said the cop. I can probably help with that.

Right away I didn't like this cop. I didn't like the way the cop
was eating his Mars bar or slouching in his chair or talking in his
relaxed way. I said, Actually, you got someone here named Casey,
right? A lady cop?

A lady cop, said the cop. Heh. I think you're asking about
Constable Casey. She works in Community Relations.

I said, Yeah, that's her. Can I talk to her?

You want to talk to Constable Casey specifically?

I inhaled through my nose and held it. I exhaled slowly, under control, like I was on the upward part of a heavy rep, and I said, I do want to talk to her. Specifically.

Okay, said the cop.

She's the only one I really know here, alright? No disrespect but I don't know you.

Let me see if she's here, said the cop. I think she's back on day shifts now but I'll have to check.

The cop got up and went through a door behind the front desk. I wanted to take some time to get myself calm again but the cop reappeared no more than a minute later, now carrying a fresh mug of coffee. He sat down and took a sip and said, Yeah, she's here. But she's on a conference call. Might be a while. Can you wait it out or do you want to talk to somebody else or what do you think?

I said, Ah, Christ, I guess I'll wait it out. Think it'll be long?

Hard to say, sir. Have a seat and I'll let you know.

I went back into the little waiting area and sat down. There was a small table strewn with newspapers, and a rack of pamphlets, information about auto theft, elder abuse, robbery prevention, drunk driving.

Across from my seat, a bulletin board was mounted to the wall. I hadn't noticed it when I came into the building. The board was covered with notices and photographs of missing persons, maybe two dozen in all. I found myself reading the details of every single notice on the board, looking at every face. The longest open case was thirty-five years old. The pictures were all candids, the kind people had taken at birthday parties and holidays and graduations. The kind where they're grinning, not thinking about anything, like the one of me and Chass and Darren giving the middle finger on the last day of high school. One of the notices showed a picture of a little blond boy holding a fish. Like the boy, most of the missing were kids, but a few were women, one or two of them close to Chastity's age.

That oldest case, I thought. Thirty-five years. Thirty-five years and where the fuck are you?

I got up and moved to a chair where I wouldn't have to look at the bulletin board. I was sweating. I dug through the newspapers on the table until I settled on yesterday's sports section. I picked it up and tried to be interested.

The minutes passed. Five, then ten. I heard a phone ringing in another room. I heard quiet conversation. The boring sounds of any office. I looked up at the desk cop, who had his chin propped on his hand and was reading from his binder. There was no sign of Constable Casey yet.

I turned back to the sports section and read part of an opinion piece about drugs in sports. The writer used the words performance-enhancing, and went on to talk about the hazards they posed not just to the user's health but also to the legitimacy of sports and to this and that. I rolled my eyes. I switched to an article about hockey.

I was halfway through the article when a raised voice, speaking near the front desk, caught my attention. I looked over, saw the back of a tall, skinny man. The man, wearing dirty jeans and a huge dirty sweatshirt, was talking to the desk cop, saying, I'm serious this time, I'm serious. I can't take it no more. She's crazy, you hear me? She'll burn me alive one of these days. She keeps saying she will. And when it happens, what'll you guys've done about it?

I'll have someone talk to you in a minute, said the cop. Just have a seat and try to relax, okay? You know how it works here.

I can't take it no more, said the skinny man.

I know you can't. Go on. Sit down. It'll just be a minute.

The skinny man turned around. I recognized him right away. The scabby skeleton face, the lank hair, the birthmark beside the eye.

One question, said the cop. Did you have a shower today, Junior?

Junior's eyes, red and wild, met mine. He frowned. Behind him, the phone at the front desk rang. The cop picked it up and traded a few words with someone and then put the receiver back down and said to me, I'll take you back to see Constable Casey now.

Junior had stopped walking, midway between the front desk and the waiting area. His eyes were still fixed on me. His frown had become deeper. He was starting to say something.

Sir, you coming? said the desk cop.

I stood up from the chair. I didn't go to the front desk. Instead I weaved past Junior, catching the stink of the man, and made for the front door. The cop gave me a puzzled look. I said, You know what? I just remembered I got this doctor's appointment.

Hey, said Junior. I think I know you.

I said, I can't miss it. I've been waiting to see this guy for weeks. I'm sorry to take up your time.

You okay? said the cop.

I think I know you, said Junior.

I said, I'll come back sometime.

I SPENT THE NEXT FORTY MINUTES AT A DOUGHNUT PLACE up the street, not touching the coffee I'd bought. I'd sat down where I could watch out through the front window. I was certain that within minutes of my arrival here every cop in Altena would come down on me.

But I didn't end up seeing even a single patrol car go by. I calmed down slowly.

I wasn't going to go back to the police station. Out loud, I said, Fucking Christ.

A couple of old men two tables down stopped their conversation and looked at me. I shook my head and closed my eyes. I counted to ten. I opened my eyes and got up and left my untouched coffee at the table. I went outside and got on my bike and got out of there.

BACK AT TREY'S I HAD THE HOUSE TO MYSELF. IT WAS lunchtime but I wasn't hungry. I paced around, rattled and fucked up. I put on my workout clothes, intending to hit the weights, and instead smoked an entire blunt to myself.

Totally baked, I sat down on the couch and turned on a video game. I managed fifteen minutes of it before I passed out.

I HAD THAT DREAM AGAIN, THE ONE WHERE EVERYTHING was pitch black and my body was paralyzed. I couldn't breathe, couldn't so much as twitch my lips or move my tongue or cry out. My throat was packed full of concrete or dirt. Panic took hold.

Then I came awake, sucking in breath, and it was all so sudden and crazy and all that I fell right off the couch. I hit the floor like a sack of bricks. Pain from my hurt rib shot through my body, and then, finally, I did cry out.

For a while I lay there on the carpet, getting hold of my breathing. The TV was still on. The video game I'd been trying to play was paused.

I picked myself up from the floor and sat back down on the couch. I'd come most of the way down from my high and my mouth was dry and my gut was upset. I didn't know what time it was, but the light outside looked like afternoon. The curtains were drawn—I'd drawn them, I remembered, when I came in—and the room was dim. I blinked, still trying to get myself together.

My mind was doing that chain reaction thing again. One thing leading to the next to the next to the next, almost too fast to make any sense of it. I thought of Ramon and Bailador. I thought about their boy Cesar in the hospital. I thought about Michelle, standing in the door to her spare room, bursting into tears. I thought about Darren. And, over and over, I thought about what I'd said on the phone that night.

You're on your own, Chastity.

The longest-standing missing person case I'd seen on the bulletin board in the police department was thirty-five years old. Thirty-five years. Longer by a decade than my own life. That wasn't missing. That was gone. That was forever.

I made it to the downstairs bathroom on the run. I collapsed over the toilet and dry-heaved. When I was sure nothing more than spit was coming up, I sat down, my back against the wall.

You're on your own, Chastity.

NINETEEN

At three o'clock two cars pulled away from the house on Free Street. I was half a block up the street, sitting at a picnic table beside the chip truck in the parking lot out front of the pig slaughterhouse. The chip truck was closed and shuttered. My bike was parked behind it. I was by myself, hunched in my hoodie, watching. The first car was DB's Eldorado. It came down the driveway and turned off down the street and disappeared. The second car was Darren's. It turned up the street, bringing a bass beat with it. As it passed the slaughterhouse—and the chip truck and the picnic table, thirty feet back from the road—the car didn't slow down. I believed, or wanted to believe, that I caught sight of two people in the front seats.

I waited. Counted to a hundred. The air around me was heavy with the slaughterhouse smell, meaty shit. I could taste it.

I counted to a hundred again and then I stood up.

As I walked to the front of the house I looked at the signal on my cell phone. It varied between nothing and one bar. I thought of her call, cutting in and out, and I wondered how long I'd known I was going to end up right here.

There was nothing interesting about the front yard or the place where the porch had been ripped off. I paused only long enough to pick up the one remaining gnome from the grass. The gnome was a little less than twice the size of his fist and heavier than I'd expected.

I went up the driveway and climbed over the plywood gate, wincing at the pain in my ribs. The first place I went was the shed. It had a padlock on it, but I was able to press the sheet metal door in a few inches. I peeked in as best I could, saw the edge of a mountain of black plastic garbage bags. Coming from them was this thick chemical smell, something like cat piss and burnt plastic. Stronger than the slaughterhouse, enough to make my eyes water, but I didn't catch any stink of flesh or blood.

Next I went up the back porch to the steel door. It was locked fast. I knocked on it softly, then harder, saying in turn, Darren . . . Seth . . . DB . . . Nothing.

I looked down and saw I'd lifted the gnome to a level just above my elbow. My fingers were tight on it. I let it down slow, as if I were performing the downward motion of an arm curl.

I came down from the back porch and walked out onto the overgrown lawn, thinking, Fuck it, fuck it, this is craziness. Thinking I would just go home and be done with it, be done with all of them, her in particular, this time for good. I'd even gone back to the gate before I stopped, feeling bitter and weird.

I put one hand out and leaned against the wall of the house. I said, Goddammit.

Half a minute later I was crouching down in the low space underneath the back porch. The dirt underfoot was hard and dried-out. There was no sign of it having been turned or dug up or anything. Down here was a small window, set at ground level in the foundation wall. The glass was dark and dirty. Nothing could be seen of the inside.

I hung around in the low space and the dirt for longer than I should've. Way longer. Then I rolled my sleeve up over my hand and turned my face away and thrust the gnome into the window. The glass broke with a sad scraping noise, not nearly as loud as I'd been afraid of. I saw I'd knocked out a crescent-shaped hole. The gnome, still in my hand, was chipped but intact. I used it to tap out the rest of the glass, and then I carefully picked out the remaining shards. My fingers were shaking.

I tightened the drawstrings of my hood around my face. I got on my belly and put my boots through the window first, then shimmied my legs through, hoping I hadn't missed any jutting glass. My hips and ass fit, but just. My feet groped around in the dark, and then touched on something hard. Too high to be the floor, whatever it was. I thought it was the toilet in the bathroom, where as a kid I'd hated to have to go in the middle of the night. Hated because of the crawlspace door on the other side of the rec room. I worked my upper body and head and arms through the window.

Balancing on the top of the toilet, I tried to turn around. I got halfway before my footing slipped and I fell over, sucking in breath as I went. I passed through fabric and pulled something down and landed hard, mostly on the left side of my body, in a position halfway between sitting and lying down.

The pain in my ribs was unreal. When I was finally able to stand up and shake off the fabric, I groped with my hand in the dark until I found a wall and a light switch. When the light came on, I saw I'd fallen off the toilet and through a shower curtain. I'd pulled the curtain and the rod right off the wall. They lay in a jumble in the bathtub where I'd landed. I had this strange urge to straighten up the mess I'd made of it.

Instead I reached for the knob on the bathroom door, and it came to me, like, fully, right at that point, in that motion of reaching for the knob, that I was committed now. I was past the point of no return.

There was nobody in the rec room. One lamp was on, shining over the stereo in the corner. There was just enough light to make out the laminate walls and the all-weather carpeting. The air was heavy with the same stink as the shed, the not-quite-cat-piss odour.

I turned off the light in the bathroom and crossed the rec room, trying to keep my breathing under control. The door to the crawl-space was locked, as I'd figured it would be, but the door itself was wood and the lock seemed to be set only in the knob. I looked at the gnome in my hand. It was heavy but wouldn't be enough. So I stepped back and then drove my boot heel into the door, just beside the knob. It didn't give, but it didn't feel like I was kicking against a deadbolt either. I kicked again and heard wood splintering. Three more kicks, and with each one, despite the pain in my ribs, something inside me—something mean—was waking up.

There was a final, splintering crack, and the door clapped open, taking the strike plate and a chunk of the frame with it.

On the other side, the crawlspace was dark.

When I paused to catch my breath, I caught a full blast of the smell. My throat tightened. My eyes felt like they were catching fire. I reached around the door frame and felt for the light switch and turned it on.

I'd expected this, their set-up, their equipment, their lab or whatever the fuck it was, but the sight of it upset me in a bottom-of-the-gut kind of way.

I saw a bunch of plastic buckets connected by loops of garden hose. The joints in the hose were wrapped with duct tape. There were four cans of Coleman camp fuel standing against the wall and a bag overflowing with rags in the corner. Set on sawhorses above the bag was a little work table. On it I saw a hot plate and a coffee pot. The glass of the coffee pot was cloudy and ugly-looking. Surrounding the hot plate was a small stack of glass baking dishes, a box of AA batteries, a digital scale and a couple of empty baggies.

I picked one of them up and looked at the familiar little elf on it. I flicked the baggie away and wiped my fingers on my pants.

The rest of the crawlspace was taken up by things that had always been there. The water heater and an old stone sink. Past the cinder-block knee wall, a slope of exposed dirt led all the way up to the underside of the main-floor joists.

Bringing a shovel hadn't even occurred to me, maybe because I hadn't really believed I would be doing what I was about to do. But . . . point of no return. I wasn't stopping now.

I THINK I WOULD'VE DUG THAT WHOLE FUCKING FOUNDA-tion up. I was using one of the glass baking dishes, pulling up at best a couple handfuls of dirt at a time. But once I got going, I would've dug all the way to fucking China, tiny scoop by tiny scoop, looking for her, if I hadn't taken one quick break to let the pain in my ribs settle down and to get the sweat out of my eyes. And in that moment, standing there in the crawlspace that used to terrify me, I heard the door upstairs open and close. I heard the squeak of weight against floorboards.

I put down the baking dish and picked up the gnome and slipped out of the crawlspace, pulling the damaged door shut behind me. I heard footsteps coming down the basement steps.

The all-weather carpeting on the rec room floor kept my own footsteps quiet. I would never have thought I could move that fast. I made it into the darkness of the bathroom in three paces.

I closed the door almost all the way, left myself a narrow crack to watch out of.

Funny thing is, I wasn't scared just then. I was wet with sweat, and I was kind of shaking all over, but I wasn't scared. I was just . . . tuned in, bro. Maybe you know what that's like and maybe you don't.

Through the cracked-open bathroom door I saw the person who came into the basement was Seth. Seth by himself, carrying a bulging plastic bag with *Altena Co-op* printed on the side. He walked over to the crawlspace, not realizing that the door was busted all to shit and the light was on behind it until he was right in front of it.

I heard him say, Hey, what the fuck.

By then I was coming back across the carpet. I lifted the garden gnome. Seth turned around. He frowned his little pig-eyes at me, not recognizing me in the semi-dark, and looked like he was about to ask a question. He didn't even raise his hands.

I hit him in the head, hard. I felt the impact all up my arm. The gnome shattered. Seth did a spin like a ballet dancer—a bailador, you could say—and fell over, crashing the crawlspace door back open on his way down.

I took a step. Seth, sprawled on the poured concrete floor, wasn't moving. He'd dropped his shopping bag at a spot near his feet. A couple of plastic jugs had rolled out of it.

I kind of thought I'd killed him. Consequences would follow, consequences in the big legal sense. But for the moment, I didn't care.

Then Seth shifted and muttered something. He turned his head. The hair above his ear was matted and dark. I dropped the pieces of the gnome. Lowering myself to the floor, I pushed my knee into the base of Seth's skull and grabbed a roll of duct tape off the little work table. I tugged the tail of the tape with my teeth, enough to get it started, and then I pulled Seth's wrists together and started wrapping the tape around them. Seth stiffened beneath me and tried to move. I pushed my knee harder against his skull and I bent his arms up until I felt resistance. I said, I'll break them, motherfucker, I swear to god.

We got the message, said Seth. Honest, man—Jesus, that hurts—you don't have to go through all this. We're doing it. Fast as we can.

I told him to shut up.

I was having a hard time getting the tape around Seth's wrists. My own hands were shaking pretty bad by then.

Wait, said Seth. I'll make for you guys. My dad showed me how. I don't need him no more. Tell Kinkaid, man, tell him I'll work for you guys direct. Honest. It isn't my business or nothing, but you could've cut DB out a long time ago. He's not much of an old man, you know? Like, he's not much of a father or nothing. I got no real loyalty to him. You don't have to do it like this . . .

I said, Shut the fuck up.

I'd managed a fifth and then a sixth pass of the tape around Seth's wrists. It was crude, but it was tight.

Seth tried to turn his head. He said, Wait . . . wait. You sound like—

I dug my knee into Seth's skull until he squealed. Then I stood up. My mouth was bone-dry. I licked my lips. All I could do now was stay on the offence. I turned Seth over and sat him against the wall. Seth gaped at me.

Ashley. What in the fuck.

Where is she, Seth?

Where's who?

Where's Chastity?

How the fuck should I know?

I said, Because you and DB and Dar— you guys all are in on this. I know you are. I know about the Amigo, the one who ended up in the hospital. I know she lost her shit over it too. I know she came here, Seth, to make it right. I know she did. So where is she?

He said, Do you know what my dad is gonna do to you when he finds out? We tried to tell you to back off, Ashley . . .

I know she came here, Seth.

I don't know what you're talking about, you cocksucker, and I don't know what happened to that crazy bitch after—

Seth snapped his mouth shut.

I said, After what?

I didn't say anything.

I reached down and picked up one of the plastic jugs that had fallen out of the shopping bag—940 ml of Drano. With unsteady hands I unscrewed the cap and drove my thumb through the inner seal.

What are you doing with that? said Seth.

I jammed my knee up against Seth's jaw. With one hand I clasped Seth's forehead and pried open his eyelid with my thumb. With my other hand I tilted the jug above his rolling eyeball. Seth tried to thrash his head away.

Tell me, Seth.

Seth gnashed his teeth, trying to bite at my hand. The eyeball rolled. The jug-neck tipped a little lower.

Okaaay, Seth hollered. Okaaay . . .

I leaned back and set the jug of Drano down between my thighs. I didn't say anything.

You lost your fucking mind, said Seth, not looking at me, sounding on the edge of tears.

I said, Chastity was here, wasn't she. A couple weeks ago.

Yes. Fuck, yes. It was, like, the middle of the night. Later. I don't know. We were working hard, man, like, we were on a dead-line, and we can't . . . I mean, we can't cook fast like they want us to, because, like, look at it down here . . . And now a pound a week? We can't—

I don't give one shit about any of that. Tell me about Chastity.

It went bad with those wetback assholes, said Seth. It wasn't her idea to start selling to them. It was DB's. Part of his whole local-earnings thing. But she was the in, right? Like, Darren had all his normal customers in the books already, and it wasn't real hard to switch half of 'em over, but he didn't know any Amigos. She was the in with those guys. It was DB's idea . . . And since her and Darren, since they were already, like, hitting it regular by then, they weren't too hard to convince or nothing. DB just had to talk to her when she was fiending. She was easy to convince when she was fiending. I seen it first-hand.

Seth was blubbering, as if this was some kind of, like, confession. Maybe, to him, it was. Anyways, he was telling me way more than I'd figured on hearing. And thoughts were coming to me one after another. The missing pieces. Chain reaction. Weirdest of all was how little it surprised me.

. . . selling them half an ounce a week, said Seth. Those guys were sucking it up, more than anybody Darren had in his books, 'cept maybe Junior. But then one of the wetbacks gets fucked up. Blows out his heart, ends up in the hospital, and we're thinking, like, we're screwed, royally. We're thinking it's gonna blow open. But it doesn't. It doesn't. The wetback keeps his mouth shut. Doesn't rat. None of his buds rat either. So nothing blows open. 'Cept her. Chastity. She blows. Because first she tries to make peace with them, like they're all old friends and let's say sorry and go back to normal, but that doesn't work, does it, because they pull a knife on her and run her off. And she comes back to us, to me and Darren and Dad, and she's like, I quit, I'm out.

I said, But I'm guessing it didn't happen like that, did it.

You think my dad would've let her, just like that? With everything going on?

You tell me.

No, man, said Seth. No. She was bringing in cash. He wasn't gonna let her quit. He told her he'd, like, *kill* her if she tried . . .

So . . . did he?

I said it in this soft voice, letting it hang, feeling the strangeness of it.

Finally Seth looked at me. The full whites of his eyes were showing. His face was shiny and sweat was coming through his shirt.

I don't know. I swear to Jesus. But . . .

But what?

But Darren . . .

I said, Tell me, Seth. Tell me or I swear I'll stomp your head into the fucking floor.

I don't know.

You're lying to me.

No. Jesus. I don't know. I got here late, and by then it'd already went down.

I said, What'd already went down?

She tried to shoot him.

What?

She tried to shoot him, said Seth. That crazy bitch showed up here in the middle of the night and tried to shoot my dad. With Darren's gun. She jacked it from his car.

I said, What are you talking about?

Look, alls I know is I was at my girl's place, other side of town, because we'd been going hard down here, day after day, like I said, and I needed a night off, and I was at my girl's place, and it's the middle of the night, and Darren calls up my girl's phone and she gives it to me and Darren's all whacked out and he's talking real fast about how Chastity came over and tried to waste our dad, our father, man . . .

You didn't see it happen, though.

No, no, said Seth. By the time I got back here, it was over. Dad was putting all those Band-Aids on his hand, right? There was some blood on the floor up in the kitchen but he'd used sawdust to get it all. And he wouldn't go to the hospital or anything. And he was mad. I never seen him so mad. He was so mad he was quiet. You don't even know . . .

I said, Where was Darren? Where was she?

Gone. They were gone. Dad said Darren was manning up. Darren was taking care of it. Taking care of her, like he should've when she first started to flake on us. It was his responsibility. He was taking care of her. From there that's all I know. I don't know nothing about how he did it or got rid of her or where or what. That's all I know, man . . . Ashley . . . I swear to Jesus. I'm like you.

I said, You're like me *how?*

It's better not to know, said Seth. Always. Right?

Then I was on top of him again. I hauled Seth away from the wall and stretched him out on the floor and took up the jug of Drano and this time squeezed Seth's mouth open and held the Drano above it. Let it burn, I thought. Let it all burn black, starting with this fat weak motherfucker who used to smack me around when I was a kid. Let him be the first to burn.

Seth gagged.

And just like in the garage, covering Kinkaid and his boys, I couldn't go any further.

I let go of Seth's head and I stood up and threw the jug away from me. I was shaking, hard, and I was cold all over, like all that sweat was just freezing solid on my skin. For some reason I thought about my dad's garage, all his well-organized tools and the warm way the afternoon sunlight slanted in through the windows.

Jesus fuck, said Seth.

I said, You aren't anything like me.

We should've done it. Man, we should've done it.

I said, Done what?

When you came here with Darren's car, you know why my dad brought you in here? You know why he didn't just come outside and get the keys from you? Because he wanted to, like, *prove* that nobody coming in here would know that anything was wrong, that anything had gone down the night before. He wanted to prove it. And he did. But you know what? He said if you had've figured anything out, if you had've got panicky, we would've done you ourselves, him and me, right down here.

I said, Bullshit.

Seth, his hands still taped behind him, managed to get up on his elbows. He showed me a vicious grin. He said, We should've, because maybe you act crazy, and you get in bar fights and you pump iron and when you need to you sucker-punch a guy, but you don't really have the balls, do you. You should've just stuck around with the pussies and the faggots—

I kicked him in the head, my boot on his skull making a thick sound. I'd pulled the kick, on purpose, just before it landed, but it was still enough to lay Seth flat out, blinking up at the light bulb.

Out of nowhere, I felt sick. I turned and leaned against the wall and closed my eyes and held my head.

I DREW LOOKS WALKING THROUGH THE MALL. I COULD FEEL them. I was dirty and my hood was up. I was walking with my shoulders squared and my chin forward, walking like I had purpose. People gave me lots of space.

It was all happening. It was set in motion and it couldn't be stopped. There was one more thing to do.

At the front of Pro Choice Electronics was a display of stereos and big-screen televisions that were all showing the same golf game. Darren was in the middle of the store, leaning against a long shelf of computer accessories. His work uniform consisted of a tucked-in button-up shirt and a name tag and a pair of pleated khakis. The clothes were hanging from him, way too big for his thinned-out body.

I was standing in front of him by the time he looked up. His eyes burned in their deep, dark hollows.

I said, Don't say nothing. I just came to see your face. I know you took care of her. I know she went over to the house that night and tried to shoot your dad and then you came over and got her and you drove her off somewhere and you took care of her, and I know. All this time you played me and everybody else like fucking fools.

There were three customers in the store and three other employees. No one had caught on yet, because I wasn't talking much louder than a whisper. I didn't trust my voice enough. Darren stared.

I said, I've never really been what I pretended to be. That's true. But this is real. This time. I made it right. And I came here to see your face before what happens next.

Ashley, said Darren. What did you do?

I said, I kicked the shit out of your brother and then I called the cops and told them what you guys have been doing at your old house. What you got going down there. I don't know where you got rid of her, so I couldn't tell them that, but they'll put it together before long. That's what they do. So guess it's all on you now, brother. It's all on you.

Darren opened his mouth. Nothing came out. He closed his mouth again. His face was completely blank. That was how he looked as I left him standing there.

TWENTY

At suppertime the clouds broke open and the rain came down hard on Altena. Time passed, first in minutes and then in hours. I didn't know exactly what I'd expected to happen by now, but whatever it was hadn't.

Trey was gone to work at the club, so I was alone in the house. So far Trey hadn't asked me what I was going to do for a new job, how I was going to make rent. I wasn't sure what I'd say, anyways. Those kinds of concerns seemed so far away that they had to belong in someone else's life altogether.

I put some leftover food on a plate and heated it up in the microwave, then took it into the living room and sat in front of the television. I fixed on a show instead of a video game and pushed my food around on my plate. When I found myself surrounded by shadows I realized the only light in the room was coming from the television screen.

At seven-thirty my phone vibrated. I grabbed it up. My dad was on the other end. He wanted to say thanks for when I'd helped Greg in the gym the other day. Dad wanted to catch up, too, see how the last couple days had been, did Darren and I have a good time on our trip to Detroit, what did the week ahead look like for me. I answered in single words. Every time I spoke I felt something twisting tighter inside me.

You okay, son?

I said, Yeah. I am.

I told you once, I told you a thousand times. Don't try to pull one over on your old man.

I had an urge to let everything out. From the first time I'd ever gone with Darren to collect money from someone to the first time I'd fucked Chastity to Junior in the motel room to the phone call from Chastity to the Amigos to Michelle to Detroit to DB at the gas station to the basement of the house on Free Street, the crank kitchen in the crawlspace and Seth laid out on the floor, to Darren standing empty-faced. I wanted to scream it all into the phone. I wanted to beg my dad to make it right, to make it alright, to make everything safe again.

I said, It's all good, Dad. Everything. It is what it is.

I'll take your word for it, said my dad. Talk soon, okay?

Okay.

As I put the phone down, it vibrated again, and I swear I jolted. Man, was I wrapped tight.

I looked at it. *Michelle*. I answered.

Rosco? she said.

I didn't totally trust my voice, but I managed to say her name.

Rosco . . . Holy shit, man, things are happening. I was out for a run an hour ago and I saw a bunch of cops at Darren's mom's old place, the one near the slaughterhouse.

I closed my eyes and held them shut. I said, Did you see Darren?

Well, I saw his car, said Michelle. That stupid blue Subaru he drives the shit out of. There's no way I would've remembered he used to live there except his car was out front. So I stopped my run and kind of hung around for a bit. There were cops all over the place, Rosco, and every fucking neighbour down there was out on their porch, watching, you know? Like it was a hockey game or something. And all these neighbours are talking about how they'd seen Darren's brother—what's his name? Seth?—getting hauled outside by a couple cops. They say Darren was there too, and his dad, and one lady says she even saw Darren's mom getting packed into one of the cop cars.

I had enough sense in my head to doubt that Barb Braemer had been anywhere near that scene—all kinds of details get added and made up and whatnot when neighbours are gossiping—but I did think about the guy I used to call my best buddy. I thought, They got him.

Rosco? said Michelle.

I'm here.

I didn't stick around for too long, said Michelle. After, like, five minutes down there I ran back home. Fuck, man, I practically sprinted. I wanted to call you as soon as I saw . . . Because, this is you, right? You did this . . .

Whatever was in my gut, wrapped so tight, felt like it would break. They got him, I thought.

I said, Yes, it was me.

Whatever it was, Ashley, you did right.

Yeah, I said.

Look, I better go, okay? I'm feeling kind of completely fucked up here. I just figured you needed to know, and you needed to know that whatever you did, you did right. But if you need anything, man, you call me, okay?

I will.

There's one more thing, said Michelle. She wasn't there. Not that I saw, anyways. And I still haven't heard a thing from her.

I nodded, not that Michelle could see me or anything, but because I couldn't do anything else. After a second or two of silence, I guess she figured me out, because she said she'd talk to me soon.

I put the phone down. I was kind of expecting another call. I didn't know who the fuck the third caller might be, but no call came.

SOME TIME PASSED. MAYBE FIVE MINUTES, MAYBE FIVE HOURS. I couldn't really tell. I got up from the couch and went upstairs to the bathroom and took my clothes off. I stepped on the scales. They told me I was 230 pounds exactly.

Earlier, when I'd called the cops and made the anonymous tip, I couldn't bring myself to give up any names. Not Seth's or DB's or Darren's or even Chastity's. All I'd managed to say was the address and to tell them what was in the crawlspace. The crank lab, right? Not a body.

I stepped off the scales and looked in the mirror. The mirror told me I'd never looked like I did now, and this in spite of how little work I'd really been doing for the last week, how much shit I'd been eating. At last the pad of belly fat had thinned away and the shapes of my abs stood out. I touched the dark bruise over my ribs.

They got him, I thought again.

I guessed it wouldn't take long for them to figure me into everything. Maybe I'd go down hard, an accessory or an accomplice or whatever to all the shit I'd always tried not to know much about.

The cops would come get me . . . or maybe I could go to them. On my own. My own terms.

I'd forgotten to gear that morning for the first time since I'd started the cycle. I did it now, part one of the Ritual: 30 mg of d-bol for the mass, milk thistle to keep my liver clean, Nolvadex to keep away the tits. Do it right, bro, do it scientific.

When I finished gearing I got up and looked in the mirror and slapped myself in the face. Weakness, I said.

I GOT TO THE GYM AT NINE O'CLOCK. I PARKED MY BIKE OUT front, hung my helmet from one of the handgrips. Some big spotlights lit up the greenhouses on the opposite side of White Bike Way, and there was a low hum of machinery or ventilation, and I could hear the highway in the distance. The rain had quit but everything was still wet and the air smelled damp.

The only person inside the gym was Chris Hagar, who was finishing a mop-up. The radio had been shut off. Chris looked up, said, Oh, hey, Ashley. I was closing up.

I said, I know. Listen, could you let me get a workout in?

I'm not sure, man. Last time, you forgot to lock the door. Janet almost fired me for it.

I said, I'm sorry. I just really need to burn off some energy, bro. I'm all wrapped up, you know?

Chris rocked back on his heels, sucked his teeth thoughtfully. He said, Ah, okay. Just promise me you'll lock it up, okay?

Hey, thanks.

For sure, Ash. I know the feeling. Sometimes you gotta rep it out, right? Hit it hard? My girlfriend makes me do yoga with her from time to time, because it's supposedly good for relaxing you, but sometimes for guys like us nothing beats the iron, am I right?

I smiled and nodded. All I could think about was throwing the weights around. I wanted to be burned into exhaustion when I rode back to town and turned myself in.

. . . Echinacea, Chris was saying. You ever take that shit?

I said, What?

Echinacea. It's natural shit. Really good for your immunity system. I mention it because—and no offence—you don't look a hundred percent. Like, maybe you're coming down with something. Anyways, you know, Echinacea. Check it out.

I said, I will.

Chris nodded. I slipped past him and went into the deserted locker room. The concrete floor was dark with drying mop-water and the locker doors all stood open.

I picked a locker. I peeled off my hoodie and hung it up. I put my cell phone on the shelf. It hadn't gone off since I'd talked to Michelle. I opened up my gym bag and got my water bottle and filled it at the sink.

Back out in the weight room, I got on one of the treadmills and set myself on a jog to get my pulse working. Chris was over in the corner, putting the mop and bucket away in the supply closet. My shoes whapping along the treadmill belt and the hum of the mechanism were the only sounds. I pumped my arms and breathed in and out in a steady, slowly increasing rhythm. The pain in my ribs was sharp and constant, but I'd already made up my mind to work through it.

After twenty minutes on the treadmill I had a good sweat going. I got off and went over to the bench press. Holy trinity, I thought. Bench, dead lift, squat. Then some abs. Then some stretches. Then back to town . . .

I pumped my body weight on the bench press. Every breath hurt my side, but I ignored it. After I finished my second set, I found Chris loafing around nearby. I sat up from the bench and said, Are you taking off now?

Yeah, I am, said Chris. I locked the front door, but I'll leave the back unlocked. All you got to do is turn the handle before you go, and the door'll lock behind you. Oh, and the lights in the locker room too. Promise me you won't forget, right?

I won't forget.

Good. Okay. I'll see you. And Echinacea. Help yourself out, brother.

I'm not your fucking brother, I thought. I'm not anybody's brother.

I watched Chris head to the back. Before he left he shut off all the lights except the one in the men's locker room and the set of fluorescents over the middle of the weight room. The shadows that fell were thick in some places and divided in others. I heard the back door open and close. The sounds were loud in the quiet.

I leaned back on the bench, relieved to be alone. I breathed in the smell of rubber and metal and sweat and disinfectant.

I was about to do another set of my body weight, but then I stood up from the bench. I loaded more plates onto the bar: 315 pounds in total. I got down underneath it and wrapped my hands around the metal. I breathed deep. Held it. I pushed the bar off the rack and let it slowly down to my chest. I drove it back up. My ribs felt like they were shattering. I screamed at them, screamed at the bar and the empty gym.

Fuck you fuck you weakness fuck you weakness.

Three clean reps. A struggling fourth. I pushed it to the top and dropped the bar back onto the rack, watched it bounce as it landed. I savoured the hard, metal-hitting-metal sound of it.

I got up, looked at myself in the mirrors. My arms were filled with blood. I flexed them, watched my biceps contract into thick balls. The flesh was overlapped with rigid veins. I extended my arms so that I could flex my triceps. They were hard and sculpted.

I didn't have much else, but I had this, and I had all of this.

I went back into the locker room and opened my locker and

got a protein bar from my bag. As I was unwrapping it, my phone went off. This time it was Trey.

He said, How you feeling, dude?

I said, Not too bad.

I didn't tell Trey where I was.

Hey, there was a cop at the club, said Trey. I don't know, like, an hour and a half ago. Looking to talk to you.

I said, A cop.

Yeah, that woman cop who sometimes comes in. She asked if you were working and if she could talk to you. I said you were taking some time off.

There was a beep in my ear. An incoming call. I said, Thanks, Trey. I—

He said, But you know, dude, in fairness, I don't want trouble.

I said, I know.

The beep went in my ear again.

Oh shit, said Trey. One more thing. I almost forgot. About half an hour ago, your buddy came here to see if you were around.

I went cold all over. I said, My buddy?

Yeah, dude. The hook-up guy. Darren. I didn't talk to him, but I saw Brice talking to him down on the lower patio, and then Brice told me he was looking for you.

I forced my voice to stay flat. I said, Oh. Was he alone?

I don't know. I didn't see anybody with him.

Okay. Okay. No big deal.

The beep in my ear, a third time. They got him, I thought. But what was this that Trey was telling me? Why wasn't it, like, computing that they hadn't got him?

I guess it's one of those nights, said Trey.

I guess it is. Look, I have a call on the other line. I gotta go, okay?

Okay, dude. I'll see you at home.

I lowered the phone from my ear and switched to the other call. I was expecting the cops. Or Darren. Or anybody.

Ashley? said Chastity.

All the colour went out of the locker room around me. I put my hand against the wall to keep from falling over. I said, What, and then I said it again. What.

She said, I've been trying you over and over. It's all gone crazy. Everything. Everybody. Jesus. I didn't exactly want any of this to happen, okay? Not like this.

I tried to speak. I couldn't even get the word *what* out this time. Everything was spinning.

I heard her saying, . . . don't know what you did. Seth got picked up. But Darren, I don't know. And DB . . . Jesus Christ, Ashley. DB. Where are you? Can you tell me where you are, because—

I heard the back door of the gym open and then close.

The world quit spinning.

From somewhere outside the locker room, I heard DB's voice: Ashley, hey, we've got to talk to you.

We've got to talk to you. We. We we we.

You got Darren real confused and upset, said DB. Not to mention what you've done for me with all this horseshit.

Ashley, said Chastity.

I hung up on her.

Seconds later, the locker room door was kicked open. Darren, not DB, stood in the opening, staring in. His right hand was holding something in his jacket pocket. After a pause, he stepped into the room, looking around.

I watched him from where I was pressed flat on top of the double bank of lockers in the middle of the room. The space was thick with dust and shadows. An abandoned shoe, a hairbrush, a used bandage. I was just able to peer over the edge, watch as Darren moved past me below. On my way up and over the top of the lockers, I'd sliced open the side of my hand on a jagged edge of metal. The cut was deep enough to not even hurt. It was bleeding onto my T-shirt and into the dust around me.

For a second Darren passed out of my view. Then he reappeared near the sinks and urinals. With his shoe he pushed open the door of each cubicle in turn. He swept aside the shower curtain. I held my hand to my chest, feeling the blood seeping between my fingers.

From outside, in the weight room, I heard DB's voice again, saying, Whatever you think you're doing, Ashley, is a pile of horse-shit. I know what's true, my friend. I tried to tell Darren . . .

Darren moved back among the lockers. He picked up my cell phone, which I'd left on the seat beside my locker.

DB's voice: I tried to tell him about you.

Darren turned and looked back, into the open area of the room, then to the double bank of lockers.

I jumped down, landing heavily. Pain blasted from my ribs and now my ankle, the kind of pain you know you're going to pay for later. I looked straight at Darren. He took his right hand out of his jacket pocket. He was holding the pocket rocket. Of course he was.

I turned and ran. As I yanked open the locker room door, I smacked the light switch, throwing the room into darkness. Darren hadn't said anything at all.

Out in the weight room, the only light came from the single set of fluorescents Chris had left on. I didn't see DB. I turned and bolted across the floor, jumping over one bench, stumbling over a second. I hit the front door at a flat-out run and I pulled on it hard, wondering why it wasn't opening, then remembered it was locked. I pawed at the deadbolt, bleeding all over the metal.

Behind me I heard DB's voice: Where the fuck are you going?

I heard the locker room door open and close.

I turned the deadbolt, pushed open the front door and rushed out into the night air. It was raining again, a light but steady drizzle. A shoddy wet halo hung around the light over the parking lot. I made for my bike, stopped, turned around, and grabbed the end of the bleacher below the gym's front window. I pulled. The bleacher was much heavier than it looked. Its steel legs screamed across the pavement. I dragged it across the door and kicked it tight into place.

A little hole punched through the glass of the front window, making a crunchy, icy sound. I gawked at it. Another hole appeared, two feet from the first. Shots. I was being shot at. A third hole appeared, and with this one a big section of glass fell out of the window and shattered across the pavement. I threw my hands over my ears and cried out.

For a second or two I could see Darren and DB, under the flourescents, coming across the weight room floor. I couldn't make out who was shooting. The expressions on their faces were exactly the same—mouths squeezed shut, foreheads creased. I turned and ran. I heard a gunshot behind me and I flinched.

My bike was parked on an angle away from the window and front door, out of what would be their direct view. At least my keys were in the pocket of my warm-up pants. It took me three kicks to get the bike started. I revved it too high, almost stalling it, as I swerved out of the parking lot and onto White Bike Way. The drizzle lanced my face, cold and hard. I took the bike up to 130 kilometres per hour, feeling it surge. The strip mall fell away behind me. On the other side of the road, the greenhouses streaked past. In my headlight, the white bicycle of the dead Amigos briefly appeared, and then it too fell behind me.

I HAD ENOUGH REMAINING SENSE TO PULL OVER AND STOP five or six kilometres farther on. On either side of the road were dark and empty fields. Not far ahead was the crossroads where White Bike Way intersected the service road, and some ways past the service road were some farm buildings and a smaller greenhouse. The lights of town stood against the sky in the distance.

I was soaked to the skin, shaking badly. My hand was still bleeding. I pressed it hard against my thigh and turned to watch the arrow-straight road behind me. A set of headlights appeared, a long way away, but they were high up off the ground and looked to be the lights of a delivery truck or a tractor-trailer. Not a car.

I was about to call the cops, right there from the side of White Bike Way, when I remembered my phone was still in the locker room. I sank down on the seat of my bike, never having felt as bad and strange and fucked up as I did just then. I kept seeing him come across the weight room toward me, that blankness in his eyes. And I kept hearing her voice in my head.

I took my helmet off the handlebars and slipped it over my head and buckled the strap. I rubbed my hands together in an effort to get some feeling back into them. I didn't want to look at the cut.

I started the bike back up and put it into gear and pulled back onto the road. The delivery truck or tractor-trailer was still a good distance behind me.

I accelerated more smoothly now, gearing up, watching my gauges: *70 . . . 85 km/h.* I was approaching the service road intersection. The farm buildings and greenhouse were about five or six hundred yards farther on. I figured I would stop up there and knock on the doors and windows until somebody came.

90 . . . 100 km/h

I was almost to the intersection when a short distance up the service road I saw the dark shape of a car. They'd taken the 7th Concession, the parallel route. They must've driven fast, their headlights off the whole time. You can't turn the headlights off on a new car, even during the day, but an old one, like some old pimpmobile Eldorado . . .

Now the car's high beams flashed to life.

I was looking right at them. They seared my eyes and I couldn't see anything and I was still moving forward and my ears were filled with the screaming sound of my bike as it accelerated. There was a sharp screech of tires—I was squeezing the brakes without even thinking about it—and the wet roadtop was moving in a fucked-up wrong way beneath me, and just when I could see again, the high beams were barrelling down on me.

The front fender of the car caught the rear tire of my bike.

I was spinning, spinning, the bike leaning too far, the engine screaming like a devil. Then I wasn't on the bike at all. I was hanging in space. Waiting for the world to come crashing back up and swallow me whole.

WHAT BROUGHT ME AROUND WAS THE RAIN LANDING ON MY visor. I was on my back. Asphalt beneath me, cold and wet and hard. I still had the helmet on. Something below my right elbow hurt so bad it made me feel sick. The rest of my right arm, from shoulder to wrist, and my right leg, from knee to ankle, felt like they were on fire. I was aware that I'd lost a shoe.

I heard an air horn and the engine brakes of a truck. These were hard, angry sounds, not very far away. I rolled onto my right side, pressing whatever was broken in my arm against the roadtop. The pain was unreal. I heard myself scream. My bike lay on its side twenty feet away, surrounded by shattered bits of plastic and chrome. I'd made it past the intersection, probably spinning out the whole time.

On the far side of the intersection, the truck—it was a tractor-trailer—was stopping hard. I wondered that it didn't jackknife. The truck was stopping for the car, which was manoeuvring back from the service road onto White Bike Way.

In the haze of the truck's headlights, the side-on shape of the Eldorado was perfectly clear.

It righted at the intersection and then turned down White Bike Way. The truck managed to come to a stop behind it. The Eldorado still had the high beams on and the light made bright white streaks of the rainfall and long shadows of the busted pieces of my bike.

I turned onto my stomach, there in the middle of the road. I pressed my left hand onto the pavement and started to push myself up. Dizziness hit me and I went back down. I tried to crawl, clawing the road with my left hand.

I could hear it coming, the Eldorado. Coming for me. The light around me was building.

There was nowhere to go. I tried again to get up and this time managed to make it into a crouch. I looked down, at my left hand, at my knee. The right leg of my warm-up pants was tattered and dark with blood. The light was all around me now.

Would I feel it at all?

The light turned pure white. Everything else turned black. I closed my eyes.

Then there were squealing tires.

Through the skin of my eyelids I saw the light change, lessen. I opened my eyes and spotted the Eldorado still thirty yards away, weaving like crazy now. It grated hard across the shoulder of the road and onto the wet field, and from there straight toward the distant greenhouse, spewing up twin rooster tails of muck behind it.

The car came to a stop a good distance away, not quite as far as the greenhouse wall. The tail lights glared back at me.

THERE ARE ONLY A FEW THINGS I REALLY REMEMBER ABOUT what happened next. I remember knowing the Eldorado meant to run me down, and I remember the way it weaved off the road and cut across the field. I must've managed to get to my feet, and I remember some stranger—the driver of the tractor-trailer—hurrying up to me, panting hard, asking what the hell was going on.

I remember telling him, Can you call the cops?

Jesus, kid, said the trucker. I think your arm is broke.

It is what it is . . .

I only partly remember walking out into the field, following the ruts the Eldorado had left behind it. I don't remember the distance I crossed, but I remember the way my legs felt light and unsteady. My one sock-foot slopped along on the wet ground. With my left hand I clutched my right forearm to my belly, and when the fingers of my left hand touched along something hard and jagged, poking out from the skin, I stopped and vomited and dropped to my knees, my vision going dark.

I don't remember getting back up, or crossing the remaining distance to the car. But I do remember coming up to where the Eldorado was stopped in its tracks, its engine still running. The high beams were shining yet, reaching out and lighting up the side of a sheet-metal shed. The car's interior light was on, the passenger's side door was open, and the little door-ajar chime was going off.

I stumbled around the side of the car, leaning on the hardtop. I looked through the open door.

DB was in the driver's seat. His right hand was gripping and ungripping the steering wheel. His head was upright but canted over to the side, as if he were trying to touch his ear to his shoulder. A dark spot like a mole was on his right cheekbone, a little below the corner of his eye. A fine stream of blood had run out of the spot, down DB's face and neck and under his collar. It wasn't as much blood as I'd have thought, you know, based on what you see in the movies. But past DB's head, the driver's side window was white with cracks and in the middle of the glass was a hole a couple inches across.

Darren was nowhere to be seen. Not in the passenger seat, not in the back. I looked in the direction of the greenhouse and farm buildings. From that way, there was only the sound of a dog barking.

I looked back into the Eldorado. DB's head was turned. He was looking straight at me. His eyes were raw, and sticking out from the left side of his head was this ugly mess of skin and hair and bits of other things. He was trying to say something. The words weren't coming out right.

I said, Fuck you, Don.

Then I remember turning against the side of the car, pressing my back into it, and sitting down. I remember the cold water soaking through my sweatpants and freezing my skin. I remember being sick again.

And then, of that time and place, I don't remember anything else.

TWENTY-ONE

Passing the monument in Missionary Position Park, what comes into view is a playground, another fifty feet away. The playground is new, all bright colours, no more than a year or two old I'd guess. It didn't used to be here. This is where we'd agreed to meet up.

I can see one little kid climbing up the side of it. Not far away, watching the kid, a woman is sitting on a bench. I squint at her. She's got short dark hair now. When did that happen?

I make my way forward. I can't help but go slow. I've been out of the cast and the boot for a month now, but doing anything physical is almost out of my league. Physiotherapy for another five or six months, they tell me. So much for the August show I'd had in mind. I think back to that sick man, the one who'd called me a leg-breaker, and I laugh a little. It's a bitter laugh. What would that man say if he saw me now? Something about karma?

A sharp throb is building in my arm and in my ankle. A general pain is rising through the rest of my body. This happens a few times every day. I have medicine for it. Percocets, funnily enough. I let my dad hang on to them, because, you know, they can be dangerous or addictive or whatever, but it won't be long before I need a hit.

Halfway to the bench I see her looking at me. She's wearing nice jeans and sneakers and a light white jacket. I cover a few paces more and she stands up and comes to meet me halfway.

We don't hug. She stands a full arm's length away, looking me up and down. There's sadness in her eyes. I don't believe I'm imagining that. She's put some weight back on herself and she's got some real colour in her face. Her hair is cut to just above her shoulders and dyed almost black. It's full-out summer, hot as hell, but she doesn't look at all overheated in the jeans and the jacket. She looks, I don't know, protected, somehow. Protected, and put-together too. Sorted out.

I say, You cut your hair, Chass.

I'm pretty sure I saw her before today. I say pretty sure because if I did see her, it was when I was in the hospital, and, trust me, bro, I was fucked up that whole time. Broken bones and internal bleeding will do that to you. I was always in and out of consciousness, and I was pretty doped up. You know when you're coming out of a dream, enough to know it's a dream, but you're not quite awake either? My time in the hospital was like that. I kind of remember a lot of people coming and going. The cops, for one thing, trying to interview me, not getting much. Other visitors were my mom, my sister, my co-workers from the club, Michelle, Greg, my old man, mostly my old man. I remember him sitting by my bed for what seemed like days on end. I think I told him I was sorry, and I think, for some reason, that made him cry. I never like seeing him cry.

But I also remember other visits in the hospital, visits that I seriously doubt actually happened. First there were the Amigos, Bailador and Ramon. It's possible they came, of course, sure, but how I remember it is they were surrounded by a bunch of other Amigos, the ones I always used to see hanging around the sidewalk bench outside the club. And they were all of them sitting on white bicycles. After the Amigos I was visited by all the kids I'd ever fought, all through high school. They came with the black eyes and bloody noses I'd given them, and they just stood around my bed and kept saying, It is what it is, it is what it is. Another visitor, worst and most impossible of all, was DB, standing in a corner of the room with that mess coming out of the side of his head, just standing there, staring at me . . . I think I ended up screaming for my dad, until either he came or a nurse came or someone came and turned the goddamn lights back on and maybe gave me more meds.

So even though I remember Chastity in my room at the hospital, I can't be a hundred percent sure. If she did come, and if I do remember it right, two things happened. One is she held my hand for a while. The second is she talked a lot, and I don't remember anything she said, except for this, What did you really think was gonna happen? Seeing as that's the same thing she said when we were kids, after we burned down the porta-potty, it makes me wonder if she was there in the hospital at all.

Either way, she wasn't buried anywhere, not in a shallow grave, not down in a crawlspace.

She says now, You look rough.

I say, Yeah, I know.

Ashley, for Christ's sake . . .

I have some news to tell you.

I know you do. You said so when you called me.

But I'm not ready to tell you yet, okay? I need to work up to it, if that makes sense.

Suit yourself, she says.

A breeze blows across the park, picks up a little force, bends the grass down. From the playground, Nevaeh calls, Watch this!— and slides down the slide.

Great job, says Chastity, waving to the girl.

I say, Chass.

She doesn't look at me. She says, Come on, let's sit down.

I follow her over to the bench and sit down beside her. I say, My dad's driving around the block a couple times.

Ha, says Chastity. Yeah, my mom's in her van in the parking lot, reading the newspaper. She probably saw you guys when you got here.

It's like we're kids again. Like we need the supervision.

I almost think we do. Don't you?

I don't know. I have no idea what to think anymore. Anyways, it's good to see you.

Chastity doesn't reply.

She's been back at her mom's for the last few weeks. This I know, along with a lot of the other things I've found out, mainly from my dad. Whether or not I saw her in the hospital, I can't say for sure, but I can tell you there hasn't been any other contact between us until now. I guess, one way or the other, there's been too much collateral damage.

Meeting up in the park was her idea, but meeting up in the first place was mine. I wanted to tell her in person, this news that's been burning me up, so I had to break the ice between us.

I'd gotten the news from the cops, just yesterday. I'd been called in to see them. It was my second interview with them this week, my thousandth interview with them since I'd come out of the hospital. In the beginning I'd met mostly with Constable Casey. She was alright. She was understanding, and she talked to me like we were on the same level. I could respect that. But before long there were a bunch of provincial plainclothes detectives on the investigation. They're another matter. When I see them they break my balls endlessly. They talk down to me. They talk to me like I'm a knucklehead.

My interview yesterday was with one of these detectives, a big guy who dresses like a biker, complete with a beard and a patched-up denim cut. This guy had given me the news, and then he'd said, So now that that's taken care of, don't be thinking of a vacation anytime soon. You're still one of my favourite persons of interest, chum.

To fill the air I say, I hope it's okay, seeing me now.

I'm not sure, says Chastity.

You're not? What's that supposed to mean?

It means I'm not sure. This is me being straight-up with you, me being honest about where I'm at. I haven't always been like that, I know. But I'm making a daily commitment to honesty.

I say, A daily commitment to honesty. That sounds like, I don't know, a line or something.

Well, it *is* a line, says Chastity. It's part of the contract you sign at Silver Lake.

I nod. It feels weird to hear her talk about that place. Silver Lake is a rehab joint outside of London. And that's where she'd been, since the Sunday after she called me in the middle of the night. Her mother had taken her there, checked her in, signed off on the financing.

She says, Lines like that, they work for me. I don't care if they sound corny. They work.

I say, I didn't mean to offend you.

You didn't. And, honestly, it is good to see you too. I mean it. Anyways, how're you coming along?

I say, Not bad. I guess. It's still pretty tough to do anything. Obviously I can't do the show in August now.

Do you really care about that?

I don't reply and I don't look at her. I know she's right but all the same I do care. I care about the show and I care about what's become of my body. I haven't been able to bring myself to step on the scales, but I have a fair idea of what they'd tell me if I did. The sight of my belly—expanding by the day—makes me sick. The Ritual has gone by the wayside.

On the other hand, since all the shit went down, I haven't once slapped my own face. Weakness doesn't mean the same thing to me as it used to. I guess I'd always believed that pumping iron and being jacked and being a hard-ass and going into battle was the way you fought against weakness. But those things don't count for much when you're getting shot at or when you know you're about to be bounced off the front of some guy's car.

Nevaeh is partly out of sight on the far side of the playground. We can hear her singing to herself. Chastity lights a dart and says, Take this for me if Nevy comes around, will you? I don't want her to see me with it.

I say, I won't. Put it out or keep it but I won't take it. It's yours.

Chastity's eyes flash over to me, but there's a small smile on her lips. She sits back and lets out a stream of smoke and says, That's fair.

Even now, everything between us has to be done in little wars. Little wins, little surrenders.

She smokes her dart. The smell of the smoke on the air isn't all bad. I kind of want a dart for myself. I find myself doing the talking, but still not letting out the news. I tell her I've moved out of Trey's and am living at my dad's house for the time being. I tell her I'm finished at the Balmoral, finished in that whole industry, and that when I get mended up I'm going to start working for a friend of Greg's. A good job, I say. I don't tell her what the job is, but I do tell her about the benefits and the paid vacation. She nods along, working on her dart, keeping one eye on Nevaeh.

I finish up all the small talk I can make. I lick my lips. My body is hurting all over. I really want a Perc. I think about Darren saying, You want to get well with me, brother?

For a second I'm almost ready to tell her, but instead I hear myself saying, I told you to fuck off that night, when you called me. I started thinking about it the next day, and I couldn't let it go, and it just got worse and worse. And I kept calling you, all the time, like I was crazy—

I know, says Chastity. I know. The only person outside of Silver Lake I was talking to was my mom. I wasn't even talking to Da— to anybody else. I'd gotten rid of my phone and tuned out of everything on purpose, because I thought I needed to.

I say, I went to your mom's house. I asked her if she knew where you were.

She was covering for me, says Chastity.

You'd been giving her money for a while.

Yeah, I had.

Real financial responsibility. Isn't that what you called it?

Ha, says Chastity. Yeah. That's exactly what it was. All the money I was giving her was going into a trust fund for Nevy. College. University. I don't know, med school. All the things me and you always used to laugh at, because we didn't know better.

You know something? I saw a brand new ATV in your mom's driveway. And a new TV in the living room.

Chastity stands up from the bench. She makes fists of her hands. She says, Do you think I don't know that? I can't make excuses for it. I can't. But there's already five grand in the trust fund, and on top of that, I'm seeing my little girl again. If my mom feels like she has to take a cut, well, that's how it stands.

I say, I'm sorry.

Goddammit . . . Don't be. I've started to believe that you can't ever make a deal in this life without it getting a little dirty, somewhere along the line. That's what they call human nature, I think.

I say, You're right about that.

Chastity walks a small circle and stops and relaxes her hands. She lights up another dart and says, I was far gone, okay? By March me and Darren were going through a gram every two days. We'd stay awake for two, three days on end. I can't describe it and I won't try. Anyways, I've been totally clean now for more than a month, but don't think I'm not aching for it. Why do you think Glenna isn't so far away?

This last bit she says looking over at Nevaeh.

I say, That night.

What about it?

I want to know, Chass.

She says, You do already, don't you?

I want to hear it from you.

She says, I don't know what to say, Ash. Jesus. After Cesar ended up in the hospital, man, I just couldn't take it anymore. I told them I was quitting. DB said he wouldn't let me. He said he'd kill me. I was far gone, okay? Please understand how far gone I was, what that shit was doing to my head. I thought it was all I could do . . .

Kill DB.

Yes, says Chastity. I called you and I called Michelle and you both told me to fuck off, and I don't blame you. I can't. Anyway, I went to the house. Darren's car was in the driveway. I got the gun out of the trunk and I went into the house. I saw DB and I tried. I tried. I even shot him once. He was in the kitchen, right? And I came in, and he was in the middle of drinking a beer, and he was looking at me, and before he said anything I shot him. In his fucking hand, not that I was aiming at it or anything, but that's what I hit. And he drops to the floor, and he starts screaming, and there's blood everywhere, and . . . and I couldn't. I couldn't finish it.

I say, I guess Darren was there.

Yeah, he was. I guess he'd been in the house somewhere. Maybe in the basement, in their . . . workspace. I don't know. I hadn't seen him in a few days. But there he was. I was a mess by then, and so was DB, obviously. I thought for sure the world was coming to an end. But there was Darren, Ashley. He took the gun away from me. DB kept telling him to fucking kill me, Ash, but D didn't give him any attention. You know what? DB was a fucking coward. He came on like the biggest and the baddest and the smartest, right? But he was a coward. Think how many times he got other people to do his work for him.

I say, Don't I know that.

Something else? says Chastity. DB wasn't just a coward. He was afraid of Darren. I could see it in him every time he and Darren were together.

Looking at the grass, I say, I guess in the end DB was right to be afraid of Darren, wasn't he.

I don't think DB knew, says Chastity. I really don't. I think DB thought he had everything wired tight. I think he thought he had his own kids and . . . and everybody else right there in his hand, doing exactly what he wanted them to do. But I don't think he ever once thought about what Darren was really capable of. When it came down to it.

You mean when it came down to DB or you?

Or you, says Chastity.

I don't know what to say to this.

I should've killed DB myself that night, says Chastity. I was *close*, Ash. I just . . .

She watches Nevaeh for a few moments. I keep quiet, and finally she goes on with her side of the story: Anyways, after everything got calmed down at the house, after what I *didn't* do, Darren drove me back to my mom's place. It was the middle of the night. We didn't tell her everything, but we told her enough. And for once? She didn't turn me out, Ashley. For once she said she'd help me, she'd help me get clean, that we'd get through this together. The next day she took me up to Silver Lake.

Did Darren know that's where you went?

Yeah, says Chastity. He did.

So all those times I asked him—

I'd made him promise not to tell you, says Chastity.

For fuck sake. Why? Were you afraid I'd show up there or something?

Chastity doesn't answer. She doesn't have to. Maybe it should piss me off or, like, offend me or something, but it doesn't. All it does is make me feel like the air's getting let out of me.

I say, Darren crashed his car that night. Fell asleep at the wheel, I guess, or was too burned out or whatever.

I know he did, says Chastity.

I saw him the next day. And you know something? It was business as usual when I saw him. It was a favour he needed. Like nothing at all had happened the night before. Nothing like what really happened.

I honestly don't think he knew any other way to be, says Chastity. I begged him, Ash. I begged him to come with me to get clean. But he wouldn't do it.

Since all the shit went down, I feel like I notice the tweakers and pipeheads and junkies in Altena pretty often. Not exactly all the time, and not everywhere, but enough. I notice them hanging around certain parks, including Missionary Position, or collecting empty bottles from the gutters and the alleys, or dirtying up some of the cheaper stores and fast-food joints and motels, like that dive where Junior and his old lady lived. And when I see the tweakers, Darren's own pale skin and sores come into my mind, Darren smoking that goddamn pipe. I wonder how far gone he really was, which makes me wonder how he could've got anywhere. In the movies you can lock yourself up in a room for a couple days and get clean, beat your addiction to whatever shit you're hooked on, but something tells me it doesn't really work like that.

Chastity says, I begged him, Ashley. God. I don't know if he had that in him to begin with, like, that *sickness*. Or maybe his dad brought it out in him. I don't know. There's a lot I'll never understand about him.

I say, And there's a lot he never understood about you.

That's true.

I almost say I'm the only one who understood her, just like she'd told me once, but I don't say it. I can hear those words for how they sound. I can hear how they belong to another time, to something I can't get back, no matter how much I wish it was different.

A few minutes go by. We watch Nevaeh on the playground. I ask Chastity for a dart. She gives me one and lights it for me. I take a deep drag, and right away I cough. But when it hits my head it isn't bad. It makes me forget, for the moment at least, how much I want a painkiller.

I say, So, do you want to know what I have to tell you?

She says, Yeah, but first let me tell you something.

What is it?

We're moving, says Chastity. Me, Nevy, my mom. We're bringing my dad with us. When this is all over, when the legal shit is done, we're moving. We're going out east, I think, maybe to where my dad's family is. It's gonna be hard, Ash. But so is everything else, and at least it'll be a new start. One we're doing together.

I can't really think of anything to say to this. Altena without Chastity, really without Chastity . . . it's the same as Altena without Darren. It's the Altena that I don't know at all. In a way, this hurts. Way more than I would've expected. This actually pisses me off. I make my way through a couple more drags of the dart.

I say, Moving. Just like that.

Well, says Chastity. Not just like that. Like I told you, it's gonna be hard. But we need it.

Maybe I'll move too.

Maybe you should. Maybe it would be the best thing for you. I don't know.

I really am pissed off. I can't explain why. I grind the dart out on the bench and toss the butt into the grass. By now, there's nothing more except the news. It's all I've got left. I say, I guess it's my turn, then. So here goes.

Wait, says Chastity.

I say, What?

I look at her. She gives me a funny little smile, one I've never seen on her before. And before my brain can even make sense of what my ears are hearing, she's saying, I already know, Ashley. I know your news. About Darren.

My mouth goes dry. My head spins.

I hear her say, He made it as far as Alberta, which is fucking incredible. He was trying to do pipeline work . . .

This is almost the same as what that big plainclothes cop told me yesterday. D had been picked up in some shitty little town called Peace River. He'd been working there without any papers or ID.

And can you imagine? says Chastity. Can you imagine Darren

trying to do work like that? My god. I bet you'd last longer on a farm than he would doing that kind of shit . . .

I close my eyes. I feel her hand on my arm. My head stops spinning. When I open my eyes again I see she's looking at me.

She says, You okay, Ash?

I say, How did you know?

It doesn't matter.

Yes it does. How did you know?

Well . . . we were talking, says Chastity. Not every day, but almost. And before you even ask, no, the cops don't know we were talking. I guess you can tell them. If you want.

Everything she's saying hits me like a punch. I came with this news in my pocket. How fast, bro, how fast everything gets turned around on you. I say, I . . . I'm not gonna tell the cops.

It got bad for him at the end, Ash, says Chastity. I mean, it was bad all along. But the last week was the worst. Nobody can run. Not really. Yesterday morning we talked for two hours straight. We talked right up until the time he walked into whatever police station they've got there and turned himself in.

They picked your buddy up in Peace River, was what the plainclothes cop had told me. He hadn't said shit about Darren turning himself in.

It was that, says Chastity, or he was gonna do something bad. Real bad. To himself. I think he was ready to when he called me. He was at the end, you know? He was as far as he could go. I told him to go to the cops. And you know what? I think, in a way, he was glad to hear it.

She's crying a little, but not enough to make her unsteady or anything. She wipes her eyes dry. We sit there for a while without saying anything, watching Nevaeh on the playground. I hurt all over, and Jesus Christ do I ever need a Percocet.

I'm about to say her name, when she says, It's four o'clock. We've gotta get going.

I say, Already?

I have a meeting with my sponsor in an hour.

Okay, I say.

Nevy, calls Chastity. Time to get going, baby.

Nevaeh's voice comes back to us, quiet but clear: I'm not a baby, Aunt Chasty.

I know, says Chastity, not loud enough for the kid to even hear. I know you're not.

Chastity stands up. Before she can just take off, I get up too, feeling wobbly on my feet. I say, I'll walk you out.

You don't have to.

I know. But I want to.

She nods. Nevaeh has come over to us. She's looking at me. Chastity reaches out to give her head a little rub, but the kid ducks it, frowning.

Attitude, says Chastity.

I'm just not feeling like it, says Nevaeh.

Fair enough. Remember which way we came here? Can you lead us back that way?

Nevaeh heads off, fifteen feet in front of us. I limp along at Chastity's side. I'm trying to keep up.

I say, You knew.

Yeah, I did. And I knew it was what you had, Ash. That it was maybe all you had.

So how come you didn't say anything?

She says, Well, no offence, but I wanted you to have it.

Bitterly, I say, I don't need anybody's sympathy. I don't need yours.

Then we'll put it behind us. That's all we can do.

We make our way past the monument with the yellow spray-paint on the missionary's crotch. Before long we come to the gravel parking lot at the edge of the park. I see a minivan parked a little distance away, Aunt Glenna at the wheel. My dad's truck is now parked beside it. And here's a thing. I can see him leaning partway out his window. I can see him talking to his sister.

Well, says Chastity, kind of in a whisper. There you go.

Her mother and my dad see us on the other side of the parking lot. They speak a few words more, and then they actually smile at each other. Then Aunt Glenna starts up the van and drives forward.

All of a sudden time is going by too quick. I need it to slow down. It's running out through my fingers. I say, Wait, wait. I need to ask you something.

What is it?

I say, All those times you talked to him, did he . . . Did he ever talk about me or anything?

No, says Chastity. He never did. But everything you need to know, he showed you, didn't he? When it came time, when it really came time, he showed you.

My eyes are starting to sting. The old me, bro, this is the part where the old me would've wanted to give my face a slap, say, Weakness. But it was never really the right word, was it? Never even the right idea. I say, Okay. Okay.

Chastity moves close to me. This time we do hug. It feels like a full minute we're together, but it isn't near long enough. She kisses me on the cheek. As we pull apart I see her glance at something. I look. She's left a little bit of makeup, foundation or whatever, on my shirt, close to my collar.

She says, Sorry about that. It'll come out.

I say, Chass, I love you.

She says, I love you too, Ashley. I guess I'll see you around, okay?

She takes a few backwards steps and then turns around. I watch her go, leading her daughter by the hand. The stinging in my eyes is worse. Everything I see is double. I watch them make their way up to Glenna's minivan. Before they get into it, Chastity doesn't look back at me but Nevaeh does. She waves. I wave back. Then the two of them are in the van, and a second later they're gone.

My dad's truck pulls up beside me, but for a little while I don't move, I don't even look. I stand there with the whole thing playing over and over in my head. Every part of it. Everything that happened, bro, every fucking choice that was made.

I stand there at the edge of the park where one time, way back when, me and my best buddy and the girl I loved did an act of minor arson. Funny, it isn't the fire that comes clearest to me now. It's those black cats exploding, bang bang bang. The little red flashes in the dark grass.

I'd take it all back, do it over again. Do it different. No I wouldn't. I wouldn't do anything different. I wouldn't know how to. It's not on me. It's all on me. It's both things at the same time, because that's exactly how life fucks with your head.

I hear my dad beside me. Son, he says.

I don't really trust my voice, but I manage to say, Yeah?

It's all gonna be okay, you know.

Okay.

Come on, son. I'll take you home now.

ACKNOWLEDGEMENTS

Craig Davidson
Jennifer Lambert
Martha Webb
Anna Maxymiw
Jane Warren
Noelle Zitzer

MATT LENNOX is the author of the
story collection *Men of Salt, Men of Earth* and
the novel *The Carpenter*, which was published
to critical acclaim. He was a captain in the
Canadian Armed Forces Reserve Force and
was stationed in Kandahar between 2008 and
2009. He completed an MFA at the University
of Guelph and lives in Toronto with his wife,
Natalie.

COVER PHOTO © DEN READER / ARCANGEL IMAGES
AUTHOR PHOTO BY JOHN BRISBANE

HarperCollins*Publishers*Ltd
WWW.HARPERCOLLINS.CA

FICTION ISBN 978-1-44343-252-8

62299

9 781443 432528